THE PLANNING COMMITTEE

David Berardelli

THE PLANNING COMMITTEE

GRAVESTONE PRESS

PART ONE

Chapter 1

He sat by himself in the small, air-conditioned room, staring blankly at the widescreen while struggling to shake the notion of superstition invading his thoughts.

He was not a superstitious man; entertaining this semblance of reasoning made no sense. Many thought along the same lines, but that didn't mean he should include himself. Superstitions, such as bad things happening in threes, just didn't belong in the mind of an intelligent, educated man. The concept was silly and largely unfounded. Three strikes and you're out. The third time's the charm. Celebrities died in threes. Other nonsense followed, but he just wasn't in the mood to remember it all. Even so, why would he think all this had to do with his stumbling upon the same beautiful woman three different times in the same afternoon?

At thirty-eight, Arthur Sills had only been married once, and very briefly. Sandi, his first fiancée, had shattered his dreams seven years earlier when she announced her pregnancy by another man just three weeks before she and Arthur were to wed. Denise, his second—and final—love, destroyed their future together just four months after the wedding when a twenty-year-old idiot with drug

5

issues slammed his stolen BMW into the driver's side of her Honda Accord, killing her instantly.

Though he had only known Denise less than a year before their wedding, the sudden loss had still been devastating. Their plans for buying their own home in Winter Park were, naturally, scrapped. So were their reservations for a weekend in Honolulu during the Christmas holidays, as well as the two very expensive tickets to see Denise's favorite group, The Pentatonix, in Orlando.

For the last few months, Arthur directed his grief inward, avoiding as much interaction with people as possible. Since he had never been a particularly outgoing person, this depressing "adjustment" didn't even seem like an adjustment at all. Nothing in his routine needed to be changed, and he discovered that, except for Denise no longer being in his life, his existence had reverted back to what it had once been.

Arthur preferred being alone. A quiet man by nature, he operated his online computer consultation service in the study of his Winter Park condominium, working through the mornings and afternoons and spending his evenings in front of his 48-inch widescreen, watching movies on Netflix while enjoying a glass or two of bourbon on ice, or a Manhattan. It was a quiet, uncomplicated existence and, except for occasional phone scuffles with abrupt, arrogant Indian techs speaking poor English, one that Arthur considered as perfect as it could possibly get.

***

The first of three strange circumstances happened that afternoon at the corner liquor store.

An attractive woman stood at the end of the aisle, blocking it. Arthur had just picked up his bourbon and would have already paid for it and left, had she not trapped him so suddenly.

She was impossible to ignore. Tall and slender, with long black hair. A model's face and large, proud breasts. Black sunglasses concealed her eyes. In her mid-thirties, most likely, wearing a sleeveless black silk blouse with the top two buttons undone, and a cream skirt about an inch above the knee. Gold necklaces, bracelets, and rings decorated her tanned flesh. Shiny black pumps with three-inch heels, making her only a hair shy of his six-foot height, accentuated her muscular calves.

"Have you ever tried this?" She held up the small, squat bottle.

He struggled to ignore her strong lavender scent. He didn't like cognac, thought it tasted like cough medicine.

"I don't drink cognac."

"A friend of mine told me the aged ones have quite a kick."

"It's strong, all right." Briefly he wondered what color her eyes were behind the shades. It bothered him when he couldn't see someone's eyes.

"Is that why you don't drink it?"

"Can't get past the taste."

Two tiny dimples appeared on her cheeks. "I guess I should just stick with bourbon, then." She lifted her glasses, resting them on top of her head so she could study the bottle. Her eyes were blue. A deep blue, like the ocean. A moment later, the blue orbs lifted, focusing on him. That steady gaze made him uncomfortable. He never liked it that women were allowed to stare at a strange man, but when a man did the same thing to a strange woman, he was considered a stalker, or pervert.

"Well, thanks." She replaced the shades, and the deep-blue orbs disappeared behind their twin black round shades. She replaced the bottle on the shelf before leaving the store.

He hurried over to the cashier, paid for the bourbon, and left. There was no other vehicle parked beside the Caddie. He wondered briefly how she had gotten to the store. A moment later, he decided he didn't care.

***

He saw her again at around six that same day, at the local 7-Eleven.

He had just finished supper before getting in the Caddie and driving to the store for gas and a six-pack of dark beer.

"Hello again." She was standing beside a shiny white Lexus one pump over. She'd changed into maroon shorts and a yellow sleeveless tank top. Open-toed tan sandals for her feet. The same necklaces and bracelets embellished her tanned flesh, and her sunglasses were pulled up, resting on top of her head.

She twisted around to get the nozzle, then twisted around again to replace it. Watching him as she worked but not making it obvious. She said something, but he couldn't hear over the low-rider pulling in. He just shrugged.

She came right over as he was replacing his nozzle. She stepped up on the island then stepped back down, making it look graceful, her hair sliding across her shoulders as she moved. Some of it swished across her arm, stopping in front of her. She stopped about three feet away, nudging it back over her left shoulder while giving him that same unsettling look as before. "I just said, it gets busy here in the afternoons."

"It sure does." He wondered why she walked all the way over just to say something trivial like that. It didn't make sense.

She tilted her head as if she could study him better. Some hair slid down her arm. She didn't seem to notice. That told him she had done it deliberately. "You're shy, aren'tcha?"

He shrugged. He didn't want to tell her that he was still grieving over Denise. He didn't want to talk about it, for one thing, and didn't want to share his grief with a total stranger. He wondered why she was so interested. A woman as great-looking as her should have men swarming all over her. "I guess you could say that."

She shook her head, obviously confused. "Haven't met anyone like you in a while. The guys I usually bump into? Well, they talk. A *lot*."

"I don't have too much to say." He half-turned to the Caddie, hoping she'd take the hint.

She reached up and pulled the shades back down over those big ocean blues. A strong whiff of lavender drifted his way. "Nothing wrong with that. Quiet works for me these days, too."

"I like it," he said flatly.

A nod. He figured she understood.

"Well, nice seeing you again." She raised an arm, turned, and pranced away. Got in the Lexus, eased away from the pump, went over to the curb, and vanished in the heavy stream roaring past.

The lavender stayed with him a while longer, lightly rubbing his cheeks as he got back in the Caddie.

***

At eight o'clock that evening, Arthur crossed the front lot of the complex and approached the strip mall directly across the street.

The Moonglow Lounge sat at the far end of the mall. It employed a pianist during the week and a small four-piece band specializing in music from the sixties on Saturdays and Sundays.

He chose a table not far from the small crescent-shaped stage, and the waitress brought over his Manhattan just a couple of minutes after he came in. A set of drums sat in the rear of the stage. In front, an alto sax rested on a metal stand beside a bass guitar. In the middle sat the piano, its bench tucked neatly beneath the keyboard. The pianist usually showed shortly before nine.

"Want some pretzels or beer nuts?"

"I just had supper, thanks."

"I'll be back to check on you in a few minutes." She whisked back to the bar.

The juke finished with Elton John and moved

10

on to Shania Twain.

He sipped his drink and noticed the familiar sight at the far end of the bar. His mind went right back to his superstition notion, which had been bothering him all afternoon. Three times in the same day. Coincidence? Had she just moved into the area? Or was she stalking him?

His thoughts looped wildly. He was being silly. And paranoid. This was how paranoia began, wasn't it? *Someone's after me. Following me. Hunting me.* The idea was ridiculous. The woman came here for a drink, plain and simple. She was already here. She didn't even know he'd come in.

She finished her drink and shifted on her barstool while the barman took her empty glass and went to fix another. She still wore her maroon shorts and yellow tank top. The bar lighting was dim and smoky, but he could see the reflection of her face in the mirror. She sat, legs crossed, back arched, enjoying her drink. Probably thinking about whether to dye her hair or change manicurists…or whatever else women like her thought about. With Sandi, it was age-lines. She spotted them everywhere. Around her eyes. Her mouth. Her neck. Even her hands. The vertical one between her brows really bothered her. She was convinced it looked like a crack, a gash. A lightning bolt. Makeup barely touched it. She looked fabulous at thirty-two, yet she thought she looked old whenever she frowned or went pensive.

He decided to finish his drink and walk back to the condo without waiting for the pianist to show.

He couldn't relax, not with her here. He'd come here for a few drinks and to listen to the piano player, but now he was obsessed with the brunette. And sex. This wasn't how the evening was supposed to go.

He dropped a ten-spot on the table, finished his drink, and got up. His gaze betrayed him, shifting back to the bar. His blood instantly grew cold.

She was staring at him. Their eyes locked. He felt exposed and vulnerable, wanting to disappear. He wondered if this was how a deer felt the moment its gaze locked onto the rifle scope.

He was being silly again. This was a woman— not a hunter with a rifle. And he certainly was no deer. She wasn't about to shoot him, was she? She would probably just climb down, walk over, say hi, smile, then leave. He could deal with that, couldn't he? Of course. If he couldn't deal with that, he might as well barricade himself in the condo.

His pulse hammered as she slid down off the stool and crossed the room, heading straight for his table.

***

"Small world," she said.

"Sure is."

She watched him and he could feel her taking him in. "You seem nervous, uncomfortable."

She had obviously found something in her quick mental examination. He didn't know if his eyes had given him away, the slight trembling in his limbs, or how he was careful to keep the table separating them. She could obviously sense *some*thing.

She stepped back. "Did that help?"

It only made him feel worse. Silly. Like a child.

She shrugged. "If I step back another foot or so, we won't be able to hear each other."

He smiled even before realizing it.

She smiled as well. "You're really good-looking when you do that," she said.

"Do what?"

"Smile."

He had nothing to say about that. He could feel his wall trembling, ready to fall right in front of her.

"You don't do it very often." She said it as if she actually knew what was going on inside him.

"How could you tell?"

"It's obvious you didn't want to, but you did. It turned out all right, didn't it?"

She was confusing him, manipulating him, distracting him. "I…guess so..."

"What brings you here?"

"I come here pretty often."

"Live around here?"

He didn't want to give her anything personal. When you told someone about yourself, it gave them power. The more you revealed to them, the more power they had. "I live pretty close."

"What's your name?"

"My name?" The room had suddenly grown warm and stuffy. He needed fresh air. He could feel the shakes coming on.

She laughed. "You have one, don't you?"

"Of *course* I have a name."

"I don't have any secret motives." She crossed her arms beneath her breasts, and his eyes lowered despite his resistance. "I like to know people's names, especially when I'm talking to them. And when I know I'm going to like them."

"Arthur Sills." He wanted her to stop the questions and thought it was the only way to get her to do it.

"Aren't you going to ask what my name is?"

He didn't want to know anything about her. If he asked her about herself, she'd want to know more about him in return.

"It's Vanessa. Vanessa Campeon." When he made no comment, she said, "Are you always this…friendly…when someone approaches you in a bar?"

"No one's ever approached me before." He cursed himself for telling her. He should have told her he had someone waiting for him back at the condo. He didn't know why he didn't. He supposed it was because he was so distracted.

"A nice, quiet, good-looking guy like you?" She shook her head. "What's wrong with the females around here?"

He glanced at his empty glass and suddenly wanted a refill. He was furious with himself for coming here. For not drinking the bourbon in the kitchen cabinet. For not putting on one of Dad's old jazz LPs. For not getting up and leaving as soon as he saw her sitting at the bar.

"Buy me a drink."

"I was…just about to leave."

"How about if I buy you one?" She reached up and pulled some black hair away from her face.

He was about to say no, but another quick burst of lavender made him forget what he had meant to say.

"One drink?" The blue eyes grew, searching his.

He felt lost and vulnerable in them—a small boy trapped in a dark, frightening world of strange shadows. All he could think about was this woman's scent.

"One drink." Her voice jerked him out of his darkness. She pulled out a chair and kept her eyes on him as she sat.

***

The waitress brought them two strong Manhattans and then hurried back to the bar.

Arthur took a large pull of his drink. It sent a fire plunging down his throat, relaxing him but not doing much else. He was uncomfortable in her presence, growing more nervous as she watched him. Her large, long-lashed blue eyes held him fast. Her heavy lavender scent intoxicated him more than his drink, and he soon realized that his surroundings were not exactly helping him overcome his fear of the sexy woman sitting across the table.

What was happening to him? Was he no longer in control of his own thoughts or actions? Had she done something to his head? Willed him to do whatever she wanted?

The concept was absurd. No one possessed this sort of power. It reeked of the supernatural, and he never fully believed in such nonsense. But he couldn't help suspecting something strange had indeed happened.

"So…what's the problem?" she asked. "You obviously don't want to be bothered. Is it me? Or females in general?"

He didn't want to tell her about Denise or his miserable love life. She would probably make him feel worse by being sympathetic. She might even try to improve things for him. He didn't want that. He had the strong feeling that she could complicate things as well as the rest of them. "I usually keep to myself."

"Then it isn't me?"

"No."

"I won't feel slighted, then."

He had more of his drink.

"You're the first guy I've ever met who didn't want to jump my bones as soon as I started talking to him."

He caught himself looking at her breasts and immediately shifted his focus to his glass. "I can imagine."

"So then, what's your story?" She'd placed both elbows on the table. The valley between her breasts deepened.

He struggled to ignore them, but his eyes wandered anyway. It seemed the most natural thing in the world, yet it made him uneasy.

"There must be someone," she said. "Or maybe there *was* someone." When he didn't reply, she said, "Ex-wife? Ex-girlfriend?"

A sudden coldness cascading down his spine made him shiver. This woman was getting way too personal. He finished his drink and made a move to get up.

"I've said something wrong." Her eyes grew. "I'm sorry. I didn't mean--"

"It's all right." He could tell she truly felt badly about bringing something up he didn't want to talk about. She obviously meant to be friendly. Now she was chastising herself. "I really do have to get back home." He got up and dropped another bill on the table between their drinks.

Her hand covered his own the moment he released the bill. Her touch was cold. He figured it had something to do with the glass. Denise's touch had always been warm. "This was on me."

"No. It's all right--"

"I insist." She pressed his bill into his palm and dug into her own bag, pulling out a twenty and dropping it on the other bill on the table.

The action caught him off-guard. He felt guilty again. She wasn't as bad—or as evil—as he'd originally thought. She was nice. He had a feeling she knew something was wrong.

"Thank you. It's been nice." He turned to leave.

"Want some company?"

"It's all right. I really like being alone."

"Something's very wrong." She moved closer, and he was suddenly engulfed in lavender. It brushed lightly against his face, warming him. The deep-blue eyes bore into his, making everything dark again. "Sometimes it helps to talk to

17

someone."

She just didn't understand. "No. Really. I don't want to--"

"Why not?"

"Talking…won't help."

She shrugged. "How do you know?"

"I just do."

She reached up and touched his cheek. "Maybe I won't talk, then."

***

His head was trapped in a cloud, everything dark and muddled as he crossed the street and stepped onto the mowed grass that would take him back to his place.

He knew he wasn't alone, that there was a strange woman walking beside him. He just didn't want to look her way; it would make her real, tell him he was no longer imagining things. It would tell him he was bringing a strange woman home.

He honestly couldn't remember how this had happened. How he let her manipulate him so easily. He went into the Moonglow for a couple of drinks; now he was bringing home a strange woman.

His mind went blank again, staying that way even as he slipped through the doorway, closed the door, then turned to face her.

"I think we both need another drink," she said, her voice soft and unsteady.

She was right. He was still shaking, still clueless about everything. Two drinks at the Moonglow hadn't relaxed him at all. He went to the kitchen and opened the cupboard. He managed to

18

grab the bourbon bottle without dropping it. He successfully pulled two clean glasses from the drainer without chipping them and poured a couple of inches into each without spilling any. He even managed to pick up the glasses, cross the living room, and hand one to her—all without incident. She took hers, brought it to her lips and drank half, all the while watching him. He took a sip himself, closing his eyes as the whiskey trickled down his throat.

His thoughts began spinning, telling him things that made sense and blending them with things that didn't. The superstition notion came back. Along with it, that persistent feeling of vulnerability that took over whenever this woman crossed his path. He wanted solitude and quiet, yet each time he stepped out of his condo, this woman had been right there. There was something about her, too. Something that made him feel better. Something that told him she somehow understood what was happening to him and wanted to help.

Something about her suggested that she really *could* help.

"Sometimes being by yourself isn't the best thing," she said.

"I'm just not good company anymore."

"Why not?"

He couldn't look at her. Her eyes made him feel strange.

Her gaze stayed on him as she pulled her tank top over her head and let it drop quietly to the floor. He watched her in numbed silence as she squirmed out of her skirt and let it fall to the floor between her feet. Her sandals came off next, discarded and forgotten as she stepped out of them.

She approached him and stopped just two feet away, her eyes locked onto his. She reached up and pushed her heavy black mane away from her face. Her lavender scent, mixed with her own sweet fragrance, engulfed him.

He opened his mouth, but no words would come. He found it impossible to grasp what was happening. None of this seemed real.

"You want it, too, Arthur. I can tell."

He tried once again to speak, but his throat felt as if it had been scraped raw. He could only nod.

"I know you do, so say it."

Once again he tried. Once again the words remained trapped in his throat.

"*Say* it." She moved closer.

He opened his mouth, and the words suddenly came right out. "I want it, too."

She pressed her warm flesh against him, wrapping her arms around his neck and kissing him passionately. Waves of hot dizziness took hold of him. He closed his eyes and surrendered to the passion.

Chapter 2

The slivers of light peering through the horizontal gaps in the blinds told Arthur it was morning.

He was alone in the bed, yet the lingering lavender scent on the pillows and sheets told him someone else been here recently, perhaps the night before.

However, he was alone.

He closed his eyes and tried remembering. Strangely, everything was cloudy. Shadows and shapes, but nothing tangible. He struggled to bring back the images, to clear up the shadows and shapes, taking his day all the way back. To the liquor store. And her.

Black hair, beautiful blue eyes, long limbs, perfect body. And then the 7-Eleven. And then--

The familiar neon sign flashed briefly in his head. The Moonglow Lounge. She was there, too. Sitting on a barstool, having a drink. Staring at her reflection in the bar mirror. Turning on her stool. Looking straight at him.

She came over to his table right after. Smiled. Convinced him he shouldn't be alone. Just a few minutes later, she left the bar with him and came back here...

Had they had sex? A drink?

Where was she? Had she left? When? And why?

Why was he having such trouble remembering?

And why were things so cloudy? Was he drunk? He remembered having two drinks at the bar. Two drinks weren't enough to get him drunk. Did he have anything else once they came back here?

He remembered pouring drinks, handing a glass to her, and drinking as they stood in the living room, staring at one another. Then another, but only later on. This time, she left the bedroom and came back moments later, handing him a glass and watching him as she drank from her own glass.

He got out of bed and straightened, wincing at a heavy tingling sensation just above his buttocks. He had either slept wrong or moved wrong—which was usually the case during sex. A damned shame he couldn't remember the previous evening very well.

He stepped into the shower stall. The thick, warm spray tumbling down his back immediately turned his lower back into sizzling jolts of hot blisters. Howling in agony, he backed away and waited for the heavy throbbing to pass. After what seemed an eternity later, the pain ebbed into a distant throbbing.

He toweled off very carefully and stepped out of the stall to examine his back. The mirror helped. Two trails of cuts ran along his spine, just inches above his tailbone.

Cuts? Made by fingernails?

Had this woman made them?

How else could he have gotten them?

He soaked some cotton balls with hydrogen peroxide and applied them gently to the cuts. The pain rushed back hotly, like beestings. He gritted his

22

teeth until the tingling subsided. He decided not to bandage them. A loose-fitting shirt would protect as well as hide them.

While facing the mirror, he wanted to scold himself about the previous night. His memory was still cloudy about what had happened. Other than bringing home a strange woman, he could find no reason for beating himself up.

After shaving and blotting his cheeks with cologne, he went into the kitchen to make coffee and a little breakfast. Food would make him feel better and also stimulate his thought processes. He got the coffeepot going, then cracked an egg and dropped it in the skillet with some butter. Just as he grabbed the whole wheat bread from the fridge and dropped two slices into the toaster, the wall phone rang. He turned off the heat and grabbed the receiver.

"Have you recovered?" The breathy, low-pitched voice perked him right up.

"I beg your pardon?"

"You had quite a night."

Was it her? The woman he'd brought home?

"I'm sorry, I don't know what you--"

"Are you having trouble remembering, Arthur?"

"Actually, I just woke up."

"I'm afraid I taxed you too much. But you needed release. You were wound so tight, I had to do something. I was worried about you."

Everything rushed back. He closed his eyes and tried focusing on the blackness that had filled his head earlier. Memories of Denise floated in, adding to the fog. He wanted his quiet and solitude back. He didn't want another woman up there, changing the status quo, upsetting his isolation.

Despite his efforts, the images swam toward him mercilessly.

"Arthur? Are you still there?"

He suddenly hated her, what she'd done. She had invaded his privacy, his solitary life of quiet desperation. He didn't want to see her again. He wanted to slam down the receiver.

"Arthur?"

"Everything's…fuzzy."

"It should be. You were quite anxious. You obviously haven't had sex in a long time."

Despite his rage, a much more serious matter rose to the surface, eclipsing all else. "Why'd you mark me up?"

"I'm sorry, Arthur. I guess I got excited."

"Obviously."

She laughed. "You didn't seem to mind at the time."

He picked up the skillet, took the egg over to the sink, and dumped it in the garbage disposal. More rage thrashed through him. He wanted to tear the phone out of the wall and toss it.

"Arthur? Are you all right?" She sounded sincere—which made him even more upset and confused. How could he be so angry at someone who sounded like she really cared? But he was.

"I don't know."

"I think we should talk more. Let me come over

there later this afternoon and we can--"

"No." The thoughts of her invading his home a second time made his pulse race.

"What's wrong, Arthur? I thought we had a good time last night. *I* did, anyway."

He didn't reply.

"Is there something I did to upset you? Was it those scratches?"

"I just...don't feel like seeing anyone today."

"Not even a nice, quiet lunch?"

"No."

"Arthur, we had fun last night. You know we did. It did you good, admit it. You need to get over whatever is eating you up. Both of us do."

He remembered her saying something about losing her husband. Something about a heart attack. Last year. After ten years of marriage. She'd been through a lot, too. He knew exactly what she'd gone through. Yet he couldn't bring himself to share his grief with anyone.

"Would you like to meet me somewhere? I think it'll do us both some good."

"No." Why the hell couldn't she accept no for an answer?

"Please, Arthur? I need just as much help as you do."

He didn't reply.

"How about the Steak and Ale, on Colonial?"

"No. No. I don't want to--" He opened his eyes and looked around. The smell of coffee, of burnt butter. Something pressing against his ear. The phone. He gawked at it as if he'd never seen one before. Why was he holding the phone? Was he talking to someone? Why was he in the kitchen?

"Arthur? Still there?"

"Yes." Who was he talking to? The brunette from last night. Vanessa, her name was. Something about the Steak & Ale for lunch. He hadn't wanted to go at first but had reconsidered. "All right."

"One o'clock a good time?"

"Fine." He tried to remember why he had changed his mind. The reason wouldn't come.

"Meet you there."

He hung up and remained staring at the phone. His pulse raced as he struggled to figure out what just happened.

***

At twelve-thirty, he tried relaxing in the living room, listening to one of his father's old Coltrane LPs.

He liked Coltrane, especially when something was bothering him, and he wanted to soothe his nerves. Coltrane's moody sax always seemed to do the job. He kept thinking of the brunette and hoped the music would take some of the edge off his anxiety. The situation just didn't feel right, and he could not convince himself that the encounters had been random. Yet he could find no reason for other motives.

He had no intention of meeting her at the Steak & Ale or anywhere else. He intended to stay right here all afternoon. When "*Resolution*" ended in just a few minutes, he decided to grab a beer and eat the rest of the submarine sandwich he'd bought the day before.

He had no explanation for what happened on the phone. Why he'd agreed to meet her, when only moments earlier, he'd told her he didn't want to. It had happened as quickly and as suddenly as one of the blackouts he'd experienced when he had learned about Denise's sudden death. Nothing else could explain why he would change his mind so unexpectedly.

Why hadn't he just hung up? Vanessa was a stranger; he owed her no explanation. Other than a single night of sex, he figured he shared no other memories with her. Had he experienced a strange bond with her? Or was it a sort of comradeship formed from their mutual grief? Some degree of gratitude brought on by her sincerity? Her desire to help him?

Whatever the explanation, it had come up quite suddenly, long before he realized anything was developing. But even so, he didn't want anyone else in his life right now. He just couldn't handle it. And he certainly didn't want a sudden relationship with someone he'd met by chance, who had interrupted his life on three separate occasions, talking her way into his home and seducing him.

When "*Resolution*" ended, he got up from the couch to grab his sandwich and beer. Halfway to the kitchen, things clouded up again, this time much worse. He stopped moving, closing his eyes while waiting for his blood pressure to stabilize. He'd obviously gotten up too fast and needed a few moments to let his body recover.

But when he opened his eyes again, he found himself behind the wheel of his car, pulling off the main stretch of Semoran Boulevard and into the front lot of the Steak & Ale.

***

The white, chalet-looking building sneered at him.

He gawked at the large hand-painted brown wooden sign over the entrance as if it were some horrible nightmare. STEAK & ALE. That's what it said. No matter how hard he tried to force his eyes to change it into something else, it remained STEAK & ALE.

He struggled to comprehend what had happened. Only moments ago, he sat in his living room, listening to Coltrane. Then he'd gotten up from the couch to walk into the kitchen to grab a beer and the last half of his submarine sandwich. But just then, some strange force had taken control of him, forcing him to leave the condo, get into his car, and drive here.

Had he suffered another blackout? Perhaps a memory lapse?

Something didn't make sense. He'd *never* suffered such a bizarre blackout, returning to a different place and in a different situation.

He couldn't accept this. It wasn't real. Things hadn't been right since he'd met Vanessa. But he was confident he possessed the power to set things straight.

Just pull back out and head north, and in no time you'll be back home--

28

A tap at his window.

He jerked his head around and gasped.

It was her. He didn't want to believe it and tried to convince himself his eyes were deceiving him. Beautiful women abounded in this city. Tall, slender, black-haired beauties were a dime a dozen these days. This was obviously some strange woman who had come over to ask him to move his car.

"Why aren't you getting out?" The familiar voice told him he'd been wrong. This *was* Vanessa, and she had somehow summoned him here despite his objections.

His pulse hammered as he searched his brain for a suitable reply. Once again it failed him, and he realized he had nothing to say. As he had learned years ago, it was best to rely on the truth when bluffing was not possible. What else could he do?

"I don't want to," he said flatly.

"What?"

He just shrugged. He felt much safer in the car, and hoped she'd soon tire of this and walk away. He knew how absurd that notion was, but he was upset and distracted, and wasn't thinking right.

She motioned for him to roll down the window.

His finger stayed away from the button. He wouldn't do it. He didn't have to roll down the window. She couldn't possibly force him to, could she?

She said something else, but he couldn't hear. She said it softly, frowning as she did so. He assumed she had cursed at him or uttered something in frustration. It made him feel a little better. In fact--

His thoughts clouded again. When they cleared, he found that he had already reached for the door and that the index finger of his right hand had pressed the button on the arm rest. The window slid silently down, and the safety of his sphere quickly evaporated as her abrupt foulness invaded his space.

"Aren't you getting out?"

"I'm...not very hungry."

"You agreed we meet for lunch."

He didn't reply. He was trying to determine why he lowered the window even though he was determined to keep it closed.

"C'mon, Arthur. I'm starving. You must be, too."

He had been hungry a few minutes ago, when he'd gone to the kitchen. Now he was more upset than hungry, and wanted to roll up his window, pull away from her, and drive back to the condo. But for some strange, inexplicable reason, he discovered that he couldn't move. This woman had somehow mysteriously gained complete control of him. The idea was absurd, but he had no other explanation of why he hadn't told her to go to hell and just drove off without another word.

"Park your car so we can have lunch."

Despite his misgivings, his desire to get away from this woman as quickly as possible, he grabbed the gear shift. Once again he considered slamming it into reverse. But he knew better. With this woman, his desires no longer belonged to him, and his mind no longer functioned. He pulled into the vacant space just a few yards ahead. As he turned off the ignition, he wanted to call himself a coward, but decided to leave that for later, when he was by himself.

Then he could try once again to figure out what was happening to him.

***

The waitress led them to a corner booth in the rear of the large, dark, air-conditioned room.

It was a little past one, but the place wasn't very crowded. Ordinarily, Arthur would have preferred such a quiet setting, but the present circumstances made him feel more isolated. He did not feel safe in this woman's presence.

She stared at him in her unsettling way, making him feel even more uncomfortable. He sensed she expected him to say something, to perhaps explain why he hadn't wanted to come in with her. When he said nothing, she turned to the waitress. "I'd like a martini. Very dry."

"Yes, ma'am." The waitress held her notepad out in front of her. She waited patiently for his order.

A drink was the last thing on his mind. He wanted to be back in his condo, listening to Coltrane and having his lunch. Staring at the widescreen would even be preferable to this. Or walking around in his undershorts, enjoying the a/c. It didn't really matter, as long as he was alone and safe in his solitude. The condo was his Happy Place; he would have given his left nut to be back there.

"Arthur? She's waiting."

Vanessa was right. The girl's patience was wearing thin. Her cheeks had already relaxed, dimming her smile from around a hundred watts to no more than sixty. He felt sorry for her being brought into this, but it couldn't be helped. Ordering a drink wasn't important at all to him. He wanted her to know that he didn't want to be here, that the woman with him had somehow forced him to come.

He decided to try to inject his thoughts into the waitress' head. He had never before tried such a bizarre thing, but this would be a perfect time to find out if he possessed such powers.

Help me. Please. I'm here against my will. Just walk back to the bar, grab your cell, call 911, and tell them one of your customers is in grave danger.

The waitress didn't move.

"Arthur..."

His mind spun with all sorts of excuses, but when he opened his mouth, he heard himself say, "A Manhattan," as if someone else had manipulated his vocal cords.

The waitress's smile flicked back on full. His heart sank heavily as she rushed back to the bar.

"What's wrong?" Vanessa's eyes had become swollen glacial pools. "Since I met you out in the parking lot, you've been acting really strange."

"Strange? Me?" Hopefully, she'd elaborate.

Her jaw tightened, and she sighed. He could tell she was trying to decide what was going on. "You're the one who suggested we have lunch

32

together. But now you're acting like you don't even want to be here."

The waitress, thank God, came to his rescue. She set her tray carefully on the table, slid Vanessa's martini in front of her, his Manhattan in front of him, then picked up the tray and straightened. "I'll be back in a few minutes to take your order."

"We're in no hurry," Vanessa said, and something cold and heavy settled around his shoulders when she said it.

He picked up his drink and tasted it. Thank God it was strong. He downed half of it eagerly. Three or four more of them would make some of this confusion go away. He might even be able to regain his former confidence and self-control and summon enough courage to tell this woman exactly what was on his mind.

"How's your drink?"

"Excellent." He finished it and signaled for the waitress.

The waitress quickly brought over a refill. As he raised it, he reminded himself to give her a healthy tip for her promptness.

"What's wrong, Arthur?" Vanessa asked when they were alone again.

"I don't want to be here." It came out automatically, perhaps because of the booze. And once it was out, he felt a hundred percent better.

"Where would you like to be?"

"Back home in my condo."

"Why didn't you tell me when we were

discussing our lunch plans?"

He had more of his drink and felt even more of his confidence rushing back. "*You* were the one discussing our lunch plans."

"Arthur, what are you trying to say?"

"*You* arranged this—not me."

"If you remember, I wanted to come over to your place, but you didn't want--"

"That's right. I didn't."

"Is there something you're not telling me?"

"I just told you. I didn't want to come here."

"But you're here. What does that tell you?"

"I don't know. I wish I did. All I know is that I was sitting in my living room, listening to Coltrane, and in the next moment--"

"Arthur..." She moved closer on the padded seat. When their thighs touched, a jolt of intense heat raced up his leg. His heart hammered wildly as her face drew closer, until it was only inches away.

Her hand found his thigh, and his blood heated up and gushed through his veins like a ruptured dam.

No. This was not happening. He couldn't allow this. He wanted—needed –to get away from her, get out of...

He didn't want--

"We're going to kiss. Right now. Understand?"

Her hot, moist lips met his. A fire ignited within him, and everything quickly turned dim. And hazy. And hot.

And black...

Chapter 3

He awoke to the smell of bacon and coffee.

He was alone in his bed. A quick glance at the bedside clock said 4:10.

He sat up, rubbed his eyes, and fought hard to remember the last few hours. He vaguely recalled driving to the Steak & Ale, then returning to the condo with Vanessa following him in her white Lexus. That happened at around two. Just two hours ago, yet he felt as if he'd been asleep for days.

He swung his legs over the side of the bed and stood. The sudden wooziness forced him back down. He sat bent over, his head in his hands, his elbows on his thighs. He closed his eyes. Took a couple of deep breaths. Rubbed the back of his neck. Once the waves of dizziness had ebbed, he got up slowly, put on his pants, shrugged into his shirt, and staggered down the hall.

Vanessa stood in front of the stove, flipping the eggs. She wore the light-blue housecoat Denise had given him for his last birthday, with his initials ornately embroidered in silver over the pocket. He didn't approve of Vanessa wearing it. It looked good on her but made him feel somewhat violated.

She didn't appear tired at all as she busily worked the spatula and tended to the bacon. "Hungry?" She slid the eggs onto a plate.

"My wife…bought me that housecoat."

"I'm sorry, Arthur. I just slipped it on. I hoped you wouldn't mind."

He wanted to pull it right off her, take it back to the bedroom, and hang it in his closet, where it belonged. The fact that this woman, this stranger, had gone into his closet bothered him even more than her wearing the housecoat. She made herself at home, and he didn't like it.

"You look hungry," she said. "We skipped lunch. Remember?"

He tried to remember when he had last eaten and realized it had been the evening before. He plopped down onto one of the two barstools at the counter and forced himself to ignore the housecoat issue. She wouldn't be here very long.

She picked up two plates and placed them on the counter, returned to the oven, picked up the plate with the bacon, and brought it over as well.

He grabbed a strip of bacon. As she poured coffee and slid the cups closer, he tried hard to remember exactly what happened once they had returned from the Steak & Ale. He knew they had had sex--he just couldn't remember the details.

"You look confused." She climbed onto the other stool.

His mind raced. He had fallen asleep after sex a few times before, but it hadn't happened in years. The most notable example took place on his honeymoon night with Denise. That incident had been helped along by a bottle of champagne, two joints, and half a dozen sessions of sex. He was in love and had been running on all eight cylinders for more than twenty-four hours. He often wondered why he hadn't suffered a heart attack that day.

This situation was much different. He wasn't in love with this woman, hardly knew her at all, and hadn't even wanted to fool around in the first place. But the demands of his body had obviously won out. "Did I pass out?"

"You honestly don't remember?" She watched him as she sipped her coffee.

"Nope."

"I'd say around an hour ago. I tried to bring you around, but you were gone."

He drank some coffee. He remembered the passionate exchange in the living room, then the frenzied groping all the way down the hall. Then the heated foreplay on the bed. But little else.

"You seem troubled, Arthur."

"My memory keeps failing me."

"You remember making love, don't you?"

"Vaguely."

"Then what's the problem?"

The problem, of course, was trying to decide why he'd driven to the Steak & Ale in the first place. Closing his eyes in the living room and opening them in the Caddie just before pulling into the eatery. And before that: Bringing this woman here even though he planned to come home alone. Something was wrong, yet he had no idea what it was or even how to discuss it. He strongly suspected this woman had caused it all. He just didn't know how—or why. "I've never had a problem remembering things before," he said.

"Everyone has memory lapses."

She had a valid point, but it still didn't wash.

Too many factors were involved. His brain, along with his self-control, hardly worked at all since meeting this woman. This frightened him, made him wary. Nothing she could say would convince him this had nothing to do with her.

After breakfast, she picked up the plates and put them in the sink. She ran hot water. "By the way, you don't have my creamer."

"What?"

"I prefer the Italian sweet cream. Most 7-Elevens have it. I don't like my coffee without it. Sugar's all right, but I'm not wild about it. Pick me up a bottle, would you? I'd like to enjoy my next cup with my creamer."

He gawked at her, trying to determine if he'd heard her correctly.

"You don't mind, do you?"

He didn't reply. There were more important things on his mind. One of them involved asking her to leave without insulting or angering her. Nothing he was thinking involved a quick trip to the 7-Eleven.

"I'd really like to enjoy it now, while the pot is still hot."

He watched her as rinsed off a plate and placed it in the drainer. Then she washed the forks, the knives. Not once did she look his way. Not once did she smile and say she was kidding. She was obviously serious.

He knew right then that it was the perfect time to tell her he had no intention of going shopping or anywhere else. He wanted her to leave. To get out of his life. Completely.

But before he could say anything, everything turned black.

***

When he opened his eyes, he was standing in front of his front door, holding a brown paper bag.

He opened the bag and pulled out a container of creamer. Italian sweet cream, just as she'd wanted.

Behind him and to his left, the silver Caddie was parked in its space. He stepped down from the stoop, went down the walk to the drive, and pressed his palm to the hood. Warm. It had obviously been used recently. His keys were in his pocket, but that didn't tell him anything. The only way he was going to learn what was going on was to ask the source.

He went back up the walk, to the front door. It opened. Vanessa stood in the doorway, still wearing Denise's bathrobe. "I was wondering where you were." She eyed the bag and snatched it. "What took you so long? I told you I wanted this while the pot was still hot." She hurried through the living room, past the archway leading to the kitchen.

He remained in the doorway, confused and stunned. It was his place, all right. He didn't remember leaving, but the evidence told him he had. Logic also told him that he had just come from somewhere. He didn't remember getting out of the Caddie...or driving anywhere...or stopping...or coming back...or getting out of the car.

This was no different from the episode at the Steak & Ale.

"Aren't you coming in?" Vanessa appeared in

the dining room archway, coffee cup in hand.

Not knowing what else to do, he turned and closed the door.

She sat on the couch and put the cup on the end table. Her hair fell down her front, some of it sliding down the V of the bathrobe and hiding in there. She flicked it back and patted the cushion beside her. "C'mon over. Stay a while. This *is* your house, you know."

He chose the recliner on the other side of the coffee table. He didn't want to be in her space. He feared that if he sat too close, he wouldn't be able to think clearly. He also feared that he might black out again.

"Something wrong with the couch?"

"I need my space."

She frowned. She stared at him, trying to read him, sense what was going on. She only gave it a couple of seconds before giving up. "That's not a very nice thing to--"

"Something's been happening to me and I'm pretty sure you know what it is."

She tilted her head. "Whatever are you talking about, Arthur?"

"My brain hasn't been working right since I met you, and I think you're the cause of it."

"Really?" Her clueless expression wasn't convincing.

His pulse hammered. There was no other way of saying it. "Did you do something to me?"

"Pardon me?"

"You know what I'm talking about."

40

"I really wish I did."

"I'm talking about this sudden lapse of memory."

"We've already discussed that. I thought--that is, we both thought--it was because you overexerted yourself."

So much for subtlety. There was only one way of asking it. "Did you put a spell on me?"

"Arthur, are you all right? Did you hit your head when you went to the 7-Eleven? You could have tripped when you got out of the car."

"I don't know if I hit my head. Everything's a blank. A lost memory. It's almost like a badly-edited movie with too many scenes missing."

She blinked. "You think I'm a *witch*?"

"I think something's happened, and you're the cause."

"Why?"

"The blackouts. The memory lapses. And whenever I try recalling specific events, there's a big void filling my head."

"What else?"

She had to be kidding. "Isn't that enough?"

"Tell me everything." She leaned forward, sitting with her elbows on her thighs. She was obviously very interested.

This irritated him. He felt like some sort of laboratory experiment.

"Tell me what you remember."

"My drive to the 7-Eleven, for instance. I was talking to you, and then I was standing outside, and I didn't even remember anything!"

"Well, you did leave in a hurry." She chuckled. "It was kind of flattering, really. A girl likes to be waited on, but you didn't have to rush off like that."

"You *saw* me leave?"

"You were standing out in the hall, talking to me, and when I turned around to say something, you weren't there anymore."

"But did you actually *see* me leave?"

"I saw the door close."

"But you didn't watch me get in my car and drive away."

"Arthur, what are you getting at?"

She was either a damned good liar or honestly didn't know what was going on. Her innocent face appeared legit. Even so, he suspected her. He had to. Nothing else made any sense.

"Ever since I met you, my head's been in a fog."

"And you think I actually put a spell on you?"

It sounded ridiculous, but he had no other ideas that would explain this. "Well, yes..."

"But not because you might be, well, falling in love with me?"

He didn't even want to get into that. She was totally wrong, but like most women, wouldn't be able to accept any sort of rejection. "No."

"I hate to burst your bubble, Arthur, but I'm not a witch. I don't even believe in witches. Or spells. Or chants. Or any of that weird stuff."

"Neither do I."

"But you've just accused me of--"

"I just don't know what else to think."

42

"You might just be overexerting yourself, if you want my opinion. We've been tearing up the sheets quite a bit lately. It's obviously been too much for you." She got up and pulled back her hair. His robe had shifted slightly, moving down her right shoulder and revealing a portion of her right breast. She made no effort to straighten the robe. He could tell she had something in mind, and it didn't include any more discussion. "I suggest we go a little easier." She suddenly stopped, turned around and smiled. "But not *too* easy."

Despite his fears, his reservations, he followed her down the hall.

***

He sat bolt upright in his bed.

"Bad dream?" Vanessa's voice heavy with sleep.

"It was so...so *real*..." He was sweating, shaking all over.

It had been much too vivid to be a dream. He was in a dark, unfamiliar room. A man lay on his side at his feet. Slender and angular, the man wore a wrinkled white lab jacket, black slacks, and shiny black loafers. He was around seventy, with thinning white hair, a long beaky nose, and a white mustache. He didn't move. A pair of large-framed glasses sat on the tiled floor a foot away. Both lenses were cracked. A dark circle of blood had gathered on the steel floor beneath the man's head.

Did I kill him?

The metal paperweight gripped in his right fist suggested he must have. He gazed at it in shock.

Spots of blood on it told him the horrific truth. He had bashed in this poor man's skull.

A dream, Arthur. It was a dream. It wasn't real.

But *was* it a dream? His dreams were generally hazy, detached. They consisted of images of people he had known, things he had done. They made no sense. During the last several months, they were usually snippets of Denise, their life together. Things they had done together before her tragic end. Several images were of her smiling at him, laughing. One image was of her shaking her head. Several were of him looking for her in their house, sobbing, wondering why all the rooms were pitch-black.

This one was too real, too detailed. He remembered entirely too much about the corpse, the room, everything. Filing cabinets. A table of laptops and hard drives. A desk lamp on the desk in front of the window. The tile floor.

Most of all, the paperweight. It was cold and heavy, about the size of a baseball, with the rough texture of a rock. It was bronze-colored, with tints of red and yellow intermixed with it in jagged layers. He could still feel its texture, its imprint, and stared at his palm in the darkness.

"You're staring at your hand."

He didn't reply. He kept expecting it to reappear.

"Arthur?"

"Did I…say anything?"

"You were talking too fast. Did you hurt your hand?"

"Did I mention anything specific?"

"Like what?"

"I don't know." He didn't want to confide in Vanessa. He still didn't trust her, not even a little. "I wish I knew."

"Go back to sleep."

Something nagged at him, and he raised the sheet. Naked. Good. Of course it was a dream. Otherwise, he'd have his clothes on. He didn't remember dressing or undressing.

"See something interesting in there?" she asked.

"I didn't get out of bed, did I?"

"When?"

"Forget about it."

"Do you always wake up from a bad dream and spend the rest of the night trying to analyze it?"

"I've never had a bad dream before. Not since I was a kid. This one was a doozy."

"What was it about?"

"I dreamed I killed someone."

"Wow. Who?"

"An old man."

"Who was he?"

"I have no idea."

"You dreamed you killed some old man you never saw before?"

He lay down and stared at the dark ceiling. "I hope I can get that image out of my head."

"What image?"

"The old man wore a white lab coat, and I saw some sort of--"

"Go to sleep, Arthur."
"It was some sort of logo--"
"Sleep."
Blackness fell heavily upon him.

Chapter 4

He awoke the next morning alone.

Denise's bathrobe was draped across the arm of the chair in the corner. Vanessa's lavender smell clung heavily to it. He dropped it back onto the chair.

Suddenly suspicious, he checked the condo thoroughly. No sign of Vanessa in the kitchen or living room. Still somewhat wary, he peered out through the living room curtains. The space beside his Caddie was gloriously empty. Relief washed through him. He closed his eyes and bathed himself in the warm sensations of blissful solitude. The heavy silence in the apartment contained a strange sweetness. A refreshing warmth.

He collapsed in the recliner and enjoyed the wonderfully warm silence. She was really gone, and he was alone once again. He was happy. And greatly relieved.

What puzzled him mostly was that he had no idea when Vanessa had left. He must have been sound asleep when she got out of bed. He heard nothing, felt nothing. All memory of her departure had eluded him. All he remembered was his horrible nightmare the night before. The dead man. The paperweight. The blood. Vanessa telling him to go back to sleep. And, of course, how quickly he'd fallen asleep at her command.

Once again she had been in complete control. Once again she had told him what she wanted. Once again he had obeyed. Just how she managed to put him to sleep wasn't the question. The only thing that mattered was her ability to do it in the first place. And to send him to the Steak & Ale. And to the 7-Eleven.

But if she had such complete control over him, why would she leave so abruptly?

Did it have something to do with the nightmare itself?

Vanessa had dismissed it, said it was a dream. She didn't want to hear much about it, and when he tried telling her more about it, she ordered him back to sleep.

What bothered him most? Her commands? His obeying them?

Or was it something else? The fact that she didn't want to hear about his nightmare?

This, of course, led to the next important question. Why hadn't she wanted to hear about it? Was it because nightmares disturbed her? Or was it possible she already knew?

Was it possible it *wasn't* a dream? That it actually *happened*?

If this wasn't a dream, if it was an actual murder, and if Vanessa knew about it, he'd been right about her all along. She had somehow turned him into some sort of helpless pawn.

The concept was both unbelievable and horrifying. For the last two days she had successfully manipulated him, controlling him as easily as changing the channel on the TV.

Had she somehow orchestrated that murder

scene? He didn't know. That was the scary thing about all this. He just didn't know.

Now she was gone. She left without a word. It was as if she had never been here.

This should have given him some sort of relief. Instead, it made him even more uneasy. The next question, the big one, cropped up immediately.

Would she come back?

***

He spent the day quietly, staring absently at the TV while listening for activity outside his front door.

Not wanting to risk another chance encounter, he deadbolted both front and rear doors, then turned off the wall phone and cell. He knew he was being silly, as well as a coward. He was a grown man— not some stupid kid with paranoia. But he *was* being paranoid, and for good reason. He was afraid of Vanessa and felt totally helpless and vulnerable in her presence. His brain refused to work properly when she was with him. So did his body. He could not let her control him any longer.

Before crossing her path again, he needed to have some sort of strategy worked out. He had to find some way of resisting, of keeping his self-control from trickling out of his body. He knew how difficult this could be, but he had no other option. If she did have the power to manipulate him, he couldn't let himself be placed in that same position. He was still struggling to decide if the old man in the white lab coat was indeed a nightmare. He sincerely hoped it was and fought down the nausea

49

each time he feared it wasn't. But if it wasn't, he had no choice but to turn himself in.

Even so, he had to face certain facts. He had no idea who the old man was, where the murder had taken place, or what had actually happened. He also had no idea how he had gotten there. He hadn't checked the Caddie upon wakening and had been forced back to sleep by Vanessa long before he'd had the chance to investigate. As a result, confessing such a fantastic, jumbled fantasy to the police could easily earn him a padded cell.

He couldn't do anything about any of this until he discovered what was happening in the first place. He had to come up with a workable plan that would get him answers. He just hoped he had enough time to do it.

He strongly feared he hadn't seen the last of Vanessa.

***

The next morning, after two strong cups of coffee, Arthur picked up the phone and made a call to Police Headquarters in Orlando.

Harry "Skip" Muldrake worked for the OPD as Programmer in their computer room. Twenty years ago, Skip and Arthur graduated from Winter Park High. After graduation they'd gone their separate ways, Arthur studying Computer Science at UCF while Skip tackled Programming at Rollins College. They hadn't seen one another until their twentieth high school reunion two months earlier, in Orlando.

"Hey, stranger," came the familiar high-pitched voice. "Guess we both made it home all right after all."

"Where the hell have *you* been? That was two months ago."

"Wow. Two whole *months*? Wow..."

Skip's deadpan, spaced-out attitude gave everyone the impression he had actually grown up in the late sixties. He always claimed his parents had met one another naked in a mud hole during the Woodstock festival.

"Aren't you gonna ask why I'm calling?"

"To tell me you got home all right?"

"Why does Orlando's Finest put up with you?"

"I'm the only guy here who knows how to fix their systems. It saves everyone the agony of trying to communicate with those weirdo techs in India. Okay, then...why the call?"

"I need your help."

"Cool."

"I need to find everything I can on a woman."

"Even cooler. A babe. She *is* a babe, right? Or is she just a regular chick? No problemo--but if she's an actual *babe*, this might take a little, well, longer than normal--"

"Will you please listen? Or do you need hosed down?"

"A possible yes to number one, and a definite maybe to number two. So go on, try telling me what this babe thing is all about."

Even though they were old chums, he feared he couldn't tell Skip his dilemma. Even someone as crazy as Skip would have trouble believing it. Arthur wasn't sure he believed it himself. But each time he visualized the body of the old man lying at his feet, he knew he had to do something, and quickly.

"Her name is Vanessa Campeon."

"Spell the last name."

"I think it's C-A-M-P-E-O-N."

"Is she French?"

"I'm not sure."

"I'll try whatever combination comes up. Tell me more."

"That's it, basically. I have no idea where she's from or even where she lives. She's in her early thirties, tall and slender, with a perfect body. Long black hair and deep-blue eyes. Long legs--"

"Whoa... A babe, all right. I have a pretty damned good idea why you want me to look her up."

"You really don't. Do it anyway."

"This isn't a sex thing?"

"Far from it."

"Did she steal from ya? Do a number on ya? Maybe a con? She a spammer? Hacker?"

"Why is that relevant?"

"It might tell me which databanks to try."

"You might as well try them all out."

"How well do you know her?"

"Not well at all."

"By the way…on a much more serious note... How are you doing? I mean, since--"

"Taking it one day at a time, thanks."

"As I told you at the reunion, whenever you need to talk, have some drinks with an old friend, anything--"

"I remember. And I appreciate it."

An awkward silence followed. Skip wasn't comfortable about such things. He needed bailed out. "Think you can find out a few things for me about my babe dilemma?"

"I'll give it helluva try."

"It's all I ask."

"Give me a few minutes." He hung up.

Arthur paced the apartment. Went back into the kitchen. Poured another cup of coffee. Went back out into the living room and sat down, sipping the coffee. Got back up, then picked up a Miles Davis CD. Got ready to slip it into the CD player.

The cell buzzed. It was Skip.

His pulse thumped. "What did you find out?"

"Not a damned thing, my friend. Let me rephrase that. I found nothing under that name."

His heart sank. "Try anything similar?"

"I checked all variations. Then I went into PeopleFinder, Social Security, DMV, Active Files, Cold Cases, FBI and all DEA sites."

"Then the name she gave me isn't her real name."

"That's one way of looking at it."

"Is there any other?"

"Sure is. The lady you're looking for doesn't exist."

***

Arthur's thoughts looped as he paced the living room.

Doesn't exist...

Vanessa was just as real as he was. He had spent two days with her, half that time in bed. She had consumed him, marked his flesh. She existed.

He had to assume the other possibility. Hell, it was simple. She hadn't given him her real name. This, of course, raised another batch of questions, most of them much more intense.

Why had she given him a false name? What was her real name? Was she a criminal? What was she trying to hide? Had she given him a false name so he wouldn't be able to track her down?

Who the hell *was* this woman?

He went over to the large, tinted window and opened the blinds. The bright, peaceful wooded setting of the complex grounds told him life went on, totally oblivious of his dilemma, and would continue, regardless of what happened or did not happen. He wanted to shut his eyes and go back three days in time, when he had gone into the local liquor store. He should have ignored her, just turned around, went down the aisle, came up the other aisle and left. He should have stayed home, then gone to the store the next day. He shouldn't have pumped gas that afternoon; he should've stayed in the condo, listening to Coltrane—or Ellington—or Basie. Most importantly, he should have stayed home that evening and not gone to the Moonglow. He kept bourbon in the cabinet; there was no reason why he had to leave the condo in the first place.

This was ridiculous. He was a grown man, not a child. Wanting to be somewhere else, or go back three days to retrace his steps, was asinine. He couldn't barricade himself like a frightened child. Sure, he still mourned Denise, and sure, he still craved his privacy…but he had to stop feeling sorry for himself. And he had to start thinking rationally.

He decided to check out the local news. If he was right about that nightmare being real, the old man's body should have been discovered by now. It had been two days. An investigation would have already begun. Unless the old man's relatives hadn't been notified, the story would be aired.

But what if it wasn't reported? What if there was no word of the incident?

Did that mean it really *was* a nightmare? That it hadn't happened?

He picked up the remote and with a shaky hand turned on the widescreen, flicking the channels until he found the local news stations. He tried three but had no luck. The first station was reporting a plan by one of the theme parks to announce a twenty percent price hike. The second had fallen victim to a long commercial break. The third came back from its break, hinted what would be run next, then went right back to another break. He returned to the second, which was still showing commercials.

Frustrated, he flicked off the set and went down the hall, into the spare room, where he kept his computer. He brought up the *Sentinel's* web page, checking the long list of key stories and articles showing up during the last twenty-four hours. Two murders headed the list, but neither fit the scenario. The rest dealt with drug dealers, meth labs, three child molestations, six car thefts, a couple of carjackings, and a short list of convicted murderers being released early due to overcrowding.

The fact that he could find nothing about the old man's murder suggested one of three distinct possibilities. First of all, he'd dreamed it. Secondly, no one had discovered the body. Thirdly, the murder had indeed occurred, but whoever discovered the body had decided not to tell anyone.

He sat back in the chair and rubbed his temples. He didn't know what frightened him more, finding out that the strange woman calling herself Vanessa Campeon didn't exist, or that the corpse he'd seen in a nightmare might not have been a nightmare after all.

***

After more than an hour of agonizing, he decided to consult a professional.

With the help of a highly qualified hypnotist, he might be able to recall every single detail that had taken place in the last three days.

The manager of the condominium complex was a tall, slender blond lady in her mid-forties named Rhonda Silverstone. He had talked to her on several occasions and learned that she knew just about everyone in the complex. She was always well-groomed, dressed in tailor-fitted, expensive clothes, hair and makeup perfect, nails professionally done. She had been divorced three times, and her last husband was some sort of developer who owned several large parcels of Central Florida land.

Mindful of the cuts on his lower back, he took a shower, shaved, then dried and combed his hair. He dressed casually--shorts, tee shirt, and tennies--and splashed his cheeks with cologne. He didn't want to look like a bum, and certainly didn't want to give her a bad impression. Before leaving his condo, he peered through the front blinds. No sign of the white Lexus. No sign of Vanessa, either. His nerves tingled as he unlocked the deadbolt and slid the chain off the runner.

He crossed the pool area, making his way for the complex office on the other side of the courtyard. A few oldsters relaxed on inflatable rafts in the shallow end of the pool,. Two others sat beneath an umbrella, playing canasta. They didn't look up as he walked by. Neither did the three gray-haired women coming out of the laundry room next to the door marked *PARTY ROOM.*

He stepped up to the door marked *OFFICE* and knocked.

"Yes?" from inside.

He opened the door a few inches. Rhonda sat at her desk, smiling up at him. As usual, she looked like she had just come from the beauty salon. "Mr. Sills? C'mon in."

He went in and approached her desk, one cautious step at a time. He knew he shouldn't be nervous; he just couldn't help it. If this went wrong, the woman might think he was a nutcase. She knew a lot of people; the word would be out in a heartbeat.

She sat back. "I haven't seen you in quite a while. What brings you here?"

He knew to tread lightly. Since most therapists

were also trained in hypnosis, he decided to go that route. "Therapist" sounded much safer and less ominous than "hypnotist". Rhonda's social circle included a lot of people. She dined out often and went to many functions and conventions her ex-husband's company sponsored. And since she also spent a fortune on her hair and nails, this widened her circle even more. He suspected she must have come across a therapist or two in her activities.

"Um, this is kind of awkward..."

"Please. Sit down." She leaned forward, resting her tanned forearms on the green desk blotter. Each slender wrist held several silver bracelets. She wore three rings on each hand. A couple of them were made with diamonds, one with sapphires. Her nails looked superb. "Tell me what's going on. Does it involve the Association?"

"No. Not really."

"Then how can I help--"

"Where do you do your nails?"

She held them up and studied them, then showed them to him. This week they were a pale blue, with tiny silver stars painted in the center of each. He guessed they had been painted this way to match her bracelets. "At Josie's, where I've been doing them for the last five years. Why? Would you like her to do yours?"

"Not exactly..."

Her cultured brows bumped together. "What's this all about?"

"I need to talk to someone."

"About your nails?"

"My head's my present problem."

Her eyes raised to his forehead. She almost smiled. "What's wrong with it?"

He knew to be as vague as possible. "Not getting enough sleep lately, I think."

She shook her head. "You poor man. This is about...your poor wife, I take it. I understand, believe me. My first husband, he--"

"Know any therapists?"

She stopped talking and stared at him. Obviously wondering what he was talking about. "What does this have to do with Josie?"

"Just a wild guess. She does nails, so I thought she might have run across one or two--"

"Why didn't you just ask me if I knew one?"

He shifted uncomfortably, getting ready for the lie. "I guess I figured that if I asked you, you'd think maybe I'd think you were mental or something."

She laughed. "You're right! I really would've." She laughed again, then turned serious, thinking about it, considering. "I'll bet she might know one or two. And she has been having problems lately. Her husband's messing around with his secretary— or so she thinks. He keeps insisting he isn't, but Josie's convinced he is. One of her girls has got this aunt in Russia who wants to live in America and wants Josie's husband to talk to Immigration about it, since he's got a cousin working there. Josie's having problems with her daughter, too. She's addicted to cocaine and has left Rehab three times--"

"Wow." He knew he was the one who had opened the floodgates, but he really was in no mood for all this. "I take it Josie could help me, then?"

"I'm sure she can give me a name. Even if she doesn't use one herself, one of her clients probably does. Some really strange women go there." Rhonda reached for her tan leather handbag, opened it, and removed her cell. "Why don't I call and ask her?"

***

The man's name was R.L. Tannenbaum, PSYD, and he'd been handling a friend and client of Josie's for over a year.

He charged three hundred bucks an hour and came highly recommended. Three hundred bucks was a lot of money--especially for an hour, which shrunk to fifty minutes on any shrink's watch—but Arthur knew he had to find out about this and needed quick results. He didn't think he'd need much more than one or two consultations. If Tannenbaum could perform hypnosis on him and help him retrieve his memory, he'd soon discover what sort of madness he faced. If Tannenbaum didn't agree to his terms, Arthur would have to look elsewhere. It would take time, but he didn't have much of a choice.

At least Tannenbaum had agreed to fit him into his schedule. His secretary had mentioned a last-minute cancellation, and that the doc would be happy to see Arthur at one o'clock this afternoon.

He parked in the multi-level garage across the street from the Sun Trust Building on Robinson, where Tannenbaum kept his first-floor office.

Arthur had gotten there early and decided to take a few minutes to arrange his thoughts before getting out of the car. He wanted to have the particulars clear in his mind and didn't want to waste anyone's time.

He sat back in the comfortable leather seat of the Caddie and began thinking of some story that would sound reasonable to a shrink. He could fabricate some nonsense about Vanessa, telling him they'd had a row the night before, in her office. Her father came in to see what the yelling was all about. Arthur hadn't appreciated the interruption and said some things he shouldn't have. Her father said some nasty things to him in return before stomping off. Arthur felt badly about this. It had not only caused a rift with his future father-in-law, but with Vanessa as well. Arthur's rage had clouded his memory of the event, and he wanted to relive the argument moment by moment to determine if he could have done something different to keep his temper in check.

He had read that a person could not do anything under hypnosis that he wouldn't do normally. He had never been hypnotized before and had no idea what to expect. He just hoped he wouldn't incriminate himself while under hypnotic suggestion. If he could do this the right way, he might...that is, if he...maybe if he just relaxed...relaxed for just a moment, and--

Relax...and close your eyes...and sit like this for a little while...and just relax...and think of quiet meadows...and...and--

His eyes shot open.

Had he blacked out again?

Unlikely. He was still sitting in the Caddie. He might have closed his eyes for just a moment, to relax and gather his thoughts...but there was no way he'd blacked out again.

He glanced at the dashboard clock. 1:48. Damn. His appointment had been for 1:00! He'd left the condo at 11:55. Even with heavy lunch hour traffic, he had plenty of time to cover the few miles to the downtown area.

How the hell had he skipped nearly a full hour without even knowing it? He'd only closed his eyes for a moment or two.

Hadn't he?

He leaped from the Caddie and ran down the ramp, to the exit, racing across the street and dashing down the cobblestone path that led to the front entrance of the building. Once he reached the heavy glass doors, he yanked open a door and went inside. Then took two steps into the dark, air-conditioned lobby and stopped cold.

A crowd had swarmed the hall leading to the offices toward the back, where Tannenbaum's office was located. He took a few slow, uneasy steps, stopping when a small army of blue uniforms appeared, blocking the archway.

A lump formed in his throat. His gut began throbbing. His back tingled. He was being paranoid again. Whatever this was, it had nothing to do with him. It couldn't have. He'd been sitting in his car, thinking, planning a strategy.

He took a deep breath and cleared his throat. "What's happening?" he asked no one in particular, hoping no one would hear him.

Standing at the rear of a small group of men in business suits, a tall, skinny young guy in a neatly pressed dark suit gave him a grim look. "Just heard there was a murder in room one-twenty-eight."

The tingling in his back became a heavy throbbing. One-twenty-eight. Wasn't that the room number in question? Or was he hallucinating? The scrap of paper Rhonda had given him...he had shoved it down his pants pocket. The room number was scribbled on it. All he had to do was pull it out and open it.

He made a move to reach into his pocket. His hand froze. The inside of his mouth had become warm and as dry as a wad of cotton. "Who was murdered?" He barely heard his own voice.

Another guy in a suit said, "Tannenbaum, I think his name was."

Chapter 5

The drive back to Winter Park was smothered in a cold, thick darkness.

Harsh reality returned only as he eased into his palmetto-lined parking space in front of the familiar one-story tan stucco building. He didn't remember anything about the trip back. He couldn't even vaguely recall what he'd done after hearing the man's name

("Tannenbaum, I think his name was")

uttered from the lobby of the Sun Trust Building.

Had he suffered another blackout? Or was this one of those fugue states one suffers after doing something despicable, then refuses to accept it and loses all sense of reality by retreating into the deepest recesses of his mind?

How could he have done something so despicable?

Tannenbaum was apparently murdered while Arthur sat in the Caddie, organizing his thoughts. At least, he *thought* he was organizing his thoughts. There was that nagging shred of doubt hovering close by, telling him that he had blacked out again. That second or two when he closed his eyes to concentrate and experienced that same modicum of helplessness and vulnerability he felt several times before, when dealing with Vanessa. Or those first few horrible months following Denise's death. Last of all, there was the matter of that lost hour he

64

couldn't explain.

Had he blacked out during this time and murdered the man, as he'd murdered the old man in the white lab coat?

Things were making even less sense. The old man's murder was the product of a nightmare. It didn't happen. Besides, he was no killer, had never in his life entertained the notion of killing anyone. He had spent his entire life playing by the rules, avoiding trouble, and tending to his own business. Why suddenly change at this point? And how could he change without even realizing it?

This was getting more baffling by the minute. Was he still under Vanessa's spell? Was Vanessa behind all this madness?

If Vanessa wasn't, who the hell *was*?

***

He went inside and headed straight to the kitchen cabinet, where he kept his whiskey.

He found a clean glass and splashed a couple of inches of Kentucky bourbon into the glass. Once the fiery liquid settled in his limbs and warmed his gut, he decided to call OPD and tell them he was the one who murdered Tannenbaum.

He saw no other way out of this. If he *had* murdered the doctor, he couldn't live with himself. Even if he hadn't, he still felt somewhat responsible. The man had obviously been practicing for years. The fact that he should die an hour after Arthur had called for an appointment was entirely too coincidental.

Living with the uncertainty of all this was more

than he could take. Even worse was the nagging fear that he was no longer in control. A strange woman had entered his life. He didn't know if this had anything to do with his grieving for Denise, or if Vanessa was indeed some sort of witch. The fact remained: he could no longer live like this.

His fingers shook as he picked up the phone. It took several tries to dial the number. His hand trembled as he held it against his ear. He cleared his throat and hoped his voice would function.

"Orlando Police Department," said the low-pitched male voice on the other end of the line. "How may I direct your call?"

A warm, gooey lump filled his throat. The phone jumped in his hand and nearly dropped to the floor. He grabbed it and held it at arm's length--as if trying to hold on to a large fish fighting to squirm out of his grasp.

He hung up quickly and stared at the receiver, half-expecting it to jump out of its nook and smack him in the face. He stared at his hands and wondered if they would ever stop shaking. Had he been responsible for his nerves going all funny, for turning the simple act of using the phone into something as complicated as open-heart surgery? Or had Vanessa somehow envisioned what he was doing and, in her own frightening, supernatural way, forced him to hang up?

He lowered his butt to a barstool and sighed deeply. This was ridiculous. He was giving her entirely too much credit. Even if she were a witch, she couldn't possibly see what he was doing right now. He was nervous, scared, and frustrated. His hands shook. He could hardly talk because of the lump in his throat. Vanessa hadn't done *any* of that.

He knew he'd go crazy if he agonized about this much longer. He had to somehow free himself of Vanessa's control and do what was necessary. If he were incapable of using the phone, he'd have to drive to OPD and report the murder in person.

He slipped off the stool and was immediately engulfed in a wave of dizziness. He sat back down and stared at the empty glass sitting on the counter in front of him. Getting on the roads after having a strong drink would turn horrendous if he were pulled over or involved in an accident.

He rubbed his eyes and told himself he could do this. He wasn't drunk; he'd had one small drink. He could operate a car. He'd stay with the flow and be extremely careful. He was a cautious driver. No accidents, no speeding tickets. He could easily handle the twenty-minute drive to the Police Station.

He got back up—slowly, this time—and just stood there, leaning against the counter. No dizziness. Good. He went back into the kitchen, opened a drawer, took out a tin of Altoids and popped one into his mouth. The minty flavor instantly opened up his taste buds and started working on the whiskey residue. Once he decided he was ready to leave, he crossed the room and opened the door.

Luckily, traffic wasn't bad. It was at least a full hour before evening rush, and the trip down

Semoran was a snap. He turned right onto Colonial and went west. The drive continued pleasantly for the next two miles.

Just before he reached Maguire Boulevard, the flashing lights of a police cruiser came from out of nowhere. In seconds they were right behind him. The driver stuck his blue-sleeved arm out his window and jabbed an index finger to their right, at a large parking lot between buildings, as they passed the main intersection.

His nerves twitched and jumped, making the simple task of switching on his blinkers much more complicated than he could ever remember. He managed, but his head turned hot as he eased off the main drag.

**

He parked in a vacant space in the rear of the small, paved lot, facing Colonial, the cruiser stopping about ten feet behind him.

Two cops got out and crept cautiously toward the car. Both were tall and broad-shouldered, and probably went well over two hundred pounds, not much of it fat. They both wore red-tinted sunglasses and kept their hands close to the oversized grips of their holstered Glocks.

The cop riding shotgun was dark, with a neatly trimmed black mustache. He stopped about five feet from the rear bumper of the Caddie, two or three feet off to the side, and took down the plate number.

The driver approached Arthur's door. About thirty, he was fair-skinned and clean-shaven, with a thick columnar neck. Judging by the light reddish stubble extending from his service cap, Arthur guessed he had blue eyes. His nametag said *Collins*. He gestured for Arthur to roll down the window.

"Driver's license and registration." His voice sounded flat, bored.

For a moment Arthur had forgotten where he kept his wallet. He took a deep breath and struggled to collect himself. His brain was swimming with dark, abysmal images of prison life, but he told himself he had nothing to worry about. This was just a minor traffic stop, and they'd probably let him off with a warning. He reached for his back pocket, but the seat belt prevented him from getting to it. He glanced up at the cop and pointed to the buckle. The cop said nothing. Arthur unbuckled, then twisted in the seat to pull out the wallet. It took forever to find what the cop had asked for, but he forced himself once again to snap out of it. He hadn't done anything wrong. He shouldn't feel guilty and shouldn't be so damned frightened.

As he pulled out the cards, several others spilled out, dropping in his lap. He handed the cop the license and registration, picked up what he'd dropped, and stuffed them back in the wallet. The cop had already gone back to his cruiser to check the ID. Arthur wanted to ask him the purpose of the traffic stop but knew better. Best say nothing when you've got the smell of booze on your breath, however faint.

The cop came back about two minutes later and gave Arthur back the license and registration. "Know why you were stopped?"

Arthur put the cards back and shook his head. "Illegal lane change."

He hadn't changed lanes since he'd pulled onto Colonial but knew better than argue. All he wanted was to get through this so he could drive to OPD and tell them his story. He didn't want to be brought in because of something stupid and risk the chance that someone had spotted him with Tannenbaum and called it in. He was confident neither had heard anything. The cop hadn't pulled out his gun when he came back from his cruiser. Even so, Arthur didn't want to take any chances. He decided to keep quiet and wait.

The cop pulled his book out, opened it, and began writing a ticket. So much for a simple warning. "Nothing to say in your defense?"

"Not if you saw me do something illegal."

He stopped scribbling and bent forward, toward the driver's window. "Do I smell alcohol on your breath?"

So much for popping that Altoid. His heart rate accelerated. *Calm down. Tell him the truth. Cops hate when you lie to them.*

He sighed. "I had a drink about half an hour ago."

"Just one?"

"Just one."

The cop snapped his book shut and straightened abruptly. "Get out of the car."

Arthur froze.

"Out! Now!" He backed up, curling his thick fingers around the butt of his Glock. His partner had already circled the rear of the Caddie.

***

Neither cop spoke as they drove in the heavy late afternoon traffic.

Arthur expected them to call in the arrest, but neither did. It made him wonder if the guy riding shotgun had done it while the driver cuffed him. Arthur hadn't seen him use his radio but could have done it while Arthur was getting out of the car.

He sat stiffly in the back seat, staring at the backs of their heads through the heavy black mesh cage. The seat was hard and uncomfortable as well as slippery, and smelled foul and musty. He could only imagine what others had done on this very seat. The awkwardness of the handcuffs affected his balance, causing him to slide as they took the sharp left onto Orange Avenue. This cramped position had caused a sharp tingling in his lower back.

The cops hadn't given him a breathalyzer test, which made him suspicious. As far as he knew, such a test was standard procedure for a DUI stop. He had never been arrested before but had seen enough reality cop shows to know the drill. Unless a DUI suspect had physically assaulted the cop, he couldn't be arrested if the results of the breathalyzer weren't positive. Many stops even included a simple coordination test, where the suspect was told to touch his nose alternately with his index fingers, walk in a straight line, or stand with one foot extended. He hadn't been given any of these tests; he was merely cuffed and shoved into the back seat of the cruiser.

71

"Can I ask you gentlemen a question?"

No reply. They didn't even turn in his direction.

"Why didn't you give me a breathalyzer test?"

Still no response. They obviously didn't want to chat.

Something was very wrong. He'd been singled out of all the traffic on Colonial and stopped for some trivial traffic offense he hadn't even been guilty of. To top it off, the cop had smelled booze on his breath, ordered him out of the car, then cuffed and shoved him into the back without any physical test.

Were these actual cops? Or was his imagination going nutso again?

He had to keep the panic away. He closed his eyes and forced himself to stay calm.

Fear sliced through him, and he forced his eyes open. What if he blacked out again? What if he woke up later on to find himself standing over the bodies of these two cops? What if they were actually real cops? Would he be able to dump them in the trunk, drive to the Police Station and report their murders, as well as the murders of Dr. Tannenbaum and the old man in the white lab coat?

Four murders? Two of them cops? He wouldn't even make it to trial.

The cop riding shotgun was talking on his cell. He spoke softly, then hung up and turned to the driver. "East Robinson."

The driver said nothing.

The fear had made Arthur's arms go numb. He now suspected he was in the company of two men who were not real cops. The Police Station was definitely not located on East Robinson.

His inner fear growing, he eyed the door to his left. The handle and door lock were missing. The rear doors of police cars were obviously so designed to prevent them from being opened from the inside. The wire mesh was another no-brainer. So was the electronic equipment on the console between the front seats, as well as the single-barrel pump shotgun with pistol-grip clamped to the dash. This was definitely a legitimate cop car. But this didn't mean they were legitimate cops.

He couldn't open the door, but he could try to break out the window. Even if he failed, such an effort would attract attention and possibly cause an accident. In this case, an accident would benefit him the most. He stood a much better chance of surviving if people saw him.

The window was undoubtedly constructed of double-strength safety glass, but he might be able to break through it with a couple of good, strong kicks. He was confident his adrenaline would help him out as well. But he'd have to do it quickly. In this heavy traffic, it would take the driver precious seconds before he could safely pull over and react to the disturbance.

They stopped behind a long line at the red light. Arthur shifted a little on the seat so he could roll onto his back. He wanted the car to be moving at a fair clip when he tried kicking out the window. This would be a suicide move, but he had no other choice. His chances of survival were slim anyway.

He had no idea why any of this was happening or who was behind it, but he didn't have the luxury of trying to figure it out right now. If he were being taken somewhere to be killed, it would have to be on his terms.

The light changed. They began moving again.

Keeping with the flow, the driver stepped it up to about forty miles an hour. Arthur knew Orange Avenue well. It was riddled with lights and intersections. They'd be slowing down for another traffic light in no time at all. It was now or never.

Gritting his teeth and taking a deep breath, he rolled onto the seat, brought his legs up and back, and--

Everything turned black. . .

Chapter 6

Whispers...

He drifted back into consciousness but made no attempt to move or open his eyes. He feared something bad would happen if anyone knew he was awake.

Without moving around, he could tell he was in an armchair with the padded back reclined at about a sixty-degree angle. The arms were wide and also padded. Someone standing beside him held his wrist. The hand was fairly large and cold, with long nails. A woman's hand. A strong whiff of lavender brushed his nostrils.

Despite his overwhelming curiosity, he fought down the urge to open his eyes. He knew he'd be safer this way.

"Still?" a man's voice whispered from the other side of the chair.

The pressure on Arthur's wrist disappeared. "It's slightly erratic, but still in the relaxed mode." It was Vanessa's voice.

"He hasn't been functioning properly lately."

"I'm aware of that."

"He was actually going to--"

"I saw the log."

"Then you must agree what we've got to do."

"I think we should wait. They haven't finished evaluating."

Evaluating? Log? What the hell were they talking about?

"There isn't much time. If he comes to in the next few minutes--"

"The doctor is scheduled to be here shortly."

"And if the subject awakens early?"

Subject? It had become agonizingly difficult to keep his eyes shut.

"I have what I need."

"I've got to go, then. Are you all right here by yourself?"

"I'm quite capable of handling him."

The man's footsteps shuffled away quickly. Arthur counted five steps, which translated into roughly twelve or thirteen feet for the average-sized man. A door closed, clicking softly.

Vanessa moved away, her high heels clicking sharply. The floor sounded like metal. She took four steps and stopped. Ten feet, perhaps? A buzzing sound. A cell phone? Vanessa's whisper: "Yes. No, he just left. Now? I really don't want to risk it. He might--" Pause. A sigh. "I'll administer a very small dose, then meet everyone upstairs." The cell phone snapped shut.

Administer? A very small dose?

His pulse hammered.

Vanessa's heels clicked again, twice, then stopped. Still a safe distance away. Cautiously he opened his right eye halfway and turned his head no more than two inches.

A dimly lit room. A large metal desk sat about ten feet off to the right. Vanessa, in a white lab coat, crouched behind it, filling a hypodermic. Her right side faced him. Her bent position caused her hair to

76

fan out in front of her, obscuring her view of him.

You have to do something! his inner voice screamed at him.

Vanessa set the vial down, tapped the needle, and came back.

He closed his eye, turned his head, and waited tensely, hoping she wouldn't hear the heavy thumping of his heart. She gently grabbed his wrist, turning it so his hand was palm-upward. Just as she applied the cold wet cotton to his skin, he opened his eyes. The needle, just inches away, moved deliberately toward his forearm.

Panic flicked a switch, forcing him into automatic survival. His left hand shot out, grabbing a handful of hair. He tugged viciously, pulling her head down and causing her to smack her forehead against the edge of the padded chair arm. Her head jerked back. The hypodermic flew from her grasp, plinked to the floor, and rolled toward the desk.

With a tiny gasp, she collapsed to the floor.

***

Arthur forced himself out of the chair.

A hot, slicing pain in his lower back riveted through him, and he fell back into the seat. His spine flaring up again. And, of course, at the worst possible moment. He could worry about that later.

He forced himself out of the chair again, this time more gently, and dropped to his knees to examine his work. Vanessa didn't move, didn't even flinch. She was definitely out cold. He'd never hit a woman before but felt this was justified. She was going to give him an injection; he suspected he'd be knocked out for some time. He had no idea what all this was about. Judging by what had already happened, he didn't want to stick around and wait for an explanation.

He crept over to the door. His heart thrashed loudly as he eased it open.

No sounds outside the room. He coaxed it open a few more inches and stuck his head through.

A long, poorly lit hall. Small domed ceiling lights spaced at wide intervals dusted the paneled walls and dark matted floor with a dull golden haze. An *EXIT* sign beamed over a door at the end of the hall, on his left.

He had to move quickly. Once Vanessa awoke, she would make an emergency call and this area would no doubt be swarming with people.

He closed the door, rushed back into the room, and knelt beside her. She still hadn't budged. The blow to her forehead had already produced a nasty welt in its center. He found her cell in the front pocket of her lab coat and shoved it down his pants pocket. A shiny plastic ID badge hung from her lapel. It provided a frontal color photo of Vanessa, a name, V. DeAngelis, and a twelve-digit number. On the opposite side of the card, a bar code showed up faintly in black at the bottom. He took that as well.

He watched her for another twenty seconds. She still didn't budge. He went back to the door and peered out into the hall.

Despite the pain in his lower back, he managed a fairly fast clip, and reached the *EXIT* door in no time. On the other side of the tiny square window, a small alcove lined with filing cabinets led to two separate doorways. He saw no one moving about.

Beside the door, a black card-reader about six inches square jutted out an inch or so from the wall. In its center, a tiny red dot appeared momentarily, pulsing at around one beat per second. His hand shook as he held Vanessa's card in front of the reader. The sudden click made him jump. The door latch released a split second later. He eased it open.

The small area smelled of stale coffee, cologne, and a faint reek of cigarette smoke. He crept over to the doorways and stopped. The quiet clicking of someone's keyboard echoed from the doorway on his left. He slipped silently through the one on the right and immediately found himself staring at a man's large bald head.

The man sat at a guard's desk, his head lowered. In front of him, five monitors displayed several different areas, each shifting to a different section of each area every five seconds. One monitored the parking lot fronting a long brick building—first at one corner, then the opposite. The second surveyed each end of the rear lot, where twenty or so dark vehicles sat, surrounded by trees. The third covered both ends of the two side lots. The fourth was split into four separate screens, each watching a small section of a dimly lit laboratory. Three figures in white coats hunkered over a table. Their backs faced the cameras.

The fifth monitor showed Vanessa lying in full view beside the chair in the small semi-dark room Arthur had woken in. She still hadn't stirred.

Good thing the guard was napping. Otherwise, he would have already made his call. Hopefully, no one else monitored the screens.

The only way out was to slip past the guard. This area looked like the sort of station one encountered upon entering a building. With luck, the main exit would be on the other side of the doorway.

What if the guard awoke? How long would it be before he alerted Security? Five seconds? Ten? What if he decided to deal with their intruder himself? Did he have a gun? Pepper spray? A taser?

A soft, almost inaudible snore.

Arthur moved closer. When he was about three feet away, he peered around the guard. He was in luck; the man was fast asleep. Arthur crept quietly past the desk, through another open doorway, and out into a small, deserted lobby.

A revolving door served as the front entrance. A card reader was attached to the wall beside it. He applied Vanessa's card and hurried outside. Mindful of the two security cameras, he kept close to the building, head down, marching steadily toward the paved two-lane road that led down a palmetto-lined path to the paved road a hundred yards or so from the building entrance.

He didn't stop, look back, or start breathing again until he was within running distance of the road.

***

At the end of the long, winding drive, the main highway went straight.

Arthur saw no reason to turn around and waste time trying to make a mental picture of the setting. There were no signs or landmarks, and the thick foliage hid the building from view of the main road.

He had to make tracks. It wouldn't be long before people stormed out of the building, looking for him. He was tired and scared, his lower back had flared up again, and he needed a drink. His watch said it was just a few minutes before seven, which meant the bulk of the rush hour had ended. Since it was still the dinner hour, he wouldn't see much traffic.

Though he had no idea where he was, he could tell by the position of the sunset that he was heading south. He had lived in Central Florida nearly all his life but could never keep up with its constant growth. As far as he knew, he had never been on this road before. The huge palmettos, pine forest, overgrown brush, and scrub oaks conveyed no sense of familiarity. This was obviously an older section that hadn't yet been selected for development. He saw no turnoffs or rooftops mixed in with the thick foliage.

Florida roads generally all looked alike. Most ran straight and were lined with endless subdivisions in highly developed areas and overgrown brush in undeveloped ones. The Florida Highway System complicated things even more by not marking the roads properly. He expected to cover quite a bit of ground before getting his bearings.

As he continued his brisk gait, he kept his ears

pricked for sounds of vehicles slowing down behind him. He wouldn't need much advanced warning. The lush growth choking the highway would enable him to slip into the woods and disappear.

A wave of dizziness hit him, and he stopped moving. About ten seconds later, it ebbed quietly into nothingness. A tingle flared in his lower back and raced up his spine, reaching his shoulder blades, where it became a stabbing pain. He gritted his teeth and forced himself to ride it out. Fortunately, it only lasted a few seconds.

He considered using Vanessa's cell to call for a cab, but after further thought, dismissed that possibility. You can't call for a cab if you're unable to provide an address.

Two vehicles heading north passed at a fast clip. He edged over to the shoulder and waited tensely, making sure they didn't slow down or stop. They kept on, disappearing on the other side of the hill. The growing pain in his lower back had turned into a heavy throbbing. He was going to have to rest very shortly.

About five minutes later, the low-pitched groan of an approaching vehicle not far behind echoed through the trees. The sound of it downshifting sent a blinding wave of terror shimmering through him. Without pause, he veered off the road. He was amazed he didn't stumble or trip as he disappeared into the heavy brush.

The vehicle continued its approach. Arthur moved even deeper into the woods, carefully avoiding deadfalls and other dangerous obstacles.

Luckily, it was still light enough to distinguish the many shapes in the woods. But it wouldn't be long before the approaching darkness would make it impossible for him to move about.

He hurried down a leaf-covered slope for another forty feet and stopped at the foot of a tall pine. He was shivering, sweaty, and out of breath, but forced himself to keep quiet. To catch his breath, he leaned against the tree and waited.

The vehicle pulled off the road and stopped. Seconds later, heavy silence followed as the engine was switched off.

The sounds of doors slamming shut made his heart pound deafeningly.

***

Voices drifted down the path. One sounded like a woman.

Vanessa? It was a definite possibility. Knowing her as he did, she'd want to get her claws on him for what he did to her.

Careful to avoid jutting roots, he circled the base of the thick pine, pressing his back against it. The sound of crunching dead leaves and snapping twigs coming from the direction of the road made the hair stand up on the back of his neck. Warily he peered around the trunk of the tree. The woods were thick with brush and tangles of vines and low-hanging limbs, but he could see movement among the trees. The figure was tall and broad-shouldered, and wearing a dark uniform—probably a guard. He held something in his hands and was pointing it straight out.

Some sort of tracking device?

Arthur backed up. Moving silently, he maintained a straight line from the base of the tree so he could not be seen. Once he had reached a respectable distance, he turned around. A group of scrubs blocked his path. He veered around them and, crouching behind the largest scrub, peered around the twisted trunk. The tall figure kept coming.

Vanessa's phone. The damned thing was equipped with a GPS. No wonder they could track him so easily...

He pulled it out of his pocket and placed it very gently on a pile of dead leaves. The guard kept coming. He was now about fifty feet away. Luckily, he'd come alone. Vanessa and the others were probably back at the vehicle, waiting for his signal.

A broken limb lay half-hidden in a mound of pine needles about ten feet away. He carefully pulled it out. It was about two feet long, three inches thick, and fairly sturdy. He veered left, ducking behind a pine just a few yards from the cell.

The guard cautiously crept around the scrubs. He didn't pause at all, just kept moving until he stepped on the phone. Startled, he jerked back and gawked at it. He looked around, then lowered his head and stared at it again. Then he consulted his tracker and turned toward his right, in Arthur's direction.

What the hell?

Keeping the tracker pointed straight out, the guard bent to pick up the cell.

84

Before the guard could straighten, Arthur leaped around the base of the pine and brought the club brutally down, onto the center of the man's shaved skull. He went down quickly, landing with a soft thump on a bed of pine needles.

Arthur did a quick scan of the area. He saw no one, heard no one. Confident the others weren't close, he picked up the guard's tracker and pointed it at himself. It began beeping very rapidly. Damn. How the hell was it programmed?

He switched it off and hurried away, making a big circle, dodging trees and hanging vines and making sure he was never out in the open.

He had two choices. He could sneak up on them and try to overpower them, or simply wait them out. He had no idea if they had more than one tracking device. If they did, they'd find him again.

Since it was getting dark, he'd have to move through the thick brush even more carefully. He couldn't risk twisting an ankle or tripping. It took him ten minutes, but he finally reached the area where the road came into view just beyond the tree line.

The dark sedan was parked off the road about a hundred yards to his left. From this distance, he couldn't tell if anyone was in it. If they decided to help with the search, they'd also be in the woods. If not, they would be waiting in the sedan.

Briefly he considered using the tracking device as a weapon. He decided right off that it was a foolish idea. He felt much more vulnerable carrying it, and tossed it in the culvert, then crossed the road and slipped into the brush. He moved quickly, keeping his eye on the sedan and the area around it. He saw no one.

Keeping low, he crept up to the sedan. The side windows were darkly tinted, concealing the interior. He moved closer, his nerves quivering as he peered inside. The keys dangled from the ignition. No one was sitting in front or in back.

He carefully opened the driver's door, slipped inside, closed it quietly, and started up the ignition.

The car, thank God, had tremendous pick-up. He mashed down on the gas and glanced at the rearview mirror. Two figures had emerged from the woods and gathered in the middle of the road, watching him.

Vanessa was one of them.

Chapter 7

Keeping the sedan at around seventy, he soared down the two-lane country road, hoping he wouldn't encounter any cops on patrol.

His last encounter with them had not been pleasant. Vanessa and her people obviously had enough money and clout to buy a couple of bad cops and have them bring him here.

Vanessa and her people. That very phrase brought about a flurry of chills racing down his back. Now that he knew she was actually a *part* of something, and not just a strange woman with frightening powers, this situation had taken on an entirely different flavor.

They tracked him. All the way into the woods. Even after he ditched Vanessa's phone, the guard still tracked him...

He accelerated to seventy-five. Luckily, he passed no traffic.

Vanessa had probably already replaced her phone. Even if she hadn't, her companion would have one and had already called their associates, made a report, and asked to be picked up. It wouldn't be long before someone else came after him.

Retrieving the sedan would not be difficult. It would no doubt be equipped with LoJack. They could disable the car at any time with one phone call. Within seconds, the car would ease to a stop and go completely dead. He would be trapped inside.

As a precaution, he rolled down the windows. He didn't know if their system would automatically roll them back up, or if they were made of heavy-duty glass. He couldn't afford to take chances.

He accelerated to eighty. Still no other traffic.

He had to make it to civilization before they switched him off. He tried to recall how long it had been since he stole the car. Two minutes? Five? He'd come maybe four miles. That put it at around three minutes. It would take them a couple of minutes to make their call and have the appropriate person get the LoJack system working. It also depended on who they called. If they contacted Security, the process would be short and sweet, and the car would have already died. If they tried one of their cronies, it might take longer. He sincerely hoped they would call the main desk. It would take the sleeping guard precious moments to wake up and get his brain working.

Two miles later, the woods abruptly ended. Rooftops began showing behind the overgrown brush on both sides of the road. His heart leaped. A red light less than a quarter of a mile straight ahead warned him of an intersection.

As he drew closer, he guessed the highway was Colonial Drive, but he couldn't be sure. Thirty seconds more and he could merge right and blend in with the heavy traffic. He might even have time to ditch the car and disappear inside one of the restaurants, bars, or--

The gas pedal went dead beneath his foot.

The car began slowing down, and the dash lights dimmed.

His heart pounded wildly as he coaxed the car off the road and let it come to a stop in the grass. As soon as he pulled over, the steering wheel locked, and the brakes went dead.

He tried the door. Sure enough, it was locked. He climbed out through the window just as it began sliding back up. When his feet hit the ground, the stabbing pain in his lower back flared up again. *Not now, dammit. I don't have time for this.*

He moved away from the sedan.

***

The bright lights of a 7-Eleven lit up the night about a hundred yards away, on the other side of the trimmed bushes.

Six vehicles sat in front of the store. Was it possible someone had left the keys in one of them?

The brilliant lights inside as well as the large spots illuminating the parking lot prevented him from getting closer without arousing suspicion. The cash register was situated just a few feet inside the front door. Someone inside would easily see him snooping about.

Two kids around seven or eight years old wrestled with one another in the back seat of a maroon SUV. An elderly lady sat in the passenger seat of an ancient light-blue Dodge Escort, watching the store activity. Two beat-up Ford pickups sat on the other side of the Escort. Both were covered with NRA stickers, their beds crammed with livestock feed, fence posts, and loose rolls of rusty barbed wire. The huge round head of a large dog—possibly a pit bull—sitting in the back seat of one of them discouraged him from getting closer.

Someone sat in the passenger seat of a white Corvette parked at the far end, smoking a cigarette. Between it and one of the pickups, a long-haired female sat behind the wheel of a black Camaro, nibbling a burrito.

He decided to cross the lot and hitch a ride farther down. All sorts of eateries and bars lined the stretch heading west. He didn't think he'd have much of a problem arousing pity in someone.

But while he was here, he needed to get something to eat. He was famished as well as exhausted and would faint if he didn't soon put something in his stomach.

Before he could reach the glass doors, his back flared up again. The exhaustion came right back with it. He leaned against the ice machine and urged his body to recover, and quickly.

"Are you all right, young man?" The lady in the Escort had stuck her head out her window.

"Yes, ma'am." He forced out a smile. "Just tired, is all. I've been...running around too much lately, I guess."

"You need to take care of yourself, ya know."

"I sure do." He reached behind him and gently touched the cuts Vanessa had made. The skin was tender.

"Bad back?"

"I twisted it...not long ago."

"Wanna go to the hospital? My hubby and I

90

could--"

"No, thanks. I--" Exhaustion swept through him again, this time more violently. He prayed he could snap out of this. Vanessa and her people wouldn't be far behind.

"We're going right past the hospital, if--"

"No, it's really all right. I--"

"It's not out of our way at all."

"What's all this?" A tall, bulky old man shuffled through the doorway. He held a brown paper bag and kept shifting his gaze from Arthur to the lady in the Escort.

"This young man needs to go to the hospital, Howard. It's his back. I think it's seized up on him."

Howard clucked, shook his bald head. "Ya can't play around with *that*, ya know."

"Thanks. I know."

"Ya mess up your back, that's it. The works."

"Thanks. I didn't know that." He didn't want to stand here, chatting with two strangers about his physical condition. He needed a ride out of here, and these two were--

What the hell was he doing? These two nice folks had just offered him a ride. A ride was what he wanted in the first place. Why was he standing here like an idiot, arguing with them?

"We can take him, can't we, Howard?"

"We gotta get on Lake Underhill Road anyway. Hospital's right there on the way. Our place is on Conway. No problem."

Flashing lights sparked the darkness straight ahead, on the other side of the bushes, where he parked the sedan. Two cruisers had already pulled up to it. There wasn't much time.

"Maybe I *should* get checked out," he said. "That is, if you don't mind taking me--"

"Nonsense," the lady said. "We don't mind."

"Go on." Howard gestured. "Climb in back. We'll getcha there in fifteen minutes."

***

Head down, Arthur staggered over to the Escort.

On the other side of the hedges, another car pulled up to the sedan. The well-lit parking lot discouraged him from turning around and showing his face. He opened the back door and carefully eased his exhausted body inside. "Would you mind if I lie down? My back doesn't hurt as much when I'm on my side."

"You just get comfy," the lady said. "There's a pillow on the floor you can use as well. It's Molly's, but she won't mind."

"Molly?"

"Our Pomeranian. We left her at the apartment with our daughter. Sure hope she doesn't scratch up the front door again."

"Your daughter?" he asked, smiling. "Or Molly?"

The woman chuckled. Howard grunted.

"Molly sure misses her mommy," the woman said. "We really shouldn't leave her--"

"Don't start *that* again, Ida," Howard said.

The woman sighed.

"How'd ya get to the store?" Howard asked.

"Drive?"

"Yes." He arranged Molly's pillow on the seat, brushed it off, then lay down. He knew better than tell them he stole a car. Most people weren't tolerant of car thieves. Neither was Arthur, for that matter. He knew he couldn't tell them what happened.

"Guess we can bring ya back for your car," Howard said, "so long as the hospital visit don't take too long--"

"Howard..."

"Wonder what that commotion is back there," Howard said. "Don't look like no accident. Abandoned car, mebbe? Don't see no one but cops and four others standing around. Stolen, maybe. Thief musta ran off."

"Watch the road, Howard. We both know what happens when you're distracted."

"Let's not go *there* again, Ida..."

"All right back there, young man?"

"Yes, ma'am."

"How's your back feeling?"

"Better, thanks." It had quit hurting as soon as he lay on his side. The seat had instantly grown just as comfortable as his own bed. He closed his eyes and relaxed.

The next thing he knew, the old lady was talking to him.

"Young man? We're at the hospital."

He snapped awake and sat up. It took him a few seconds to get his bearings. The bright lights of the hospital entrance pushed beams of white glare at the car, clearing his head. With a deep sigh, he pushed open the door and used the doorframe to pull himself into a standing position. Once he regained his balance, he pushed the door closed. "This was very nice of you," he told them.

"We'd like to stay and see you're all right," the lady said.

"No. Please. You've done more than enough. I'll be all right. Thanks again."

"What about your car?" Howard asked.

"I can take a cab to pick it up."

He frowned. "Cabs cost money."

"I'm fine. Really. Thanks again." He waved, turned, and lumbered over to the bright front entrance.

Less than a dozen people sat in the waiting room. Still groggy, he shuffled up to the desk, signed his name on the sheet, took the forms the receptionist handed him, and found a chair in a corner. He eased his throbbing body gently into a curved plastic seat. It was a far cry from the back seat of the Escort.

He began filling out the forms, but sleep nudged him again, and his vision quickly blurred. He rubbed his eyes. They blurred again, and he became vaguely aware that he was pushing a wavy line across the page with the pen. They would think he was a nutcase or druggie and would call OPD. He'd better rest his eyes for a moment. A few seconds was all he needed. Then he'd be able to…

Chapter 8

"Time to get up, honey..."

Arthur opened his eyes. A broad-shouldered gray-haired woman in a white uniform nudged him. He stared dumbly at her and glanced at his surroundings. A hospital? It took him a few moments to remember how he'd gotten here. Then he noticed the clipboard in front of him, and the chicken scratches applied to some of the blanks. "I haven't f-finished...filling out--"

"What medications are you on at the moment, honey?"

"Nothing."

"None?" She seemed surprised.

"I'm just...tired." The yawn came without warning.

"Can you get up?" She snatched the pen and clipboard and grabbed his upper arm. She had big hands for a female. Her grip hurt like a vise. She was obviously accustomed to handling violent patients. She wasn't someone you'd want to piss off.

"Of course I can get up." He tried pulling free, but she held on. The wedding ring on her finger suggested she probably led her husband around without much fuss.

"Then show me." She let go as soon as he stood up. His arm grew warm as circulation slowly returned.

They went down a long hall. His back flared up

again, but he forced himself to ignore it. She stopped when they reached the third room on their right. "Go on in," she said. "Someone'll be right with you." She closed the door behind him.

The room was small—about ten by ten—and smelled of antiseptic. A padded table covered with a sheet of thin white paper sat in the center of the room. A metal table covered with vials, cue tips, cotton balls, tweezers, and other First-Aid supplies occupied a corner. To his left, a mirror and sink reflected the overhead light. To his right, a chair awaited him.

He collapsed on the padded seat. It was much more comfortable than the curved plastic chair in the waiting room. He squirmed into a comfortable position. The pain in his back squawked a little. He leaned back and closed his eyes, surrendering once again to the warm, dark mist.

Moments later, someone tapped him on the shoulder, and he realized he'd nodded off again. This woman was a tall, slender redhead with a sharp-featured, pretty face. She wore glasses with large lenses and was probably around forty-five. She was squinting at the chart in her large, bony hands. "You're Arthur…Si_____?"

"Just plain Sills will do."

"This is *Sills*?" She pushed her glasses up her nose a fraction of an inch, produced a pen, and scribbled something on the chart. "You misspelled your own name?"

He shrugged. "I'm tired."

"What's the problem? Mono? Chronic fatigue

syndrome? You didn't get very far with your chart."

"I must have drifted off."

"I already got that. So what's wrong?"

"My lower back."

"Specifically?"

"It hurts."

"Any history of back problems? An injury?"

"I slammed my car into a telephone pole and twisted two of my lumbar vertebrae."

"How long ago?"

"About a year."

"Does it restrict your movements?"

"I can't do cartwheels anymore."

She blinked. "Do you miss doing them?"

He sighed. "Not at all. My change tends to fall out of my pockets."

She shook her head. "Have you had therapy?"

"A chiropractor."

"How long ago was your last--"

"About eight months."

"How long were you supposed to go for treatment?"

"Longer than I went."

"And you stopped going because...?

He shrugged.

She nodded, staring at him while trying to evaluate his situation. "You're in luck. We might be able to help you tonight. It's pretty slow tonight. Stand up."

"Huh?"

"It's easier to take off your shirt when you're standing. Besides, I can't examine you when you're lounging in that chair. You'll fall asleep again."

He did as she ordered.

She circled him, moved closer, and bent. "Wow..."

Not the sort of thing you want to hear from someone checking you out in a hospital.

He swallowed. "Wow?"

"Sorry. That wasn't very professional, was it?"

"Depends on what you meant by it."

"You've got a really bad infection going on back here."

"Infection?"

"Good. You're paying attention." She wheeled over the small metal cart. "Sit down on that table. I'm gonna give you an injection."

"A *shot*?" He hated shots.

"That would be the layman's term for it, yes. This looks nasty. These are fingernail scratches, right?"

"You could say that."

"Fingernails carry tons of bacteria." She swabbed his shoulder with alcohol. "Don't move." She gave him the injection. "See how pleasant things are when you do as you're told?"

"You're right. I'm having a ball."

She applied something cold to his lower back. A hot jolt stabbed him in the same place, and he stiffened. "*Shit*."

"Sensitive?"

"What was your first clue?" The burning sensation lingered for about twenty seconds and ebbed quickly.

"Call it female intuition." She picked up some cotton swabs and began cleaning and dressing the wounds. "Interesting."

He felt he should clear this up. "If you're wondering how I got the scratches--"

"I know a little something about grownup games, baby. I've been on this rodeo a long time." She took some gauze from the table and cut it in strips, then pressed it firmly to his cuts.

He could tell she wanted to say something else. "I have this strange feeling you've got the wrong idea about me. This isn't--"

"How it looks?"

"Well, yeah. It's not."

"I've never understood why so many like it rough. I guess I'll always be the sentimental type— candy, flowers, romance, candlelight dinners, soft music. You know. Corny, old-fashioned. Romantic."

He wanted to laugh. He'd also been the old-fashioned type. Denise had always preferred old-fashioned romance. She'd seen *Casablanca* and *An Affair to Remember* dozens of times and loved candlelight dinners. She loved dressing up. And getting surprise gifts. And spontaneity. In the beginning of their relationship, he often wondered if their romance would die. Little did he know that it would never get the chance to perish on its own.

"Everyone rocks to his own beat," the nurse said. "But if I were you, I'd take it easy. I'm going to give you antibiotics for that infection. Good thing she didn't bite you." She tilted her head. "You didn't...*ask* her to do this, did you?"

"Of course not."

She shrugged. "Like I said, everyone rocks to his own beat."

He found himself getting angry again. Not at this lady, but at Vanessa. "Do I look like the sort of guy who *enjoys* being carved up?"

She smiled faintly. "I don't know, honey. We only just met. Maybe after a few dates...when we get more acquainted..."

All he needed right now. A smartassed nurse.

"If I were you, I'd let these heal before getting back in the saddle. You've obviously been trying to ride the wrong mare."

He knew better than give her any of the details.

"Is this the first time she scratched you?"

"Yes. Why?"

"Guess she wanted to spice up the evening her own way," she said. "But like I said, I'd be careful."

"Thanks. I'll try to remember."

"Your lady friend. How long have you known her?"

"Not long."

The nurse frowned. "Honey, you're a nice-looking guy. There are plenty of females out there, and not all of them need to slice you up to have a good time. Were you drunk, by the way?"

"Does that matter?"

"Just curious. But it might explain why you let her do this to you."

"I had a couple of drinks."

She finished dressing his wounds in silence.

He suddenly felt the urgent need to explain himself. "Something wrong with having a couple of drinks?"

"I'm fine with a couple of drinks. In fact, I've been known to have one or two on occasion. Sometimes three or four, especially after a couple of these wicked back-to-back shifts. But when folks drink too much, they turn stupid, and that's when they end up out there in the waiting room, making my shift a little too interesting for my taste." She snapped something shut, then went over to the sink and turned on the tap. "You're entirely too old to be acting like a silly kid."

"I guess it just got a little…out of hand."

"Even so, I'd give myself a little vacation before trying to get back in that saddle. That infection needs time to heal. You can lie face-down on that table now."

He just looked at her.

"The doctor on call specializes in osteopathic. If you lie down as I said, I'll see if I can bring him here and have him do an adjustment. Would that be all right?"

"You can do that? Bring a doctor here? Just like that?"

She smiled. "He owes me a couple of favors."

"You…don't even know me."

"I feel sorry for you. You seem like a really nice guy. Besides, I know what it feels like to have back pain." She pointed to the table. "Now lie down and I'll see how quickly I can get him here."

He did as she said.

***

The streetlamps brushed sections of the half-filled parking lot with slender bars of golden haze.

Walking normal and pain-free again, Arthur left through the main entrance. The adjustments the doc had made to his back had made him feel much better and had taken the edge off his exhaustion.

It was getting late, and there was little activity outside. Two women in white uniforms were getting in their cars farther down, near the main turnoff. Straight ahead and about two rows down, a couple of large well-dressed men got out of a van.

Although he felt better, the chaos during the last couple of hours had taken its toll. He had to continue to think logically and consider his options. He needed a cab but had no cell phone. It had probably fallen out of his pocket during his last blackout, when the fake cops turned him over to Vanessa and her people. He ditched her phone, but that was necessary because--

Because of what? Its GPS? That made no sense. Even after he had tossed her phone, the guard was still able to track him.

But how?

He couldn't worry about that now. He had to keep moving.

A row of pay phones stretched down the hall leading to the restrooms. He still had his wallet; he could use a credit card.

But where could he go? If they could track him in the woods, they could track him wherever he went.

The realization slammed through him.

They know I'm here...

He had to get away. He couldn't just stand here like an idiot and wait for them to show. He was a sitting duck. Besides, he needed rest. And a shower. And food.

The two men from the van continued walking toward the entrance. Straight toward him.

He fought down the panic. He was being paranoid again. This was a hospital. They could be doctors. Or patients. Or even visitors. They could be going inside to perform an operation. Or see a sick father, or mother...

But what if they were Vanessa's cronies?

Should he run back inside? Hide in the john? The prospect of playing hide 'n seek in a huge, brightly-lit hospital didn't appeal to him. He would stand a much better chance out in the open.

Should he just stand here and wait? If they were doctors or visitors, they'd walk right on by. If not...

He knew he couldn't wait. The stakes were much too high. He was much too tired to play their games. He stepped down from the curb and veered to his right, moving at a fairly swift pace toward the far end of the parking lot. The lights illuminated the far corners of the aisles, but large portions of the spaces toward the center remained shrouded in darkness. If he reached the center aisles, he'd have a chance to slip away.

As soon as he started down the aisle, they turned to their left and came after him.

More cold chills raced down his back. He'd

been right all along. They really *had* tracked him again.

He ran down the aisle, weaving between vehicles and ducking down another aisle. He glanced behind him. They'd separated. One of them rushed down the main thruway to the right while the other stayed on Arthur's tail. Two cars had pulled into the lot during this time. A third had pulled out of its space about ten rows down, providing some distraction.

He sprinted down another aisle, where two SUVs and a pickup truck filled adjoining spaces near the end of the row straight ahead. He stopped abruptly, stepped between an SUV and the pickup, squatted, dropped down, and rolled beneath the pickup.

It was pitch-dark. If he couldn't see, neither could they. The approaching footsteps grew louder and stopped a few vehicles down. His pursuer was probably checking beneath the vehicles. Unless he had a flashlight, he wouldn't be able to--

A slender beam of white light sliced into the space between the SUV and the pickup. The beam slid toward the left, then toward the right. Arthur rolled closer to the edge of the pickup, hoping the wide double tires would conceal him. It must have worked. The beam vanished, and the footsteps resumed as the man hurried away.

Arthur rolled out from beneath the truck, crawled down one aisle, got back down and rolled beneath another large vehicle. A moment later, the flashlight beam splashed beneath the vehicle next to the one concealing him. He waited tensely, not moving, until he heard distant voices farther down, where the two had come from.

He began crawling again, moving toward the big, well-lit building. If he could get back inside, he could sneak into one of the little examination rooms. They would think he had given them the slip and would leave. Or sit in their van and wait for him to come outside again. He could call for a cab and have it pick him up on the other side of the building.

He kept crawling, his eyes alert for the wandering flashlight beam. As far as he knew, they were at least a hundred feet down. It could be a while before they backtracked. If he could just make it to the building...

A couple of car doors slammed shut one aisle straight ahead. An engine came to life, headlight beams blazed, and a small sedan crept out of its spot, coasting quietly down the aisle, toward the main drag.

About a minute later, he reached the first row. Ten yards straight ahead, the road leading out to Lake Underhill cut across his path. The bright front windows of the hospital smiled at him. His heart leaped. Should he jump to his feet and haul ass? It was probably less than a hundred yards to the entrance doors. He could easily reach the building before they could catch him—especially if they were still checking beneath the vehicles at the other end of the big lot.

He pushed himself into a kneeling position so he could see where the two men were. At that same moment, a loud click that sounded like the hammer of a gun made him cringe.

A few feet to his right, a woman whispered, "Don't move."

106

Chapter 9

Arthur froze.

He remained kneeling, his arms to his sides. The cool night air tickled the back of his neck, but he forced himself not to shiver.

"Whaddya think you're doing?" she asked softly.

He opened his mouth, but the only thing that came out was a soft choking sound.

"*What* was that?"

He took a deep breath, swallowed, and tried again. "Sh-Shivering," he managed, and his throat closed up again.

"You're not making any sense. Look at me."

"You...told me not to move."

"I changed my mind."

Still shaking, he slowly turned his head. The sight made the hair stand up on the back of his neck. The biggest gun he had ever seen pointed directly at his face. The barrel was as large as a cannon.

"Why aren't you talking?"

"I'm...too busy trying not to faint. That's a...big gun..."

"It's a Smith & Wesson three-fifty-seven. Yeah, you could say it's big. Now start talking."

"What was the q-question?"

A sigh. "You weren't by any chance hiding underneath my car, were you?"

"W-Why would I do that?"

"Everyone knows carjackers wait underneath a car they want."

"I'm not a carjacker."

"I knew you'd say that."

"How could I do that when you're already in the car? With a big gun?"

She didn't reply right off. Hopefully, she was thinking that one over. He also hoped she would stop pointing the gun at his face.

"Then why are you crawling around out there?"

"I'm hiding."

"From whom?"

That gun was scaring him half to death. Since he was much too frightened to improvise, he knew he'd better tell her the truth. "Some really scary people."

The woman stuck her head out the window. Tendrils of light-colored hair waved wildly in the evening breeze. He couldn't see her face. It was eclipsed by the cannon. So was the rest of her. "I don't see anyone else out here."

"They're probably hiding in the shadows."

"How many of them?"

"I saw two, but there are possibly more."

"What do they want?"

"I wish I knew."

She lowered the gun, and he felt his limbs relax. "You realize how weird this sounds, right?"

A spike of anger poked through him. "If I could make something up, I'd try helluva lot harder to come up with something more believable."

"Well, I kinda think you're not a carjacker."

"How can you tell?"

"You're not the type." She pulled the gun back inside. He couldn't tell if she placed it in her lap or on the console. It didn't matter. At least it was no longer pointing at his face. "Okay, I can tell you're not a badass—which is why I haven't shot you already. I'm not sure I believe what you just told me. It sounds way over-the-edge. But I'm pretty sure you're not after my car. Tell you what. If you just get up and walk away, I won't call the cops, okay?"

"But--"

"It's the only option you've got."

He didn't want to deal with the cops again. He also didn't want her pointing that cannon at him again. If he got up and walked away, those two would catch up to him in no time. "I guess I've got no choice, then."

"But if I were you? And people I didn't know were--"

The harsh clicking sound of approaching footsteps grew louder behind them. He immediately dropped down and rolled beneath the van beside the Toyota. The clicking grew louder.

Vanessa's voice: "Excuse me!"

"Yes?"

"Have you seen someone lurking around here?"

A pause. "Lurking?"

Vanessa's voice grew louder as she drew nearer. "He's an escaped mental patient. He's dangerous, and we've just received word that he's been seen out here."

Mental patient? My God. Why the hell did they want him so badly?

"Which facility?"

"Behavioral Health Assessment Center." Vanessa's heels stopped clicking between the van and the Toyota. He could see her pumps. One of them tapped impatiently.

"Which one?"

"Florida Hospital."

"The one on Rollins Street?"

"That's the one."

"Hmmm. Which treatment program is this patient on?"

"I can't divulge that. It is extremely urgent that we--"

"You said dangerous…"

"He is a mental patient."

"What sort of mental patient? Not all of them are dangerous."

"I'm not at liberty to say. But I will say he assaulted me."

"That would explain the huge goose egg on your forehead."

Vanessa sighed. Her toe tapped again. "Yes. It would."

"What's this guy look like?"

"He's nice-looking, with dark hair. He's thirty-eight, slender, and around six feet tall."

How the hell did she know his age? He didn't remember telling her.

"Is he armed?"

"No."

He held his breath, wondering what would happen. He'd known women all his life but could never predict what they'd do or say. This woman had just caught him crawling around her car. She told him she didn't believe his story, so he had no idea if she'd hand him over to Vanessa.

Then, after several agonizing moments of silence, she said, "Sorry, but I haven't seen anyone like that."

He sighed in relief.

"You're sure?"

"I think I'd remember a nice-looking guy, six feet tall and slender, on the right side of forty."

"I thought I heard voices around here somewhere."

"Really?"

"I believe so."

He waited tensely, holding his breath again.

"If I were you, I'd have myself checked for that."

Silence. Then: "Thanks anyway."

"Hope you find him."

"Oh, we will." Her footsteps clicked quickly as she hurried away.

About half a minute later, the woman whispered, "Still there?"

He hesitated. He wanted to thank her but didn't want Vanessa to get suspicious and come back.

"She's gone."

"I'm...still here."

"Still want to get away?"

"Now more than ever."

"Think you can climb in through the back window? I wouldn't advise opening the door. If anyone's watching, they'll see the interior lights come on."

He couldn't believe his luck. "You mean you're gonna help me?"

"I guess that's what it means. Can you do it?"

"I'll manage."

The window rolled down.

Once again he hesitated. Was this woman on the up and up? Or was she just humoring him so she could turn him in and claim a possible award?

"Make up your mind. I'm tired and wanna get home."

"So am I, dammit." The anger emerged spontaneously. It had been a rough day.

"Then shut up and get in."

He rolled out from beneath the van, straightened, then dove head-first through the open window. Fear pushed him to work faster, and he squirmed through, using his hands to crawl onto the back seat.

She'd already started up the ignition, rolled up the windows, and pulled out of the space.

***

Moving quickly, she pulled the Toyota onto Lake Underhill Road, merging effortlessly into heavy southbound traffic.

He sat sideways in the back seat, gazing out the rear window. He expected to see headlights rushing up behind them at any moment. Blinding lights jumped and hopped everywhere. A small car kept close behind them but switched lanes and pulled off before he could consider it a threat.

Even so, he knew better than lower his guard. Judging by what Vanessa had told this woman, she and her friends would not stop in their quest to get him.

"Something on your mind?" the woman asked.

"What makes you say that?"

"You're not saying a word. And you're staring a hole in my window. Believe me, no one's following us."

"You honestly didn't believe her, did you?"

"About what? Your being an escaped mental patient? Or that you were dangerous?"

"Yeah."

"I could tell she was lying."

"How?"

"For one thing, if you were an escaped mental patient, you wouldn't be dressed as you are."

"I could've snuck up on someone. Knocked them out. Taken their clothes."

"Yours fit too well. Besides, I didn't see any county or private ambulance anywhere in the parking lot. An escaped mental patient makes big news. Especially a dangerous one. The entire place would've been crawling with cops."

"Makes sense."

"Besides, she wasn't dressed like any doctor."

"You're pretty observant."

"Comes with the territory. So...do you know that woman?"

He didn't want to tell her the whole story, but he didn't want to lie to someone who'd gone out of her way to help him. And she had that cannon sitting in her lap. "I guess you could say that..."

"How?"

"It's...a long story."

"Try giving me the highlights. I've got some time."

"I think you'd just better drop me off."

She turned. Even in the darkness he could see the iciness in her big blue eyes. "This can't possibly be a love-gone-sour thing, can it?"

He couldn't believe it. She'd drawn her own conclusions even without his help.

"It's more like a bunch-of-bad-guys-after-some-poor-innocent-schmuck kind of thing."

"This has nothing to do with you doing a number on her and her trying to get even?"

"Actually, she's the one doing the number. On *me*."

She didn't speak for the longest time. He couldn't blame her. Anyone would consider this mess a bit theatrical.

"What's your name?"

"Arthur Sills."

"What do you do?"

"I used to be a computer analyst."

"*Used* to be?"

"That's a long story, too."

"You've got too many long stories. Tell me about the only one that really interests me."

"Which one is that?"

"The one about the lady with the hugantic lump on her forehead."

"Like I said, I'm not really sure what's going on." He saw no point in telling her about Vanessa. "It would be a lot simpler if you just dropped me off."

"Where do you live?"

"I have a condo in Winter Park, just off Semoran."

"My place is on Michigan. We're heading there now. It's kind of in the opposite direction of where you live—wouldn't you say?"

He said nothing.

She sighed. "This is where you're supposed to say, "I've got a friend living around here who can put me up for a little while. He—or she—doesn't live very far from where we are.""

He couldn't take his eyes off the rear window. "Actually, I have no one."

"You're not married?"

"No."

"No friends? Relatives? Acquaintances? Business associates?"

"No one."

She slowed down at the next light and stopped behind a large Dodge Ram pickup. She said nothing, just stared straight ahead. Figuring he'd scared her, he slid over to the passenger's side and pushed open the door. "Thanks for getting me out of there. I mean it. If there was some way I could pay you back--"

"Shut up and get up here." She patted the front seat.

"But you've done enough--"

"Shut up and just do it."

He got out, opened the front door, and got back in. As he buckled up, he noticed her for the first time. She was small, blonde, and around thirty. She wore a white uniform and had slender arms and a small bust. The big gun remained in her lap, covering it. Its silver finish glinted in the darkness of the cab.

The light changed. At the intersection, she turned left onto East Michigan. About a block later, headlights very close behind them made him cringe. He turned in his seat and glanced out the rear window. The headlights stayed close.

"Think it's them?" she asked.

"I'm almost positive."

She glanced in her rearview. "He could be one of those assholes that likes to tailgate. For some reason, people seem to be doing that sort of thing more and more nowadays."

"I'm not sure of anything anymore."

"One way to find out." She quickly swerved into the passing lane and pumped the brakes while easing into the turnoff lane. Behind them, the van also swerved, cutting off traffic. Horns of protest wailed, and the van crept up until it was right behind them again.

"All right, asshole, let's see how far you wanna take this." She put on her blinkers and slowed, all the while coasting toward the right edge of the lane.

When a break came, she jerked the wheel sharply to the left and gunned it, making a sharp U-turn.

In seconds they were heading north on Peel. She gunned it again, swerving in and out of traffic. He watched the side mirror. Because of its size, the van had difficulty keeping up. By the time it had forced its way into northbound traffic, they had already crossed the road and turned left, onto East Grant. She accelerated, barely slowing down before making a dangerous left onto South Bumby. He closed his eyes and tensed his body, hoping they wouldn't die. She gunned it again, slowed briefly, then made a sharp right onto a residential road.

"Damn, you're good."

"I hate being followed. It's a female thing." She took them down the road at a much safer speed. Once they reached the other end, she turned off, rushed down another residential street, and made another turn. They went one block, turned off, and made a right, until they were back on East Michigan. One block later, she pulled over and stopped in front of a deserted strip mall.

She sat back in her seat and fluffed out her blond hair. "That sure was an adrenaline rush."

He sighed deeply. Only then did he realize he'd been gripping the door handle. It took him three tries to pull his fingers free. The circulation had stopped in them, making them tingly. But at least they'd lost the van. He wiggled his fingers to get the blood flowing again. "I don't think anyone could possibly keep up with--" Then he stopped.

The pavement behind them, as well as the interior of the Toyota, brightened into a blinding glare as the blinding headlights eased up to them.

Chapter 10

Tires squealed as she jerked the Toyota away from the headlights, pulling out into westbound traffic a block farther down.

She raced down the street and made a sharp right, past a gas station, then a left, and another quick left. They tore down a palmetto-lined residential area until the string of green lights swaying over East Michigan straight ahead urged them on. After making another dangerous right turn into traffic, they weaved between lanes and slipped through several yellow and red lights.

"Got anything more to tell me?" She kept glancing at him as they snuck through the red light at the intersection of Michigan and South Ferncreek.

"Such as?"

"How's this for starters? How the hell do they know where we're going? How can they keep finding us in all this traffic? Most importantly, who *are* you? I mean *really*?"

He couldn't blame her for doubting everything he'd told her. Even so, he didn't want to tell her his worst fears. He didn't want to tell her that a bunch of scary people he didn't even know were relentlessly tracking him. That Vanessa—a woman he barely knew—had obviously done something to him. That she and her people had been tracking him for hours, and he had no idea why.

"You're bugged, aren'tcha?"

119

Though he'd been denying it to himself, he realized there could be no other logical explanation. She'd already figured it out. Well, it wouldn't take a brain surgeon, would it? Even so, he didn't want to believe some strange woman had injected him with a tracking device. "I'm not a hundred percent certain, but--"

"Just say it."

"All right. I'm bugged."

Those big blue eyes shot him an icy glare. He felt as if he'd just been slugged with a barrage of icicles. "What else haven't you told me?"

"There's nothing else to tell!"

"People don't go out of their way to bug someone and track them all over Orange County, just for the fun of it."

The more she spoke, the dumber he felt. Her words poked into him like barbs, tearing into his insides.

"You're not a carjacker. That much I believe. But the other stuff?" She shook her head. "You must think I'm really stupid."

His heart sank. "Then you don't believe me."

"Tell me one thing. How'd they bug you?"

"I have no idea."

She let go of the steering wheel with her left hand and picked up the gun, repositioning it so the barrel pointed in his direction. His limbs grew cold. "You have no idea?"

"It must've been when she drugged me."

"When was this?"

"Friday night." He didn't want to go into the whole story. "This whole thing is totally strange and complicated--"

"You've got two minutes to start talking before I turn this car around and take you to the Police Station."

He told her about last Friday—from the time Vanessa had walked into the liquor store until she followed him back to the condo. He didn't tell her about the mysterious trip to the 7-Eleven. He suspected that if he told her everything, she'd consider him a certified nutcase and would take him directly to the mental hospital Vanessa had mentioned.

She remained silent, staring straight ahead. Once he had finished, she grabbed the gun and shoved it under her seat.

He sighed in relief.

"The way it sounds, this flaky bitch obviously latched onto you for some weird reason."

"Then you believe me?"

"I know all about flakes. I see them and work with them daily. They're everywhere, and they're capable of anything. Hell, I was married to two of them."

"At the same time?"

"Funny. No, I latched onto the first one right out of Nursing School, then found the other one about five years ago. As for your story? I just don't think you could make up something like that and expect me or anyone else to believe it."

"So then, where are we going?"

"You're not out of the woods yet. There are still a few things about all this I've got to know more about. But right now, we've got to lose them. We can't very well hash this all out when we've got a vanload of crazies after us."

"We *can't* lose them. Isn't that obvious?"

"We've got to. Then I need to take you to someone who can find that damned bug."

"Then what?"

The blue eyes held his. "Guess."

"You don't mean--"

"That's exactly what I mean."

His nerves tingled as they raced through another light, went a few more blocks, then slowed, eased into the turnoff lane, and followed a long line waiting to pull into the entrance of a seafood restaurant.

***

After pulling into the gravel drive, she followed the slow-moving column across the front lot, past the large one-story building lined with shuttered bay windows facing the highway.

Two pickups pulled into the first two spaces near the entrance while the others turned right at the far end and went down the bumpy side lot, where several empty spaces awaited them between the oak trees bordering the property. A long line of parked vehicles facing Michigan extended to the end of the front lot. They found a vacant space one down from the end. She eased into it and immediately doused the lights.

He watched the headlights passing behind them and wondered how long it would be before Vanessa's people found them again. "Why did you bring us here? You know it's only a matter of time before they find us again."

She sat back and fluffed her hair. Several wild tendrils brushed her cheeks, but she ignored them. She was now very close, and for the first time he noticed how striking she was. Her face was small, but sharp-featured, with high cheekbones, a short, upturned nose, and firm jawline. Her blue eyes, large and penetrating, consumed him. "We needed to find a crowd. It's easier to blend in and also easier to sneak away. I've been carting your butt all over Central Florida for the past half-hour and quite frankly, I'm getting tired. I just worked two back-to-backs. Besides, I'm hungry and want a strong drink. Now…unless you wanna be left here by yourself, I suggest you tell me what's going on."

"I…don't even know your name."

"You're stalling."

"You know mine. I feel weird, not knowing yours."

"Mandy Rhodes, all right? Now that we're all chummy and everything, why don't you take me inside that nice-looking restaurant and treat me to supper? You can talk while I eat. I've got to figure out what to do with you."

"Whaddya mean?"

"Listen. Arthur. You're a nice guy and all, but this…this thing you've got yourself involved in…I didn't exactly sign on for it."

"I know."

"I'm just a head nurse."

"I know. The white uniform sort of tipped me off."

"I'm glad it's good for something. Listen…we're going inside and you're going to tell me everything you know. And after I get some serious food in my empty gut, I'm taking you to the Police Station."

He felt his jaw drop.

"I don't know anywhere else I can take you. I don't know what or who you're dealing with, and if I drop you off just anywhere, I'll worry about what happens to you. Can't help it. I'm a nurse. I help people. It's kind of a credo. Do no harm—that sorta thing."

"What happens when…when they come in?"

"What did they do the last time they had you?"

"Vanessa tried to give me an injection."

"What sort of injection?"

"I don't know. I suspect it was some sort of sedative."

"This is sounding really weird. I suggest we try and grab something to eat before they show up again. You are paying, right?"

"It's the least I can do."

***

Dark and air-conditioned, The Seafood Shack boasted a nautical setting.

Thick wooden beams spanned the huge area. Small square tables and chairs fashioned of polished cedar covered the dark wooden floor. Fish netting hung loosely from the beams. Oars and canoes were bolted to the paneled walls. Copper lanterns in the center of each table provided lighting. Harried waitresses dressed in sleeveless white blouses, black skirts, and green aprons dodged sweaty busboys hauling gray tubs stacked with dirty dishes and silverware.

Mandy chose a table toward the back and next to a window facing the west side of the building, where she could keep an eye on the Toyota. The waitress rushed over and scribbled their orders, returning a minute later with their drinks.

Mandy downed half her vodka rocks in one swallow. "Tell me more about this Vanessa bitch."

He sipped his Manhattan. "What would you like to know?"

Mandy shrugged. "The bug thing, silly."

"We had sex."

"I figured as much. So...tell me. How'd she manage to bug you during sex?"

"She distracted me, somehow."

The waitress brought over their scampi and fried oysters. Mandy quickly devoured an oyster and sighed, then had another. "Must have been some distraction."

"Must have been."

"What exactly did she do?"

"I don't know. Everything went really hazy after that last drink I had."

"Go on."

"After we did the deed, she wanted a drink, so she went back into the kitchen and fixed one. A little while later, everything blurred and grew hazy. Then I started having blackouts."

She had more of her drink. "Tell me about them."

"They started the next morning. After she fixed breakfast, I was in the kitchen doorway, talking to her, and the next thing I knew, I was standing on my front stoop, holding a bag."

"What was in the bag?"

"Vanessa wanted this special creamer they carry in the 7-Eleven."

"And you went there and bought it, but don't remember?"

"Exactly."

"You were obviously in some sort of induced fugue state."

"Nothing else makes sense."

She ate some scallops. "Just off the top of my head, I'd say you were given some sort of hallucinogen."

He'd been right all along. Vanessa could have easily slipped something in his drink when she'd gone to the kitchen. But something didn't make sense. "Why didn't it work right off?"

"How do you know it didn't?"

"I didn't feel any different. Not until later, when she started getting rough."

"I'd say it worked pretty fast, then. You didn't feel the injection. The drug could have done several things."

"It obviously messed up my memory."

"They've got drugs that'll do just about everything now. Dull the senses. Sharpen them. Alter the imagination. Affect the central nervous system. Interfere with the memory, the order of events, how you see people, hear what they say. The drug companies are the most powerful industry in the world, believe me. They're even more powerful than the oil companies."

"I didn't realize that."

"They stay under the radar and let the oil companies, the stock market, big business, big government, politics, terrorism—everything else that makes the headlines—have the spotlight. They have to. If we all knew what they were doing, we'd start asking questions they wouldn't want to answer."

"Well, we all know they kill people."

"For one thing, their research never stops. They're like modern technology, only much more dangerous because they play with people's health. Each time a new drug is developed, they use their resources to get it passed and released to the market, then sit back and watch what it does. When an acceptable number of people develop side effects and die, they turn to their massive legal monster machine to handle the lawsuits while they work on something else to hit the market with."

"I thought each drug was fully tested before it's put out on the market."

"It is."

The realization made his blood turn cold. "You mean all this…what's happening to me…could be just one of their nasty drug experiments?"

"It's beginning to sound that way."

He leaned closer to her and lowered his voice. "I think I might have been involved in the murder of two people. Are you telling me this could be because of a new drug they're testing?"

Her eyes grew. She looked around to make sure no one was listening, then leaned over the table. "You what?"

"At first I thought it was a dream. A nightmare. At least Vanessa tried to convince me it was. But the more I thought of it, the more I realized it wasn't. Dreams and nightmares are usually hazy, and most of them make no sense. This was much too real."

"What exactly happened?"

"I was standing over this man. I had a paperweight in my hand, and there was a pool of blood on the floor beneath his head. He was an older man—about seventy, I guess. He wore a white lab coat. The room I was in was just like the one I woke up in this afternoon, when two fake cops delivered me to them somewhere on Edgewater."

"Fake cops?"

"I decided to drive to OPD to tell them what I'd done. I thought I was going crazy and couldn't stand it any longer. I was halfway there when two cops pulled me over on Colonial on a bogus charge."

"Where'd they take you on Edgewater?"

"I don't know. I was out cold. I was going to try and kick my way out through the window of the police car but blacked out before I could do anything. I woke up in a building somewhere on Rouse Road, about five miles north of East Colonial."

"How'd you escape?"

"I overpowered Vanessa and used her badge to get out of the building."

She stabbed a scallop with her fork. "How'd you do it?"

"Just before she could give me the injection, I grabbed her hair and smacked her head against the arm of the chair."

She smiled.

He shrugged. "She gave me no choice."

She ate her scallop and drank some ice-water. "What's this about a second murder?"

"The other man was a therapist in town."

Mandy blinked. "A *therapist*?"

"I wanted to see someone professionally so I could--"

"What was…this therapist's name?"

"R. D.--"

"Was it Tannenbaum?"

Something cold settled in his gut. "H-How did you know?"

She didn't speak for the longest time. Her face had turned pale. He strongly suspected he had done something even more horrible than he'd imagined.

"Mandy…did you know--"

"I knew him." Her voice had become a whisper.

He couldn't speak. He lowered his gaze to the napkin in his lap.

Mandy knew him. Colleague? Boyfriend? Fiancé? It didn't matter, did it?

He expected her to toss her plate at him. Or slap him. Or get up and storm out of the place.

After the tense silence, she found her voice. It was soft and raspy, and when he met her eyes again, he saw they were moist. "Do you honestly remember exactly what you did? You…killed him? You actually…killed Robert?"

"I don't know *what* I did. I swear to God. I have no idea I did anything. I didn't even wake up in his office. I woke up in my car. In the parking garage. I didn't remember a damned thing."

"Then how do you know what you did?"

"Like I said, I don't. But after I woke up--"

Mandy was staring at something behind him. His neck grew warm. "They're here, aren't they?"

Her slight nod sent chills down his spine.

Chapter 11

"Are you sure it's them?"

It occurred to him that Mandy could be wrong. After being followed across town, her paranoia might be working on her as well. "I mean, could you possibly be mistaken?"

"They haven't moved since they came in. They're just standing there, staring."

"Maybe they're staring at you."

"Why would they do that?"

He shrugged. "You're a babe."

She continued watching them. "Thanks for the compliment, but they're not watching me."

His throat suddenly felt raw. "How many are there?"

"I spotted three of them getting out of a van from the side lot about two minutes ago. One's out in the waiting area. The other two are in the archway, watching us."

"Are they large?"

"I'd say around six-two or –three. Yeah, they look pretty healthy."

"Dammit."

"Don't lose it. There's a chance we might be able to get out of this."

"How?"

"We could just sit here and wait for them to make the next move."

"I don't like that idea."

"Neither do I. If you've been telling me the truth about them, they'll try picking you up here and a lot of innocent people will get hurt. We've got to take this elsewhere."

"You could just leave. They want me—not you."

"I couldn't leave you like this. That wouldn't be very nice. You're not saying I'm not very nice, are ya?"

"I'd never say that."

"Good. My reputation means so much to me."

Something in Mandy's steady blue eyes comforted him. The feeling possibly came from his recollection of how easily she handled that cannon. However, her cannon sat back in the car, and right now they faced three large men who were undoubtedly armed. Mandy was about five-one and weighed a hundred pounds, soaking wet. Even so, she didn't appear scared, just angry.

At first he wondered if it was because they'd interrupted their meal, but then decided the real reason was Tannenbaum. Judging from how she reacted to the news, he couldn't gauge the nature of their relationship. It didn't matter. Even if the two had been only distant acquaintances, the fact remained. Tannenbaum was dead, and those responsible could be the three who'd just come into the restaurant.

"Put some money down on the table," she said finally, still watching the two men.

"How much?"

"Enough to cover our bill, silly. And the waitress has been working her buns off, so give her twenty percent. But don't do anything until I get up and leave."

"Where are you going?"

"To the john. Put the money down and sit here for three minutes. Use your watch to time yourself."

"Why three minutes?"

"If we get up at the same time, they'll know we're up to something. Three minutes will give me enough time."

"For what?"

"I'm not quite sure. Not yet. Just wait three minutes, then get up, walk down the hall, and meet me in the ladies' room. Don't worry, I'll make sure it's clear."

He decided to trust her. She was obviously thinking much clearer than he was.

"Got it?"

"What happens if they approach me while you're gone?"

"They wouldn't try something like that. They won't know what I'm up to and it'll make them nervous. They'll think I might be phoning someone."

"You're sure?"

"Of course I'm not sure. But remember. Three minutes—no longer." She picked up her steak knife and fork and slid them down the front of her jeans. Then got up and left.

Since he always carried his money in his front pocket, he didn't have to stand up and draw their attention. He pulled out his roll, peeled off some twenties beneath the table, put the rest back and slid the bills beneath his water glass. He finished his Manhattan and tried to keep his hand from shaking.

Once the three minutes had passed, he got up slowly. He then slipped carefully between a waitress and a busboy and headed for the hall marked *RESTROOMS*. He somehow managed a steady gait without stumbling or making a spectacle of himself.

He finally reached the door marked *LADIES* and pushed it open.

Mandy was standing in front of the mirrors, her white blouse wide open. Her white lacy bra immediately grabbed his attention. So did the tiny mole between her breasts, and the slightly larger one just above her navel. She frowned. "Do I have to slap you to get your mind back on track?"

"I'll be all right in a minute."

"We don't have a minute. Are you capable in a fight?"

"Capable of what?"

"Defending yourself—what else?"

"I'm reasonably lucky if I can get a good one in."

"You overpowered Vanessa…"

"I also overpowered one of their guards in the woods."

"Good. You don't freeze up." She handed him the knife and fork. "Take these and get into that stall. Close the door, but don't latch it. Hold it shut with your hand. Then wait."

"For what?"

"When they come in, I'll try to get at them as best as I can. If they get by me, do as much damage as you can with those."

He slipped unsteadily into the stall and pushed the door shut. He stood beside it, staring at the knife and fork. He began having second thoughts, wondering if he could carve up someone. When he thought of what Vanessa had done and how much trouble these people had put them through, he realized he was ready to face them.

The ladies' room door opened. Frenzied footsteps.

Mandy's voice: "Um, you're in the wrong room, boys."

A man's voice: "Where is he?"

Mandy: "I'm the only one here at the moment—as you can see."

The man: "Lady, we can make this easy or difficult. It's up to--"

Slap!

"Ow!"

Thunk!

"Ahhhh!"

Swat!

"*Arrrghhh*!"

Thumping sounds followed, three or four of them in rapid succession, followed by gasps, groans, and moans. There were two more gasps, followed by the sounds of something plastic clattering to the floor. A moment later, the trashcan slammed to the tile, echoing loudly.

Silence. He pulled the door open. Two large men in dark suits lay motionless on the tiled floor. Two small black automatic pistols lay on the floor between them. He gawked at them while Mandy stood beside him, buttoning her blouse. "What the hell did you *do*?"

"The room needed straightening up." She bent and collected the pistols. "You ready to get the hell out of here?"

He nodded.

"Here. Take this." She handed him a pistol and took the knife and fork and tossed them into the toppled trashcan.

He'd handled guns a long time ago, when he'd done a short stint in the Army during Iraq. He hadn't gone overseas but had stayed at Fort Benning his entire tour to give classes on computer technology.

"It's off safety, so all you have to do is--"

He flicked it on safety and pressed the clip release. When it slid onto his palm, he checked it for ammo. It was full, with one up the pipe. He slammed the clip back and clicked it off safety.

Mandy watched him and smiled. "And when did Baby learn all that?"

"I'm pretty good with guns, actually."

The door opened abruptly. The third man stood in the doorway, blocking it. The gun in his hand was held steady and aimed at both of them.

The moment the big boy shifted his gaze to his fallen comrades, Mandy's right foot lashed out, knocking the gun out of his grasp. The gun slapped against the wall and clattered to the floor. He gasped in pain, cradling his wrist. The same foot came around the other way, in a vicious counterclockwise motion, the heel of her tennis shoe catching him smartly between his legs. An ear-splitting groan sounding like the mating call of a sperm whale escaped his throat. He doubled up and began whimpering.

Arthur quickly moved toward him and cracked him on the back of the head with the gun. The thug went down hard, his face smacking the tile.

In the ensuing silence, he turned back to Mandy, who was watching him. "We make a good team," she said.

He didn't reply. He was too busy trying to figure out what she'd done. She'd just turned three big, strong men to mush in seconds. It was like watching a Chuck Norris movie.

"He's blocking our path."

"Huh?"

"Move him away from the door, all right?"

His brain finally began working. He grabbed the thug by his ankles, dragged him inside and let him lie next to his buddies. Mandy had already left the room. When he joined her out in the hall, she was carrying a yellow *Caution--Wet Floor* sign, which she placed in front of the door.

Without another word they slipped through the rear exit and raced outside.

***

Just before they reached the Toyota, Mandy turned back to the restaurant.

137

She was probably waiting to see one of the three stagger outside and come after them. Arthur almost wished they would.

But no one came back out.

Before they got in the Toyota, she emptied the clip of the automatic and wiped down the gun and clip on her shirttails. Then she tossed both in the bushes in front of her car. "I suggest you do the same. If we get stopped or pulled over, the only firearm I want in my possession is my three-fifty-seven. We don't even know if these are legal."

Without protest he ejected the clip and wiped everything down, then tossed the works in the bushes.

As they got back onto East Michigan, he sat back and stared at her in wonder. He didn't know if it was admiration or fear. Probably a little of both. It wasn't every day a guy witnessed such a spectacle. Especially when it involved a woman. And a tiny one at that.

"I'm sure you've got half a dozen questions you'd like to ask," she said, staring straight ahead.

"Just one."

"Let's hear it."

"How the hell did you that?"

"Do what?"

"You're kidding, right?"

"I'm good, but I can't exactly read people's minds."

"You're good, all right. I've never seen anyone your size beat the living shit out of three slabs of beef, all of them armed, without even breaking a sweat."

She shrugged. "They pissed me off. They interrupted our dinner."

"Where the hell did you learn to fight like that?"

"I picked up a few things here and there."

"What sort of things?"

"Some valuable tricks a vulnerable girl needs to know in today's brutal, uncompromising world."

"Vulnerable?"

"I was. Once."

"Something obviously happened."

"I learned some of that stuff in nursing school. I also took a self-defense course. My first husband helped, too. Especially when he started coming home drunk and wanted to knock me around."

"Is he still alive?"

She smiled. "I'm not a killer."

"That doesn't answer my question."

"I left him before the violence got out of control."

He decided to leave it at that. "Where are we going?" he asked.

"Home. I've got to think. Ever since I bumped into you, my entire life has turned upside-down."

He suddenly felt very guilty and stupid for bringing her into this. If only he hadn't crawled so close to her car...

Chapter 12

Mandy pulled onto East Jersey Street and passed several homes, veering over to the curb about halfway down the street before stopping and dousing her lights.

The homes were well-maintained frame houses, with small groups of oak trees and rows of bushes separating them. Front porches and carports were attached to many of the dwellings. Picket fences spanned the property lines. The streetlights illuminated front lawns, bushes, and gravel drives.

Since Mandy had parked between driveways, Arthur had no idea which house was hers. She sat in silence, watching the opposite side of the street. Several cars were parked along the street. Many sat in driveways or carports. Anyone could be hiding in a parked vehicle, watching them.

"Which one's your house?"

She pointed across the street. "Three houses down. The one with the white hurricane shutters."

"We're not going in?"

She lowered her window. Other than distant traffic sounds, they heard nothing. "I have this strange feeling my place is being watched."

"But how do they know about you? Vanessa's only seen you once."

"Since they had no trouble at all planting you with a bug, these people have mega resources. And after our party back at the restaurant, I'd guess those three big boys won't stop at anything to have another whack at me."

"What's the plan? We can't stay here all night."

"Well, we can't very well stay in the house." She put the car in gear and began moving down the street with her lights off. As soon as they reached the end of the block, she glanced at her rearview. "*Damn.*"

Arthur spun around. She'd been right to pass on the house. Headlights crept up behind them.

Mandy made a quick left onto South Bumby and shot north, running a red, then zipping down another block. Traffic was light, so she had no problem getting around. She soared down the street and stopped abruptly, pulling into a deserted garage. A double row of vehicles was parked off to the side, in front of the stall doors fronting the place. She eased around them, backing into a space in front of the alley separating the buildings.

While watching the street, she killed the ignition, then bent and pulled something from beneath her seat. It was a small metal toolbox, which she placed in her lap. She groped in the dark for the glove box, opening it. Still watching the streetlights straight ahead, she rummaged around and found a penlight, then closed the glove box. Using the tiny glow from the penlight, she opened the toolbox, removed a screwdriver, and handed it over. "We need a new plate."

It only took him a moment to assess the situation. "You want me to steal one?"

"And do it quickly. Hopefully, this place doesn't have dogs. Here. You'll need this." She handed him the penlight.

He got out and crept behind the parked vehicles, squeezing between an ancient pickup and one of those small trailers used to haul lawn mowers. Squatting, he stuck the penlight between his teeth. His fingers trembled, but he forced himself to stay calm. Stealing a plate was a crime, but he'd rather be charged with that than be hunted down by Vanessa and her gang.

He went back to the Toyota and switched the plates, then snuck back inside with her plate. "I figured you wouldn't want to leave this."

"Slip it under your mat. We'll put it back on if we ever get out of this."

Her statement riveted through him, and he felt worse than ever. He forced himself to stay silent as he slid her plate beneath the mat at his feet.

Mandy fired up the ignition, pulled back out onto Bumby, and hurried north.

***

A few minutes later, Mandy got onto Raeford and headed east, until they reached Conway Gardens. She pulled onto Lake Margaret and stayed on it until Semoran, where she made a right, heading south.

It was after eleven. Traffic had eased up, but the tight southbound group sticking close behind kept them both alert. Most of the flow eventually pulled off but were replaced by more Semoran traffic. This new batch followed them closely before

142

pulling into turning lanes as Mandy sailed through the next intersection.

She kept with the flow, constantly watching for possible tails. Without warning she pulled into a Quick Stop, easing up to the front and dousing her lights. She sat in silence for a full minute, watching the store activity. There were only a few people inside. "Got any money?"

"Some."

"How much?"

He pulled out the wad from his pocket and counted. "Eighty-seven bucks."

"That's all?"

"I can get another two hundred from the ATM inside. What do you have in mind?"

"Go inside and take out two hundred, then c'mon back out."

The ATM sat off to the right, across from the cash register and about fifteen feet from the glass doors. He pulled out his wallet and selected the appropriate card, then withdrew two hundred dollars. He hoped it was enough. He didn't know how much they'd need or what Mandy was planning. Besides, he didn't know if or when he'd be able to get to another ATM.

He found her outside, talking to a pair of young girls who had just left the store. Both were skinny, about eighteen, and were dressed in tight tank tops, shredded jeans, and open-toed sandals. Both wore their hair in long tendrils, sporting tattoos on their skinny arms, neck, and legs. He also saw studs on their faces and ears. The blonde's toenails and fingernails were painted red.

Mandy gestured him over. "I just asked these two if I could use their cell to make a local phone call. I also told them I'd pay them for it."

"How much?" he asked.

The blonde said, "Fifty."

The redhead said, "Seventy-five, but I wanna know why."

Mandy turned back to her. "Why what?"

"There's a payphone inside. Why not use it?"

Mandy shrugged. "I don't like payphones."

"Why not?"

"Germs."

The blonde giggled.

The redhead said, "Buy a can of Lysol."

"I hate the smell."

"Buy a can of scented."

Mand groaned. "Do you want the money or not?"

The redhead turned to Arthur.

Growing impatient, he peeled off three twenties and held them up. "Sixty bucks, no questions asked."

Mandy took the bills and waited.

The redhead crossed her arms across her skinny chest. "A hundred," she said, her evil smirk directed at him.

The blonde grabbed the money and thrust the cell into Mandy's outstretched palm. Mandy walked briskly away, dialing a number.

"Hope she doesn't go far," the blonde said. "That phone cost me a chunk of cash."

"You mean it cost B.K. a chunk of cash," the redhead said flatly.

"Whatever."

"Who's your friend calling?" the blonde asked him.

"Hope it's not anyone in Portugal," the redhead said.

"No questions," he said flatly.

***

"What was all *that* about?" he asked as they pulled out of the parking lot.

She shrugged. "I had to make a call."

"Why not use the payphone?"

"If I'm right about these people being involved with the drug companies, we can't take any chances."

"That bug they stuck me with can't possibly have that much of a range."

"How do you know?"

She was right. He *didn't* know. In this age of rampant world-wide technology, the only thing one could say for sure was that today's new advancement would be obsolete in twenty-four hours. "Does this car have GPS?"

"I wouldn't have bought it if it did."

"Why not?"

"I don't want everyone knowing where I am or what I'm doing. Call me weird, but I've never been very comfortable, knowing Big Brother is getting closer and closer."

"What do you do if you don't know where you're going?"

"I'll stop and ask someone for directions. Or buy a map. Isn't that what people used to do years ago, before GPS and cell phones?"

He caught himself gazing at the taillights straight ahead and wondered if they belonged to people who were about to set a trap. Then he glanced at the side mirror and wondered why the night was so dark. And if the headlights several car lengths behind them were the people after them.

Snap out of this. You'll drive yourself crazy.

"You gonna tell me who you called?"

"A very good friend in St. Cloud. She's a head nurse and has access to a bunch of things."

"Such as?"

"She's getting us a scanner."

"You mean--"

"We've got to find that bug."

He didn't reply. He felt his gut tightening up.

"And once we find it, you know what we've got to do."

His mind reeled. The fear, the disgust, the regret—everything came back. Vanessa and her hypodermic. Tracking him in the woods. Sending him places without his knowledge, his consent. Messing up his head, his memory. Forcing him to involve a total stranger. Following them. Stalking them. Threatening them with guns.

He needed to stop it right now, before things got any worse, if that was at all possible. Being responsible for two murders was horrible enough.

He could never forgive himself if anything happened to this lady. "I want you to drop me off. Right here."

"But we're right in the middle of--"

"I don't care. You don't belong in this."

"You're sure you want me to do that?"

His heart thumped wildly; his limbs had gone cold. He knew what would happen once he was on his own again, but he just didn't care. He didn't want her involved. Or hurt. "Yes."

She made no attempt to slow down or pull onto the shoulder.

"I'm serious, Mandy. I appreciate everything you've done, but I can't let you get any more involved in this. Just drop me off. Please?"

"What'll you do?"

"I guess I'll just--"

"I'll tell you what you'll do. You'll try and find your way back to your place, but before you get one mile, they'll find you and pick you up. I have no idea why they want you or what their scheme is, but I have this strong feeling you'll end up dead if they find you again."

He had nothing to say to that. Judging by what had already happened, he suspected she was absolutely right.

"And what about me? What do you think will happen to me after I drop you off?"

His mind went blank. He hadn't gotten this far in his thinking.

"I'll tell you what'll happen. I'll drive home and forget about you and the people after you.

Everything will be just peachy keen once I'm back to minding my own business. Right?"

He knew exactly what she was saying. It made him feel stupid.

"You're totally wrong and just as naïve as a ten-year-old if you think that'll happen. This is the real world, it's filled with monsters, and believe me, they're much more difficult to spot than the ones in horror novels and spooky TV shows. Take those three steroid cases who met us at the restaurant. You think they'll just forget about me after what I did to them? And what about the bitch who drugged you, marked you up, then jammed you with a bug? They all know you've told me everything by now. I've been keeping them from getting their claws on you for the last four hours. I may be wrong, but I'm pretty sure it's really ticking them off by now."

She was right. Dead-on. She helped him get away, and in doing so, had sealed her own fate.

"Enough about me. Were you serious when you told me you have no friends, relatives, or associates? Not even a wife?"

"I might have a connection who could help us. He's a high school chum of mine. A computer geek. He works for OPD."

"All right, then. Tomorrow, after we get rid of that bug, we're going to have breakfast. Then we'll need to..."

He didn't hear the rest. Once that phrase

("get rid of that bug")

drifted into his head, he froze, and suddenly realized that his right hand had moved toward the

148

door. He watched it as if it belonged to someone else…as if he had no control over it and had no idea what it was about to do…

Just as he realized what was happening, everything went black.

But not before he felt his hand grabbing the door-pull.

PART TWO

THE HUNTERS

Chapter 13

Arthur woke up in a strange living room.

His head ached, his temples pounded, and his entire body felt stiff and heavy. He tried to sit up, but an avalanche of dizziness forced him back down. A heavy throbbing seemed to be coming from an area between his shoulder blades. He tried to touch it, but his arms weighed a ton.

He felt the mattress he was lying on. A bed? Too narrow. A couch. That made sense since this was no doubt a living room.

He closed his eyes and struggled to remember what happened.

Mandy's Toyota. Yes. They were on the road and Mandy was talking about her friend. Things grew cloudy, and his right hand began doing something strange. He was reaching for the door.

Then blackness.

He tried sitting up again, then lay back down when the dizziness came back, filling his head.

He heard someone's voice. At first he thought it was a man. It was low-pitched and raspy. "He's awake."

Footsteps approaching.

Mandy stood over him. She was dressed in a red tee shirt and jeans. Her hair was fluffy and tangled. A soft cloud of minty shampoo drifted his way.

Someone else came into his line of vision. Another woman, this one tall, broad-shouldered, and about forty, wearing a nurse's uniform. Her thick red hair was tied in a bun and cut short in front, settling in uneven bangs over her broad forehead. Her cheeks were chubby, her nose broad and fleshy. Her lips formed a long, thin line. She gave the appearance of someone who didn't put up with nonsense.

"What happened?" he asked in a weak voice.

"We took that damned chip out of you," the woman said.

"Where *are* we? What happened? How'd I--"

Mandy frowned. "You tried to get out of my car."

He was right. He *had* reached for the door.

"You were obviously placed in another fugue somehow. Otherwise, you wouldn't have just gone blank and tried to open the door. Not while I was doing eighty miles an hour, anyway."

"How'd you stop me?"

"My three-fifty-seven." She shrugged. "Had no choice. I tapped you on the back of your head and you went right to sleep. Don't worry. I didn't do any real damage. I know where the good spots are."

"You actually took the bug out?"

"I met Rita at Kissimmee Hospital, outside the Emergency wing. She had everything ready, and it only took fifteen minutes. We did it right in the car. You began stirring, so we gave you a sedative to put

151

you back under. I figured the chip would be between your shoulder blades, and I was right. The scanner confirmed it. We removed it, then brought you here."

"Where'd you leave it?"

"Once we left the hospital, I stopped at a strip mall a few miles in the other direction, dropped it on the pavement, then mashed it with a hammer I keep in my toolbox. Then I turned around and brought you here."

He laughed. It made his head hurt worse, but he couldn't help it.

"Something funny?"

"I knew you'd get me with that gun sooner or later."

Mandy grinned.

Rita patted Mandy on the shoulder, then crossed the room with short, heavy steps, making the floor vibrate. She snatched up a huge tan leather handbag from the coat tree next to the front door. "Now that we've got your friend fixed up, I'd better get back. Still have eight hours to go before my shift's done."

"We'll probably be gone when you get back," Mandy said.

"No problem, just make yourselves comfortable. There's beer in the fridge, and also pizza I bought this afternoon. I only had time to polish off two pieces, so there's plenty left in the fridge. Pepperoni, sausage, and mushrooms. Just leave a piece or two for me. Gotta go."

Mandy followed her out.

He lay back on the cushions and let everything sink in. It all sounded incredible, but he had to accept the fact that it had happened. They'd removed a microchip from his flesh. The more he thought about it, the angrier he became. He'd been carrying around a *microchip*, for God's sake. A glass tube of technological data. In his *flesh*. He'd got hooked up with a woman who had no qualms about drugging him and sticking the cursed thing into his body.

Did this explain everything that had been happening to him? His memory lapses? His confusion? The blackouts? The mysterious trips? The two dead men?

His anger flared up, and he visualized wringing Vanessa's neck. Why would she do this? Was Mandy right? Was this all nothing more than a drug experiment? Had he been selected as some sort of guinea pig?

Or was this something else?

Mandy came back in, pushed the door shut, and slipped the chain on. She carried her gun in her right hand, which she placed on the kitchen counter. She came over to the couch and sat. "Angry at me?"

"For what?"

"You're gonna have a goose egg on the back of your head for a day or two."

He touched it gingerly. It was tender, and there was a lump beneath the bandage, but it would heal in a few days. "Like you said, you had no choice."

"So why the mad face?"

"I'm thinking about Vanessa."

153

"Think about her later. Enjoy the fact that you're no longer carrying around that chip. Want some pizza?"

"I *am* pretty hungry, now that you mentioned it."

She went back to the kitchen, opened the fridge door, pulled out the box, and placed it on the counter. Then got out two bottles of Corona and set them beside the box. He saw the beer and immediately pushed himself into a sitting position. His upper back flared up again. He chose to ignore it.

"How long have you known Rita?"

Mandy put a plate in the microwave. "About ten years. She trained me when I started working at ORMC."

"What did you tell her about...all this?"

"The truth."

"She believed you?"

"Why shouldn't she? She's my best friend."

The microwave dinged after about a minute. Mandy put the other dish in and flipped it on. While the pizza heated up, she opened the beer, picked up a bottle, and had a healthy sip. When she saw him watching her, she picked up the other bottle and brought it over. He took it and immediately pressed the ice-cold bottle to his lips. The tangy brew instantly brought him back around.

The microwave dinged again. Mandy brought over the dishes and some paper towels, placed them on the cocktail table, and sat beside him. He grabbed a plate and shoved the small steamy triangular end into his mouth. It tasted heavenly.

Mandy picked up a piece from her plate. "By the way, we'll probably need to steal another license plate tomorrow."

"I took that first one off a trailer. No one should miss it for a while."

"It says *trailer* on it. If a cop sees it, he'll stop us. There are a string of garages on Thirteenth Street, so it shouldn't be a problem. I'd like to get an early start in the morning before the rush hour starts up."

"How early?"

"I'd like to pick up the new plate by seven. Then we have to get in touch with your friend."

"Seven's pretty early."

"The sooner we can get this straightened out, the better. I'm exhausted."

"I'm really sorry about everything." He couldn't help the anger and the frustration drifting back.

"I know." She finished her pizza slice, sat back, and drank some beer.

"I'll give you one last chance to back out of this."

"We've been through this before. This has to be resolved. You know it as well as I do. Besides, I took out their chip. They'll really be pissed at me for doing that."

"I just don't know what we'll be able to do. What if these people are actually working for the drug companies?"

155

"It doesn't matter. We can't let them go around, sticking chips in people, can we?"

"No, but like I said, what can we do to stop them?"

"I've got no idea, but we've got to do *some*thing..."

***

After breakfast, they were on their way back to Orlando by seven the next morning.

As soon as they left Rita's small place, they stopped at a tire shop on Thirteenth Street that hadn't yet opened, removed a plate from one of the vehicles parked in the small lot beside the building, and were back on their way in five minutes.

Arthur felt extremely guilty for stealing two license plates in just twelve hours. Since bad cops could be involved, and since he had somehow been responsible for two murders, they couldn't report any of this to OPD. It would be a huge mistake to contact the FBI, as well.

He had no idea who they could trust. Because of his traffic stop, he didn't want to go anywhere near the OPD building. But they needed Skip's help. Mandy assured him bad cops wouldn't bring attention to themselves in a place filled with other cops. Her reasoning was sound, but he remained skeptical. And frightened.

As Mandy drove north, he couldn't shake the notion that he'd become some sort of laboratory experiment. He had no idea if Vanessa's implant was merely a tracking device or something far worse. The fact that it had been able to induce a fugue-like state told him the worst. It could be a new drug experiment. Or some sort of hallucinogen intended for military purposes. It might also be a new drug to be analyzed before being placed on the market. Whatever it was, Mandy had destroyed the evidence. The damage was done. Otherwise, Vanessa's people would have already found them.

Even so, he suspected the worst of all this hadn't yet happened. Due to Mandy's quick thinking and invaluable help, he was no longer a laboratory subject. However, he had become a loose end. If he was right, the future had become unbelievably bleak.

They reached South Hughey Avenue at a few minutes before eight o'clock and parked in the multilevel garage across the street from OPD. He had never dreaded parking garages before, but the last few days had made him jumpy. Claustrophobia had wrapped itself tightly around him, making him feel trapped and exposed. He kept staring at the side mirror, expecting someone to magically appear behind them.

"You okay?" she asked.

He didn't want her to know he was scared, so he forced out a smile. "Sure. Why?"

"You're sweating."

He shrugged. "This is Florida."

"I'm not sweating."

"Your spray-on deodorant must be better than mine."

"You used mine after you stepped out of the shower."

"What can I say? You're braver than me."

She placed a hand on his forearm. "We're gonna be okay."

Despite his fears, the warmth of her touch reassured him.

Before getting out, they both scanned the big, dark concrete area. Several cars and pickups were parked across the aisle and farther down, but no one sat in them, nor did he see movement amongst the shadows.

Mandy tapped his shoulder. "Let's get this show started."

Outside, cops, men in suits, and women in business clothes wandered in and out of the large concrete building. Cars and SUVs cruised by, some stopping at the lights, others turning down side streets, or heading for the ramp that would take them directly to I-4. He saw no glints of binoculars coming from windows. No one peering around the corner of OPD, or behind a parked vehicle. No one staring. If someone was watching, Arthur didn't see him.

His pulse fluttered as two cops came out and went down the walk, to the far side of the building. They both glanced in their direction but kept on moving. Arthur turned to see if they'd turned around as well. Neither had.

"Stop being so paranoid," Mandy whispered.

"Can't help it. I keep expecting to bump into those two again."

"I already told you about that. The chances aren't very good for that happening."

"And if it does happen?"

She shrugged. "Then I guess we're screwed."

He should have known better than mention that. Mandy wasn't one for mincing words.

***

Skip Muldrake met them in the reception area just a few minutes after they asked the receptionist to call his office.

Skip had dropped a few pounds since Arthur had last seen him. He wore a white dress shirt opened at the collar, black slacks, and shiny black leather slip-ons. He shook Arthur's hand and slapped him on the back.

"This is Mandy Rhodes," Arthur said. "Mandy? Harry Muldrake."

"Everyone calls me Skip," he said.

They shook hands.

"You obviously didn't come here to invite me to lunch," Skip said.

"We came to see if you can possibly help us," Mandy said.

"Anything I can do for an old friend and his friend. You *are* his friend, aren't you?"

"We met under really strange circumstances," she said. "But after all we've been through together, you could definitely call us friends."

Her statement made Arthur realize once again what she had done. She could have easily turned him in to the cops or told him to get out of her car. She not only believed what he told her, she decided to help him. Only someone very special would have done that.

"So how can I help?" Skip asked.

Mandy glanced at the receptionist, who was taking a call. Three suits and two cops rushed by. More people came in from the street. "Is there a place where we can talk?"

Skip snatched up two visitor's passes from the box on the reception desk. Mandy and Arthur pinned them to the front of their shirts on their way to the elevators. After a short trip, the elevator doors opened up to a carpeted hall. They went down the hall, past the restrooms and a metal water fountain. At the end, a door marked *COMPUTER ROOM* opened to a maze of cubes. They went down a long aisle, past dozens of cubes. Arthur saw no one but heard the distinctive clicking sounds of busy keyboards bouncing off the white ceiling. They stopped at the far end, facing the doorway of a corner cube.

The cube was approximately eight by eight, with a long, narrow window in the corner facing Hughey. A table sat against the opposite wall. A copier, fax machine, percolator, Styrofoam cups, sugars and creamers covered the tabletop. Two armless chairs faced the metal desk. Skip gestured for them to sit, then lowered himself into his own chair with his back to the window. "Now," he said very softly, "what's this all about?"

"We're in trouble," Arthur said.

"I kind of guessed that. What sort of trouble?"

"We don't know," Mandy said. "There's a woman involved, and she's been after him--" she jabbed a thumb at Arthur "--for the last two days."

Skip scratched his jaw. "You mentioned a woman giving you problems when you called me a few days ago. Is it the same person?"

Arthur nodded.

"Didn't I try and pull up her name?"

"Yes."

Skip scowled. "I know this was only a couple of days ago, but would you mind refreshing my memory about what happened after--"

"You found nothing."

"Good." He sat back. "For a moment I thought Old-Timer's had settled in. Nothing was coming, and I don't usually draw a blank. Not after just two days."

"She gave me a fake name."

"That was a no-brainer. I take it you've now got some idea what her real name is?"

"Her nametag said V. DeAngelis."

"Nametag?"

"Nothing else was on it except her photo and a barcode."

"Was it a security-type badge?"

"It opened metal doors that respond only to card-readers."

"V. DeAngelis." He was already typing.

"Ordinarily, we'd assume the V. means Vanessa," Arthur said, "but since we're obviously dealing with someone involved in some scary shit--"

He stopped typing. "What sort of scary shit?"

"I'm not sure, but to put it bluntly--"

"He was injected with an implant that was obviously some sort of tracking device," Mandy said. "To me, that qualifies as scary."

Skip's forehead wrinkled up. "An *implant*?"

"They also kidnapped him."

Skip's chestnut eyes grew. "You're not serious."

"They used cops for the kidnapping," she said.

"Are you absolutely sure?" Skip's voice became a tense whisper. "Regular cops?"

"They were dressed as cops," Arthur said.

"That doesn't mean they were the real thing. Not if they were involved in a kidnapping, as well as an illegal implant. Tell me more."

Mandy told him about the incident at the restaurant.

"Three men?"

"Three *big* men," Arthur said. "They had guns, too."

"And you managed to slip by them?"

Before Mandy could explain, Arthur said, "She beat the living *shit* out of those guys. All *three* of them. You should've seen--"

"Stop it, all right?" She swatted Arthur on the arm.

"Seriously?" Skip looked impressed. "A lady *your* size?"

"You can stop it, as well." Mandy frowned.

"Yes, ma'am..."

Mandy's frown vanished. "Listen. We need to find out who we're dealing with. I'm pretty sure we've got to do this carefully. We have no idea who they are or who they're connected with."

Skip went back to his keyboard. "DeAngelis. I'll try Di, De, and D apostrophe."

Less than half a minute later, he stopped clicking and sat back.

"Something wrong?" Arthur asked.

"I just found her."

Chapter 14

His heart racing, Arthur circled the desk.

There it was, filling the screen. The woman's stats, bio, history—even a photo.

DeAngelis, Vanessa Lorraine. Height 5'9". Weight 130 lbs. Eyes blue. Hair black. DOB: 8/13/85. POB: San Francisco, California. Education: Stanford University. Undergraduate Degree, Computer Engineering. Master's Degree, Computer Technology. Master of Science in Nursing, Sacramento State School of Nursing. Married 9/1/10 to Richard Summers, divorced 7/17/13. Married 3/12/14 to George S. Bradford, divorced 3/17/15. Executive Member of Administrative Staff, Central Florida Records Storage Center, Orlando since 6/10/15.

Skip clicked on an option and pulled up the particulars.

Central Florida Records Storage Center, 11735 North Rouse Road, Orlando, Florida. CFRSC, a privately funded facility. Provides paper records, security microfilm, and magnetic media storage for the Government and private sector. Handles storage consignment primarily for Orange and Osceola Counties.

"That building's a *storage facility*?" Arthur couldn't believe this. A darkly lit room. Vanessa and her syringe. Talk about a "doctor." Something was definitely wrong.

"That would explain the security you mentioned," Skip said. "Records and storage require strict privacy and security issues. The facility would have to maintain high security status for the Government and private sectors to want to use them."

"They kidnapped me and brought me there. They even tried to give me a shot to keep me there until someone they referred to as a doctor showed up."

"Did they say what this doctor was going to do?"

"No." Arthur studied the screen. Something about Vanessa's dossier raised red flags. Stanford University. Degrees in computer engineering and technology were impressive, but the one in Nursing intrigued him the most. "Why would she need a degree in Nursing when she already had two others?"

Skip continued typing. A page populated with several rows of miniature tracking systems and microchip implants came up. "Anything on this page look familiar?"

"It was black." Mandy pointed to the models in the center of the page. "And tapered at both ends. Those are about the right size, though."

"Black?"

"It looked plastic. Or quite possibly gelatin."

"Some sort of cover, or protective coating. Was it shiny or matte?"

"Shiny."

"Maybe it was designed to make the insertion easier." Skip clicked on it. It brought up a page filled with characters that looked Chinese.

Arthur glared. "She stuck me with a Chinese chip?"

"It's manufactured in China but distributed and sold over here. And the data is generated over here. The Government uses these."

"Which Government?"

Skip shrugged. "Ours. The FBI, more specifically. They've been using them for years. They're all basically like the chips they use for pets and livestock. The only difference is the actual content. They're all hooked up to different databases. FBI chips can be hidden anywhere. Many are powerful enough to track for miles."

"My God." Arthur felt even more uneasy. "What have I gotten myself mixed up in?"

Skip rubbed his eyes. "That woman's got degrees in Computer Technology, Engineering, and one in Nursing, and she's working in a storage facility. It just doesn't add up."

"She's Administrative Staff," Mandy said. "She's obviously pretty high up."

"High up in a storage facility." Skip shrugged. "The place is nothing more than a high-tech library. Anything impressive about a librarian?"

"Maybe they pay well," Arthur said.

"So do Computer Tech jobs," he said. "Engineering positions--especially in her field—start at six figures."

"Nursing, as well," Mandy said. "A nurse on the Administrative staff of a major hospital makes six figures, easy."

"Maybe she couldn't make up her mind and decided to get three degrees," Arthur said. "Just in case the economy bottomed out, as it did, and she wanted to make sure she'd always be employable."

"That's one theory," Mandy said.

"What's yours?"

She shrugged. "Her file looks really good."

"So what?"

"I think it looks too good."

Skip attacked the keys again, entering the name Richard Summers.

"Apparently Summers came up as a software CEO for DiskWorks, Inc., based out of Tampa since 2010." Skip hit another key. "Summers also graduated from Stanford with a Master's in Computer Engineering and worked as Administrative Assistant for SanDisk, in San Francisco, from 2011 until 2015.

"SanDisk?"

Skip pulled up the stats. "One of the elite crowd from Silicon Valley. They're a data storage facility. Very high-tech. Flash memory cards, USB flash drives, digital audio players. The *crème de la crème* of modern technology."

"Summers worked for them, then moved to Tampa, and branched out on his own?"

"DiskWorks has a more efficient distribution program in media conversion and transfer. Summers probably took what he learned at SanDisk and used it to snare his former contacts. His company's client base is heavily concentrated in the San Francisco Bay area."

"This could explain why she's at the facility on Rouse Road," Mandy said. "If she worked with Summers during their marriage, she probably learned the potential in data storage."

"That facility has to be some kind of front," Arthur said.

"If it is, it's a good one," Skip said. "They've got helluva customer base. Reputable local high-tech companies, many of them with Government contracts. AT&T. Lockheed-Martin. Merrill/Lynch. Advanced Micro Devices. Oracle. Tupperware. UPS. These companies have their own storage facilities, but many of them pay for backup files in case of national emergency, or natural disasters. Hurricanes, tropical storms—you know the drill."

"Maybe their customers don't know what's going on."

"That's a stretch. Let's check out Husband Number Two." Skip entered George S. Bradford's name. The FBI screen automatically came up. A red blinking line flashed over Bradford's name. The words *SECURITY LEVEL DENIED PASSWORD CLEARANCE REQUIRED* slid across the center of the screen.

"Uh-oh. Now I've done it."

"Looks like she was married to a Fed," Mandy said.

"What's with the fireworks?" Arthur asked.

"This is definitely Eyes Only. I need my supervisor's permission for this. It's got alert status, which reports hits to other departments immediately. If my supervisor's in his office, he's probably already seen the alert."

"Apparently Bradford's high security," Arthur said.

"Or high security risk," Mandy said. "I guess that means we're dead in the water."

Skip grinned. "Under ordinary circumstances, maybe..."

"You know of a way to sneak in there and pull it all up?"

"First, I've got to get out. Someone's monitoring, knows I'm in there and is checking me out." He backed out of the webpage, then closed all his other windows. His cheeks had flushed.

"I sure hope we didn't jeopardize your job," Arthur said. It was bad enough he'd turned Mandy's life upside-down.

"I get into trouble a lot. It's unavoidable in this situation. I've pulled up sensitive stuff before."

"Any idea how long it'll be before you can go back in there and try again?"

"I'd better wait a little while. I've got a break coming, anyway. If anyone says anything, I'll just give 'em a story."

"We'd better go," Mandy said. "I don't want anyone seeing us here. It might make them ask you more questions."

"Let us know how this turns out," Arthur said.

"How can he?" Mandy frowned. "We ditched our phones."

"Dammit, I guess I forgot. We had to get rid of them so they wouldn't track us again."

Skip opened his bottom drawer and reached inside. "How about a nice, fresh, top-of-the-line burn phone?" He clicked it open, programmed a number, snapped it shut and handed it to Arthur. "My number's on speed dial. It's programmed with a re-router that'll automatically switch the line to another grid. If someone taps my phone, they'll get someone else's number."

"Thanks," Arthur said.

"We'll keep in touch," Mandy said.

When the elevator doors opened on the ground floor, they went out, making their way to the lobby through the small crowds of passersby. Mandy suddenly grabbed his upper arm and pulled him back around the corner, behind a potted plant.

"What's wrong now?" His pulse hammered as he gawked at her.

"One of the guys from the restaurant last night." Her voice was a harsh whisper. "He's standing over there, at the reception desk."

***

Arthur recognized him instantly.

The man was the one blocking the bathroom doorway when they tried to leave. Now he was blocking their exit from the Police Station, watching everyone who passed, came in, or left the building, and talking into a cell phone as he scanned the area.

To get past him, Mandy and Arthur would have to turn invisible.

"They couldn't possibly have tracked us here." Mandy sounded irritated.

Mandy was right. She destroyed the chip as well as swapped her tag twice. Unless they had scanned her VIN with some sort of ultra-tech scope, they couldn't have tracked them here. But they obviously had.

"Maybe he works here as a security guard," he said.

"Wanna just stroll on by and see what he does?"

When she put it that way, he felt silly for even voicing the idea. Still, something about this made no sense. "He can't do much in a police station, can he? He can't exactly kidnap someone in full view of every cop in the city."

"That doesn't exactly give me a warm fuzzy."

"Me, neither."

"I'm up for suggestions."

He shook his head. "I don't think we have too many. Even if we manage to get past him, his buddies are probably outside, watching the parking lot."

"And if they checked out the garage, they already recognized my Toyota. I'll bet it's the only twenty-year-old Toyota there."

"Then I'd say it would be pretty damned stupid for us to go back to the car."

"Well, we can't stay here very long. Let's try another exit."

They hurried down the hall, merging with a small group of people in business suits and turning left, down another hall. This one took them directly to the *EXIT* sign above the rear door awaiting them about a hundred feet straight ahead.

Goon Number Two stood near the door, talking to his cell.

Grabbing Arthur by the elbow, Mandy pulled him into the small alcove beneath the *RESTROOMS* sign. "I guess that solves that mystery."

"This is beginning to look kind of, well, bleak."

She sighed. "Got any ideas that could actually work?"

He reached into his pocket, brought out Skip's burn phone, and handed it to her.

Mandy stared blankly at it. "Anyone in particular you'd like me to call?"

"How about nine-one-one?"

She blinked. "And what exactly should I tell them?"

"Can you sound hysterical? They'll probably believe a hysterical woman."

She smiled. "I think I know where you're going with this." She dialed the number and began breathing heavily. "Hi…um, yes…I'm calling about a…well, I just saw this guy walk into the Police Station a few minutes ago. Huh? I'm coming to it, dammit. Don't rush me, I'm scared, and when I'm scared, my brain kinda lets loose and—yeah, yeah. Deep breaths. All right. Thanks, shoulda thought of that myself. Anyway, before this guy goes inside, he opens his coat and I see what looks like a…a…hell,

172

it sure did look like a bomb strapped to his belt. And a gun. I also saw a gun...in one of those shoulder holster hickeydoos. About two minutes ago. He's big, wearing a dark suit. He's got a shaved head, and went in through the front... My name? Oh God, no! I see *another* guy, and he's dressed just like the first guy. He's going around the back, and his hand's in his jacket pocket. Gotta go!" She snapped it shut and handed it back to him. "How was that?"

"You were great." He took the phone and frowned at it.

"Then why the furrowed brow?"

"What if they try tracing the number? They'll probably consider it a crank call."

"They take bomb scares seriously. But don't worry. Even if they try, this phone's untraceable, remember?"

"Guess I forgot. So then, I guess all we have to do is wait and see how long it takes for someone to--"

Two men in security uniforms rushed around the corner. One of them spotted them, stopped, and gestured. "Ma'am? Sir? Please accompany us to the rear exit."

"Is something wrong?" Mandy asked.

Two uniformed cops and three well-dressed women scurried by. A woman in a police uniform hurriedly pushed an elderly man in a wheelchair down the hall past them.

"No time for explanations," the security guy said, and both men nudged them down the hall, where small groups of people were being ushered toward the *EXIT* sign.

Goon Number Two had disappeared.

***

Outside in the bright morning sunlight, people milled about in small groups.

Many smoked cigarettes and chattered away while cops dropped orange cones in a crooked line surrounding the rear lot. The piercing sounds of sirens increasing in volume preceded the red bomb disposal truck and trailer, which eased to a stop in front of the building. Many in the groups scattered, heading in the direction of South Bryan Avenue. Those still watching remained frozen in place.

Mandy and Arthur joined a group moving quickly up the walk while more cops dropped orange cones across Hughey Avenue. Other uniforms waved at traffic, motioning for them to turn around or back up.

As Mandy and Arthur moved away from the OPD Building, they both watched the activity in front of the parking garage. Arthur assumed Mandy was wondering if it was safe to return to the Toyota. In the chaos of a bomb scare, it would be difficult to keep an eye on everyone in the crowd. Vanessa's people might have decided to bring in reinforcements.

"Think it's safe to get back to the car?" he asked.

"Stick with the crowd. I don't think they'll try anything with so many others around."

"They already tried to get us in a crowded restaurant."

"Only when we left the main room."

They followed two well-dressed women and a young couple pushing a stroller into the dark concrete building. While the couple with the stroller went up to the second level, Mandy and Arthur followed the women down the ramp. One woman marched right over to a sparkling red Honda while the other approached a black Audi three spaces down.

Keeping their brisk pace, Mandy and Arthur went down the aisle. When they were about six spaces down from the Toyota, the heavy clicking of heels behind them grew louder quickly.

"Dammit." Arthur immediately felt his blood pressure rising.

"Keep walking. We might have to split up if there are more of them."

Fear gripped him; he couldn't imagine doing this by himself.

The footsteps accelerated. He had the strong urge to run. Sensing his fear, Mandy grabbed his wrist and squeezed. When he turned to her, she shook her head and slowed her steps. He followed suit. Just then, she stopped entirely, let go of his wrist, and spun around. He spun around as well.

The man following them stopped cold about six feet away. He wasn't one of the three who'd accosted them at the restaurant, but was dressed similarly, in a dark suit and black dress shoes. He wore a buzz cut like the others and was around the same age—twenty-five or so. Also like the others, he had broad shoulders, a thick neck, and a large chest. His gaze shifted from Arthur, then to Mandy.

"Are you following us?" she asked bluntly.

The man said nothing.

"Nothing to say?"

He remained silent.

Mandy sighed. "If you're gonna stand there like an idiot, I guess you won't mind if we just leave."

The man's right hand disappeared beneath his jacket. Mandy took one quick giant step. Her other leg shot up, the toe of her shoe slamming into his unprotected crotch. Gasping loudly, he doubled up, clutching himself. A small handgun shot out from his grip, clattering to the pavement. Mandy reached out quickly. Her arm bent at the elbow, she shoved her extended fingers at the man's eyes. He screamed. His head jerked back. His hands covered his face as he dropped to both knees.

"Let's get out of here." Mandy picked up the man's gun.

They rushed to the Toyota. Mandy had already clicked the doors unlocked, and they jumped in. She fired it up, slammed it into reverse and pulled out.

Knowing he was going to be captured again, Arthur handed her Skip's phone. "Take it." Without a word, she shoved it down her pants pocket, flipped the car in gear, and headed for the exit.

By the time they'd reached the ticket gate, a black van waited on the other side, blocking the exit. Two large men stood in front of it, watching them grimly.

176

"Shit." Mandy checked the rearview. Another van had snuck up close, blocking their escape. "We're trapped."

"Now what?" He could barely breathe, let alone speak.

"We have to split up."

"We've got guns."

"So have they."

"But it's our only chance!" Panic gripped him. The thoughts of leaving her made him nauseous.

"Forget it. Run as fast as you can. It's been nice." She ran a hand through his hair, gave him a quick smile, and forced open her door.

Anger seized him. He kicked open the other door and bolted out of the car, but before he could manage three steps, two of them had grabbed his arms, lifted him up, and pulled him off-balance. Behind him, a man barked something. Farther down, Mandy yelled, and a scuffle ensued. The man gasped loudly, and another squealed. His anger intensifying, Arthur struggled to pull away from the two huge men holding him. He let a fist fly. It connected into soft tissue, and one of the men holding him gasped and released his grip. Arthur mule-kicked at them, catching something hard--a knee, perhaps--and heard another yell of pain close behind him.

Someone else had entered the picture. He counted at least three of them, all of them sidestepping to avoid being kicked. He fought to pull his arms free, but his left arm was immobilized in a viselike grip while his right was pulled savagely behind his back. Exhaustion came quickly, weakening him. An explosion of searing pain danced up his arm, turning his shoulder into a ball of hot numbness. A cold dab of something wet preceded the pinch of a needle applied to his neck, and he knew any attempt to struggle from then on would be worthless. He thought he heard a gunshot behind him, but just as he tried to analyze what happened, he felt himself going limp.

Blackness came quickly.

Chapter 15

He awoke lying on a couch in a dark, cool room.

A long table lined with monitors spanned the opposite wall. Behind the monitors, a large pedestal-mounted TV screen covered most of the wall. Google Earth filled the screen, brightening the room. Two male figures sat in front of the monitors, their backs to him. A small desk lamp lit up the area between them. Both wore headsets and were mumbling into small headset-type microphones while working their keyboards.

He struggled to sit up, but a wave of dizziness engulfed him, forcing him back down. Sighing, he closed his eyes and massaged his temples. Only then did he realize he wasn't tied down. Strange. Would these people go to such lengths to hunt him down without making sure he didn't escape again?

He tried a second time to sit up. The dizziness returned, but not quite as harsh. A tingling sensation in his right shoulder trickled down his arm. It was where they grabbed him in the parking garage. They had probably torn a muscle.

Resting his elbows on his thighs, he gently massaged his eyes, hoping to regain his equilibrium and adapt his eyesight to the dim lighting. Other than the Google Earth image and the tiny hazy glow from the desk lamp, he remained in darkness.

He thought of Mandy and wondered where she was—if she had been able to escape. He wondered about the gunshot he heard an instant before they knocked him out. Had she shot one of them? Or had they shot her?

A rush of warm bile filled his throat. He couldn't live with himself if they'd done anything to her. She'd gotten away—he was certain of it. She shot one of them and injured another, perhaps two of them. Mandy knew how to take care of herself. She probably blinded at least two of them. There was no way she would ever let them catch her.

Keep thinking this, he told himself. *Otherwise, depression will set in. You'll blame yourself and give up--*

Stop it, take hold of yourself, and get out of here. You owe it to her.

He had escaped before, hadn't he? This situation would be simpler because the two at the monitors were occupied. Also, since Vanessa wasn't in the room, he wouldn't have to contend with her again.

With renewed vigor, he pushed himself into a standing position. The dizziness came back. So did the tingling in his shoulder. This paralleled the morning after his first night with Vanessa. That same dizziness, that same confusion.

Keeping an eye on the two figures at the monitors, he forced himself back up. He wanted to knock their heads together, but that would require sneaking up on them. He was more interested in getting out of this room.

Ignoring the growing nausea, he tiptoed across the room, to the door, where a slender horizontal beam of orange light shone just above the floor. He stopped moving and turned once again to the two men. They remained engrossed in their work.

He took two more slow cautious steps.

A large, broad figure appeared out of the darkness, blocking the door.

No wonder he wasn't tied down. Where can you go when a mountain of hard flesh guarded the room?

The mountain pointed to the couch.

Feeling like a chastised little kid, Arthur trudged back to the couch, sat, and buried his face in his hands. Now what? Just sit here and wait? For what? For who? What was all this about? Was this actually an experiment with the drug companies? Was he nothing more than a laboratory rat? Who were those two watching Google Earth?

The door opened slowly. A vertical orange beam slowly grew thicker in the widening doorway. The shapely figure of a woman appeared in its glowing center. She came in and shut the door behind her. The scent of lavender, like a brush of forbidden sweetness, wafted gently toward him, sliding across his face.

It was Vanessa.

***

"You've been very naughty, Arthur."

Vanessa sounded like she was talking to a child. She approached him cautiously, her arms crossed, stopping about three feet from where he sat on the couch.

In the darkness, he couldn't see her features clearly. This irritated him. He wanted to see the lump on her forehead; it would have given him a sense of accomplishment, of triumph. A little self-confidence would have shown in his eyes, softening her arrogance. But the darkness had blurred out her features, giving her an intimidating anonymity. And the condescension in her voice kept both his anger and helplessness frighteningly close.

"You really shouldn't have wandered off. Look at the mischief you've gotten into." She uncrossed her arms and rested her hands on her hips. It reminded him of Nazi movies he had seen, where the women interrogators were named Ilsa and delighted in torturing and castrating men. "I still haven't forgiven you, by the way." She reached up and pushed some hair away from her face. "My head still hurts."

He remained silent. He wanted to laugh but knew it wouldn't make this situation any better.

"Nothing to say? I would've thought you'd be inquiring about that skinny blond nurse friend of yours."

He perked up. "Where *is* she?"

She sighed, and her breasts rose, obviously to get a rise out of him. It was a wasted effort. "She met with an unfortunate accident."

Heat engulfed him, and despite the dizziness, he stood up. The mountain of muscle immediately emerged from the darkness and lumbered right over. "What sort of accident?"

"Ah. A strong response. And here we were thinking you two were just--"

"What happened?"

"Are you sure you want to know, Arthur?"

"Tell me, dammit!"

"Your friend is dead."

Dead...

The horrid word ripped through him, and he collapsed onto the cushions. Suddenly light-headed, he bent forward, his head between his thighs. He wanted to cry, to scream. Mandy was dead. Because of him. And nothing he could do or say could change it. These cold-hearted bastards had killed her.

The hot rage swept through him. He jumped up again. His hands had turned into hot fists. He wanted to strangle her. He also wanted to strangle the two sitting at the screen, as well as the mountain of muscle standing beside her. These bastards had killed Mandy because she had helped him. It was his fault entirely, and he knew he would never be able to live with himself.

He lunged at Vanessa. Before his hands could get within two feet of her neck, the mountain of muscle had wrapped its powerful arms around Arthur's torso, picking him up easily. Arthur continued struggling, his feet lashing out at empty air, his pinned arms totally useless. The pressure around his chest was excruciating. The breath eased out of him, and he felt himself going limp beneath the viselike grasp. In seconds, he stopped struggling, and the pressure around his torso vanished. The floor slapped the bottoms of his feet when he was set back down. A huge hand pressed against his chest, covering it. He was then pushed backward onto the couch.

As he stirred weakly on the cushions, he wanted to jump back up and lash out again. Another hot surge swept through him. Using what remaining strength he could summon within himself, he shoved his fist clumsily into the enemy's midsection. It felt like he'd just punched an eighty-pound punching bag. The gorilla didn't even flinch; he grabbed Arthur's wrist, twisting it and pulling his arm behind his back and halfway up, until Arthur's fist rested painfully between his shoulder blades. A jagged fireball raced up his arm, settling in his shoulder. Defeated, he fell to his side. The huge hulk released Arthur's wrist and backed slowly away.

"Finished with your tantrum?" Vanessa asked. "Kraus is very strong, Arthur. I suggest you don't antagonize him further. He has anger issues he hasn't yet resolved quite yet."

Arthur carefully brought his arm around to his side. Aside from a strange tingling in his left shoulder, his right arm felt undamaged.

Tingling in his left shoulder. What was *that* all about?

He needed to focus. The issue was Mandy. "Why?" he asked in a weak, raspy voice. "Why the hell did you have to *kill* her?"

"She gave us no choice. She was quite a fighter—I'll give her that. She shot one of our men

184

and injured three others. It was a shame she had to die. She would have fitted in well with our organization."

Our organization. And they used people named Kraus. Once again he thought of the Nazis.

"What did you do with...with her?"

"Why so concerned, Arthur? Would you like to send flowers?"

His gaze focused once again on her swanlike neck. It was too dark to see it, but he could easily imagine the tiny pulse fluttering inside it and calculated just how much pressure it would take to stop it. He visualized his hands grabbing her head by the ears and twisting...and twisting again. And again...until the snap echoed loudly in the room.

The hatred plunging within him scared him. He had never been this angry before, had never felt such seething rage coursing through him. It was almost like a terrifying monster had awakened beneath his skin, growing, breathing through his lungs, seeing through his eyes.

This woman was evil. Cold. Vicious. Unfeeling. She had seduced him. Drugged him. Injected him. Forced him to kill. God only knew what lies she told him during the last--

Lies. It came to him in a bright flash. This bitch had been lying to him since he had known her. She could be lying now. If she was, there was one sure way to find out. He had to find out. Had to know for sure.

"How do I know Mandy's dead?"

"I just told you she was."

"And if I don't believe you?"

"Now why would you not believe me?"

"Because you're a lying, evil, conniving bitch."

"Such language, Arthur..."

"Let me repeat my question. How do I know Mandy's really dead?"

"Are you sure you want to know?"

"God dammit, I *need to know*!"

"Oscar." She didn't take her eyes off him. "Bring up the footage of yesterday afternoon's activities—specifically that fiasco in the parking garage on Hughey Avenue."

Oscar attacked the keyboard. Google Earth disappeared from the screen and was immediately replaced with camera footage showing the scuffle in the parking garage. The camera, working inside the van that had blocked Mandy's Toyota from behind, stayed on Arthur during his struggle with the two men. The man on his left pinned his arms while his partner removed something—probably the hypodermic—from his jacket pocket.

The scene shifted, showing Mandy from the back, shooting one of the men. The angle suggested it was coming from a camera positioned in the other van—the one blocking Mandy and Arthur from the front. The man went down, clutching his right arm. Two others rushed toward her. Mandy gouged them both in the face and ducked under the ticket gate. She dodged another man and turned the corner. Another man appeared, grabbing her around the waist and picking her up easily. She kicked him in the shin, forcing him to release her while dropping to one knee. She spun around and gouged him in the face. He collapsed, clutching at his face. Mandy began running away. Another man lashed out, kicking her behind her right knee. She went down hard and rolled, hitting her head on the concrete ledge. She lay still.

Tears gathered in his eyes.

"Satisfied, Arthur?" Vanessa shrugged.

"You bitch..." His head throbbed hotly as the rage surged through him. It felt as though the temperature in the room had gone up ten degrees.

"She gave us no choice. It was unfortunate. As I just said, she would have proved useful."

"She would never have worked for you—whoever the hell you people are."

"We," Vanessa said firmly. "You are one of us now, Arthur."

"I'll never work for you, either."

"You already are. And since we've been able to reacquire and repair you, you're back on our team."

The tears in his eyes grew hot. Reacquire? Repair? She made it sound like he was some sort of machine. "The first chance I get, I'm going to the police and telling them what you've been doing. And what you did to Mandy."

"I'm pretty certain you won't do that, Arthur."

"And what makes you say that?"

"Your past activities just might incriminate you."

"My what?"

"Oscar. Open up Arthur Sills's file--especially his last two assignments."

187

Assignments? What the hell was this psychotic bitch talking about?

The first footage that came on showed him standing over the gray-haired old man in the white lab coat. As he held the paperweight, the camera zoomed to the floor, getting a clear close-up of the huge halo of blood pooling beneath the man's head. The camera shifted, providing a close-up of the bloody paperweight in Arthur's hand. Last of all, the close-up settled on his blank face.

The second piece of footage showed him sneaking out of an office. Just before he closed the door, the camera, positioned in a corner of the office near the ceiling, focused on the body of a well-dressed man with dark hair and full beard lying behind the desk. Once again, there were close-ups of the body, followed by Arthur's face just as he slipped out of the room.

"Bring back memories, Arthur?"

"No. Not at all." He didn't know how he kept from screaming. The anger was the only thing holding him together. "I was kind of unconscious at the time. Both times."

"And that's what you'll tell the Orlando police?"

"How's that?"

"If you go to the police to report what you think we've been doing, they'll receive copies of these tapes in the mail. You realize that, of course."

They had him cold and nothing he could do would change it.

"Now do you get it, Arthur? Now do you understand who you belong to?"

"I have no idea who or what you people are. I don't understand *any* of this."

Vanessa chuckled softly. "You're wrong, Arthur. You understand all you'll ever need to."

Chapter 16

He had stumbled upon a group of cold-blooded killers and had become one of their pawns.

They now owned him. He had already killed two people for them.

"Who *are* you people?"

"You don't need to know, Arthur. All you need to do is follow orders--which you'll do because we've given you no choice."

Her words tore into him like shards of glass. He couldn't let himself give in. He could not believe anything this woman told him. It was too unreal.

"I'd like to know the names of--"

"There is no need. I am the only one you'll answer to. You're much better off not knowing who else is involved. In a worst-case scenario, if the unforeseen happens and your mission is aborted, you shall know as little as possible if you are captured by the enemy and interrogated. You can surely see how important this is to us—yes?"

The "enemy." Who the hell was "the enemy?"

"Do you understand, Arthur?"

Her smug attitude caused his blood to heat up. "I certainly wouldn't want anything to jeopardize your fanatical plans."

"I'm *so* glad I picked you, Arthur." Vanessa's smile glowed in the darkness, reminding him of some hideous beast from a vampire flick. "There was one point when I feared I'd made a mistake.

When you overpowered me last night, I actually thought--"

"Why did you pick *me*?" It had become the most important question of all.

She shrugged. "I liked you."

"That was all? The only reason?"

"Our recruitment practices might seem strange, but they usually achieve the appropriate result."

"That was it, then? You liked me?"

"There was a little more to it than that, of course."

"Like what?"

"You're damaged, Arthur. You suffered a tremendous loss, one that nearly destroyed you. As a result, you retired from society, from life."

"So?"

She shrugged. "You've become a hermit. A loner."

Loner. Like Lee Harvey Oswald. And Chapman. And John Hinckley, Jr. And Dahmer. The realization slammed through him.

"Your record substantiates your grief, Arthur. Grief can be self-destructive, as you undoubtedly know. It can cause one to do the most impulsive things. It takes over, and oftentimes the mind caves in under the pressure, causing the victim to snap."

She had mentioned his age when she was talking to Mandy at the hospital. At the time, he'd thought it odd that she knew. Now it made perfect sense. "You found my name in the *Sentinel,* in the obituaries. When Denise..." He could hardly hear his own voice.

"We've done extensive research, Arthur. In the event of an arrest, your spotless record will easily convey the message that you simply snapped. We found no arrests, no criminal activities, in your files. No evidence of drunk driving—not even a speeding ticket during the last twenty years. You're a sterling example of a fine, law-biding citizen beyond reproach."

These people were good. And thorough. They had access to his records and obviously had the time to go back to his teen years. They even used their resources to grab two legitimate-looking cops and a legitimate-looking squad car. They tapped into Tannenbaum's office and gotten footage of everything the man had done during the last couple of days. Vanessa undoubtedly did serious work at that storage facility, using her knowledge for things other than records and file storage.

"To make a long story short, Arthur, you're a very safe investment."

"Lucky me." It took two tries to find his voice again.

"We're the lucky ones. Those of us on the Planning Committee all agree that your association with us will be extremely rewarding."

"The *Planning Committee*? *That's* what you call yourselves?"

"The Committee is only a small part of our organization. We are quite large and spread out. Our mission is to make sure the correct people are chosen for the right jobs--"

"So *that's* what you are? An employment agency?"

"We also guarantee that certain events take place in their natural order. And those threatening this process are removed before anything is done to upset the balance of events."

She sounded like a psycho villain in a James Bond novel.

"We certainly wouldn't want anyone to upset that balance."

Vanessa ignored his comment. "Like I said, we're an extremely large organization."

"One that murders people."

"Assassinations are only a small part of what we do. Everything is part of the greater picture. As I've said, we make sure certain things happen when and where they are scheduled to happen."

He forced Mandy's image away. He couldn't let himself lose focus. "How long have you...has this...been going on?"

"It's really not necessary to go into that. Let's just say our organization is crucial to this modern way of life. World markets and futures depend upon certain governments operating appropriately. Otherwise, the collapse of modern Mankind would have taken place years ago."

"Sometimes I think Mankind needs to collapse."

"Enough chatter, Arthur. I've already told you too much. Now it is time for you to start back to work."

"W-Work?"

"Make us proud, now. You've got many important tasks ahead of you."

"Killing people?"

Vanessa sighed. "I know this can be difficult for the average person to understand, but an astonishing large percentage of the people on this planet simply have no value."

Vanessa was insane. So were the people she was associated with.

He needed to learn more about this. He couldn't let them turn him into a killer. "Just tell me one more--"

"No time for that. Oscar?" She turned toward the two men sitting in front of the screen. The one on the left raised his head slightly. "Arthur needs his immediate release."

Arthur turned to the screen. Beneath SUBJECT, AUXILIARY TEAM B, RCK-7, DK-2, the name, Sills, A. J., was displayed, with several vertical columns of figures filling the large blue space directly beneath it. The figures were a combination of numbers and capital letters and changed rapidly.

Following a swift series of harsh clicks, Oscar entered a long sequence on the keyboard.

Blackness immediately followed.

***

He woke up on his living room sofa.

The lamp on the end table was on. So was the kitchen light, as well as the light in the hall. The TV was playing a movie from his DVD collection—one of the Bourne flicks. He couldn't remember if he'd left the DVD in the player. It had been a while since he had seen it. If it had been left in the player, it might explain why it was playing. Otherwise, he had to assume he had selected it when he came home. The only problem was that he had no recollection of doing anything from the time he had blacked out after talking with Vanessa in the dark room.

Anyone else would have freaked over such a baffling situation, but after what he had been through during the last few days, he didn't think anything would ever surprise him again.

His encounter with Vanessa rushed back. And with it, every unpleasant detail. The dark room. The two men sitting in front of the huge screen. The mountain of flesh guarding the door. Vanessa. Google Earth. Film footage of the gray-haired man in the lab coat. Tannenbaum's office. The scuffle in the parking garage. Most of all, the horror footage of Mandy.

She was dead. The bastards had killed her.

He was "reacquired" by Vanessa and her ghoulish cohorts. He had also been "repaired." They no doubt inserted another tracking device into his flesh while he was unconscious.

He sat up slowly. The dizziness didn't hit him as hard as he expected. He immediately felt the dressings on his lower back. Still tender to the touch. He carefully pulled the bandage loose. The dark, dried blood suggested the dressing hadn't been removed.

He was convinced he was wearing a new tracker. Where had they put it this time? Did it really matter?

Mandy was dead. That was the only thing he cared about.

It was bad enough Denise had died so needlessly. So unjustly. Much too soon. But now, just one year later, he was faced with the death of another beautiful woman. This one was dead because of him. Because he had crawled too close to her car. Because she was the kind of person who helped people, who couldn't drop them off because she would worry about what could happen to them.

In his present mood, he didn't care what he'd done before he'd awakened on the couch. Didn't care why the movie was playing. Or even who had put it on. His life had become someone else's property, and nothing would change that. Nothing but his own death.

Yes. It came down to that. The only thing he could control was his own death. It was the one thing they couldn't take away from him. He didn't know if they were aware of it, but he certainly was. But he had to do it while he was still conscious. Before he was programmed into another blackout.

It seemed the only sensible solution. He no longer had control over his own actions and was doomed to spend the rest of his life killing people he didn't even know, for reasons known only to his handlers.

The situation couldn't possibly eclipse the guilt he felt for Mandy's death. It was a guilt he could never forget, and one he would live with for the rest of his life. It was this fact alone that convinced him to end their game quickly.

Since he knew he couldn't end his life by his own hand, the only option was to smear himself on the road. He had tried that same thing months ago, when the pain from Denise's death grew unbearable. This wouldn't be any different. If he was lucky, he wouldn't get out of this one alive. As grisly as it sounded, it wouldn't be that difficult. It was late; the drunks would be out in droves. If he handled this properly, a wild chase with a drunk would be all he needed to seal his doom.

He crossed the room and opened the front door. The Caddie sat in its usual spot near the trimmed bushes. It was a warm, muggy night; the mosquitoes, flies, and gnats were out in full force. As good a night as any to bring an abrupt end to this unpleasant business.

He went back into the kitchen to check the counter, where he kept his keys. Of course they were right there, where he always left them. He would have been surprised if they hadn't been there.

He went back outside and got into his car, switched on the ignition, flicked on his lights, and backed out of his space.

The last time he had done this, he ended up on Colonial and Goldenrod, and traffic hadn't been bad when he'd wrapped himself around the telephone pole that nearly broke his back. Tonight, since he was in a more composed frame of mind, he would choose his battleground wisely. His point of departure would be the strip clubs lining the Trail. The area typically crawled with drunks and frustrated men haunting the porno shops and strip clubs.

He cruised down the street and zipped right through the orange light. As he proceeded down the next block and turned onto Semoran Boulevard, the glare of headlights in his side and rearview mirrors made him shield his eyes.

Idiot. He wasn't in the mood for this tonight.

He stomped onto the gas pedal. The headlight glare continued blinding him, and he carefully adjusted both mirrors. As a precaution, he soared through the next red light. The vehicle behind him stayed on his rear bumper, tearing through it as well.

The realization ripped through him. He was being followed.

***

Despite the strong, almost overwhelming urge to hurl himself into another place and time, he kept the Caddie steady.

Perhaps it was the intense anger consuming him. Despite his depression, his decision to end his life, he wanted to get back at them. To kill Vanessa for making this happen. To strangle Oscar for having the power of life and death at the touch of a keyboard. Most of all, he wanted to punish everyone responsible for killing Mandy. To make them feel the pain, the agony, and the guilt he felt.

His brain jumped into overload, forcing his body into action. Before he realized what he was doing, he had shifted lanes and increased his speed, zipping through a red light. The headlights stayed close behind, but he continued hauling ass, taking advantage of the breaks in the heavy traffic.

His plans of suicide had completely vanished. He found it almost amusing that only minutes earlier, he had wanted some drunken stranger to kill him. Now that someone posed a threat, he was fighting to avoid a confrontation. He had no idea who it was. It could have been Vanessa or one of her watchdogs. It could have been some drunk. Or just some idiot who liked tailgating. It didn't matter. For some inexplicable reason, this encounter had triggered something in him that he had never experienced before. A warm rush had swept through him, and he wondered if this sudden euphoria was directly connected to Mandy's death.

Why didn't he just slam on the brakes and let the tailgater hurl into the Caddie? He had been managing a steady 55. Being rear-ended at this speed and forcing him into someone else would easily put him in the hospital. But now he realized he didn't want to be rear-ended. As he weaved dangerously in and out of the lanes, he wanted only to lose the tail.

Had his encounter with Vanessa changed his attitude toward life? Had the fear of death overshadowed all his former feelings of depression and self-destruction?

As he ran another red light, he found that he didn't care about his attitude or feelings. Despite all those other feelings consuming him, his seething anger remained foaming at the brim like some hazardous concoction about to overflow. He wanted blood. And revenge. And he needed to live if he wished to carry it all out. He wanted to see blind terror in the eyes of those who had ruined his life, who were responsible for ending Mandy's life.

He risked a quick peek in the rearview. He could tell there were two people in the sedan. Were they Vanessa's cohorts? If so, why the tail?

They probably didn't want him driving around late at night. They had spent considerable time and money rewiring and reprogramming him; they would not want their investment ruining their plans or future assignments.

He turned onto Colonial and headed east, then pulled into the turning lane to follow a battered pickup and two motorcycles into the front lot of a crowded bar. As expected, the sedan turned in behind him. He slowed to a crawl until the vehicles in front of him found parking spaces. Then he turned right, dodging small groups of drunks staggering back to their rides as he circled the building. He finally reached the entrance and pulled back onto Colonial, heading west.

At the intersection of Colonial and Semoran, he turned left and headed south, mashing down on the gas. The sedan followed, and they were soon both weaving in and out of traffic, until Curry Ford Road awaited them straight ahead. He cut a sharp right, smacking the curb. Close behind him, the sedan nearly slammed into a van, swerving out of danger before thumping onto the curb.

About a hundred yards later, he slowed and pulled into the strip mall behind the huge shopping center complex facing Semoran. He hurried down the paved lot, turning left and easing down the narrow road beside the supermarket, then coming out in front of the massive brightly lit building.

His plans for revenge continued unraveling before his eyes. He could circle around and head back out onto Curry Ford Road. The intersection of Curry Ford and Semoran was considered one of the most dangerous in Central Florida. Traffic remained heavy; running the red light at the intersection would result in certain suicide. If the sedan kept close, it would enter the field of fire as well.

He veered left, but the sedan zipped past, cutting him off and stopping directly in front of him. The tinted side window prevented him from glimpsing the driver. Arthur was tempted to ram him, but his gut intervened, telling him to back up. He slammed into reverse but saw lights in his rearview as two vehicles eased past. His pulse thumped mercilessly as he waited nervously for them to pass, his wet palms gripping the wheel. He needed to go through with this. Ram them. Yes. That would work. He'd survive, but the driver would be dead. Spending the rest of his life in prison would screw up their plans.

He slammed it into gear. His heart thrashed so loudly, he feared it would explode. *Take a deep breath. You can do this. Do it for Mandy. She would want you to. In fact, if she was still here, sitting beside you, she'd--*

The door of the sedan shot open. The driver jumped out.

It was Skip.

His heart leaped. He sat there, frozen. Was it really Skip? Or were his eyes deceiving him? Was the fear of what he had almost done making him hallucinate? Was it the panic? His imagination taking over again?

With a shaky hand he pushed open the door and forced his warm tingling body out into the muggy night air. "*Skip?*" His mouth felt as if it were filled with warm molasses, and no matter how hard he tried, the words wouldn't come out right. "What're you—how—what's—why're you--what's...going on?"

"Why the hell didn't you just stop at one of those fucking red lights?" Fury oozed from Skip's eyes, causing them to glint in the store lighting. "We were about to pick you up at the condo when you started hauling ass. What the fuck's going on? You almost got us all *killed* back there!"

"You were back at my--" Arthur stopped talking. Something Skip had just said nipped at him. *We*. Skip had said "*we*." He'd also said "*us*." "Did you say *we*?" His eyes drifted over to the windshield of the sedan.

"I brought a friend of yours with me. You almost killed her, too. The mood she's in, she'll be the one to put the knot on your head."

"*Her*." Skip had said "*her*." Could it...could it possibly--

202

The passenger door opened. The blond hair barely cleared the roof. The warm night breeze made the golden tendrils dance wildly. Arthur's jaw dropped as she circled the front of the car.

It was Mandy.

Chapter 17

Tears filled his eyes.

Arthur stood gawking at her, telling himself he wasn't really seeing her, he was only imaging it. Wanting to believe it was her, yet telling himself she wasn't there, she was dead, and his imagination was fabricating this, forcing him to believe she hadn't died at all.

Even so, he struggled to accept what his eyes were trying to tell him.

This was real; Mandy was alive. And the only thing that made sense was that Vanessa had lied to him. About everything.

"M-Mandy?" left his lips before he realized he'd opened his mouth.

Then, incredibly, she nodded.

He rushed over and wrapped his arms around her, hugging her and clinging tightly to her. He was surprised when her arms encircled him as well. The tears kept coming.

Long before he wanted this special moment to end, Mandy lowered her arms. Her eyes were also moist, sparkling in the reflection of the shopping mall's spotlights, but her face held that same deadpan expression he remembered so well.

Then reality thundered back, spewing forth its unpleasantness. The events of the last twelve hours returned. He had seen it on a large screen. Mandy had been slammed to the concrete. She hit her head and lay there, not moving. Even if she hadn't died, she would have been captured and taken somewhere else to be killed...or turned into another killer.

He couldn't let his imagination run wild. Mandy was *here*. She was *alive*. As he stared into those big, beautiful blue eyes, the only thing that made sense was that she *had indeed survived*. She was here, safe and sound.

"You're...okay?"

Her brows came together. "Amazing, isn't it? Since you went *way* out of your way to kill me!"

"I had no idea. I—"

"As well as your friend!"

"I--I didn't know...I thought...the sedan...Vanessa...they chipped me...I thought...I was afraid they—"

"What exactly are you trying to say, Arthur? Your sentence is sort of, well, confusing, among other things." She seemed amused by his puzzlement.

"You're...you're okay!"

"Aside from a few cuts and bruises, I'm just fine. Why the tears? It's only been a few hours. Were you that worried?"

He wanted to hug her again. "You're *alive*. You're...actually *here*. You're not dead. You're living. Breathing."

She glanced at Skip, who just shrugged. "I got away. It was tricky, but I managed."

It still didn't make any sense. "I saw them going after you. They showed you tripping. Hitting your head. You didn't move. Vanessa told me you were dead."

"And where did you see and hear this?"

"Everything was on film."

"Film?" Skip asked.

"Where did all this happen?" Mandy asked.

Confusion set in, this time in a different direction. Mandy obviously had no idea what he was talking about. He briefly wondered about the blow to her head. If it had-- No. He didn't want to go there. "In the parking garage. On Hughey. When they blocked us in."

She shrugged. "I got away, like I said."

This still didn't make sense. "I heard a shot right before they knocked me out."

"I winged one of them. I tried to get more, but there were too many. They grabbed my gun, but I managed to hurt a few more before I got away."

"This makes no sense. None at all." He found that he just couldn't grasp what happened.

"We need to talk," Skip said. "The sooner, the better."

He was right. They needed to find out what was going on. He suspected Vanessa had told him more lies than he could even imagine.

"Your place," Mandy said. "Let's go. Now."

Arthur nodded.

"This time, *I'm* driving." Mandy's expression was fierce.

He knew better than argue.

***

Mandy slid in behind the wheel while Arthur got in the passenger's side.

As soon as Skip got back into his own ride, she pulled behind him and followed him back onto Curry Ford Road.

Arthur sat tensely, hoping he wouldn't black out. It only took twenty minutes to get back to the condo, and he needed to tell Mandy and Skip everything he knew while he was still able to.

Keeping close behind Skip, Mandy made the left onto Semoran and stayed with the solid columns of traffic. "Now tell me why you thought I was dead."

"I saw you die."

"How?"

"They had cameras in their vans."

"Interesting. Makes you wonder why, doesn't it?"

"Apparently they film everything."

She stiffened. "Everything?"

"They have film of me standing over the old man I told you about. Apparently they're able to get hold of the building's security cameras. They're extremely well-connected."

"What about Robert?"

His mouth went dry, but he managed to get the words out. "Him, too."

She went back to concentrating on the traffic, but he knew what she was thinking because he was thinking the same thing. He had killed two people, and one of them was someone Mandy knew. Someone she obviously liked-- perhaps loved.

She finally said, "The film...it was taken from the building's security files?"

"I can't think of any other way they got hold of it."

"And it actually showed you killing Robert?"

"It showed me leaving his office."

"Nothing *before* that?"

"He was lying on the floor as I left."

She fell silent again, staring at the taillights moving in front of them. "What about that other man? The elderly one?"

"I was standing over him with a paperweight in my hand."

"But you didn't see yourself actually *hitting* him with it?"

"No."

More silence. He could tell something was bothering her because he quickly discovered that he felt the same.

"Tell me what you saw in the parking garage."

He told her, but even as he did, he wondered why it suddenly sounded so wrong. So concocted. A short time ago, he had agonized over Mandy hitting her head on the concrete and dying. He didn't know what she was thinking right now, but he suspected it was similar to what had entered his own mind when he first saw her emerge from Skip's sedan.

"Judging by what you saw on their film, I should be dead or in a coma. As you can see, I'm neither. I was knocked around quite a bit, but as I've already said, I escaped. Right after I shot one of them and got away, I rolled underneath a pickup and crawled between it and another car, dodging them until I reached the main street. Then I cut through traffic until someone stopped and asked if I wanted a ride. I called Skip when I was a safe distance away, and he met me about fifteen minutes later, on Robinson. He took me to his place on Edgewater, where I could get cleaned up. I told him what I knew, and we decided to head on over to your place to see what was going on. We parked three buildings down and watched your place for at least an hour. We finally saw a dark van pull up to the curb in front of your door. You got out and walked rather stiffly up to your porch, unlocked your door, and went inside. We waited another half-hour, but the van didn't leave. Skip wanted to call you, but we both knew better. The van still hadn't budged, and we both thought someone would eventually get out and pay you a visit. Quite frankly, we just couldn't figure why they let you go in the first place. It seemed suspicious—you know?"

"You mean, *I* seemed suspicious?"

"We couldn't help feeling that way. Anyway, after nearly an hour, the van

finally left. We waited fifteen minutes, just to make sure they didn't come back. We wanted to check things out. I was halfway to your place when you came out and got into your car. You didn't even give me time to call out your name. Before I could get close enough to wave you down, you had already pulled out. Skip picked me up and we followed you, until we stopped you in front of the shopping plaza. I take it you thought we were them?"

"I didn't know *who* you were." He didn't want to tell Mandy about his plans of suicide. "I was kind of, well, depressed, and didn't want anyone following me. If I'd known it was you..."

She nodded but said nothing.

"I wonder why the van stayed so long in front of my place."

"I guess they wanted to make sure you didn't leave."

"Maybe they wanted me to have a good night's sleep. Apparently they've got more assignments for me."

"What kind of assignments?"

"Guess."

"You mean...?"

"That's right. Assassinations."

"Any ideas why they picked you for all this?"

"Vanessa said she picked me because she liked me. And because I'm damaged. And a loner. Apparently this fits the profile of the average psycho killer when he's finally caught. The fact that I've got a spotless record helps, somehow."

"Strange."

After some thought, he decided to tell her a few things. He hesitated, but felt he owed Mandy an explanation. "I guess you're wondering why Vanessa considers me damaged. It's kind of a long story. When you asked me if I was married--"

"Skip told me," she said quickly.

He sat back. "He told you? About Denise?"

She nodded. "I'm sorry, Arthur. That was something no one should have to go through. These

210

are obviously vicious, nasty people. To prey on someone who has just suffered a horrendous loss is something only a monster would be capable of."

He stared at his lap, his mind once again returning to those dark, gloomy days, but strangely coming right back this time. To the present. To Mandy. And to the people responsible for all this. "I'm still trying to figure what they really did in the parking garage."

"That's simple. They altered the film."

"Obviously. But why?"

"I'll give you something even better to think about. With what we both know right now, what makes you think you actually killed *anyone*?"

Chapter 18

As Mandy pulled into the paved drive leading to Arthur's condo complex, his thoughts continued to spin.

Vanessa wanted him to believe Mandy was dead. She also wanted him to believe he killed Doctor Tannenbaum, as well as the white-haired man in the lab coat. To make certain of this, they altered the film footage in the parking garage. They were obviously professionals and had done a terrific job. This made him fear the obvious: they were masters at whatever they did.

It was very late when they returned to the condo. He was tired, angry, scared, and confused. And thirsty. He headed straight for the kitchen cabinet. He grabbed a bottle of bourbon, poured two inches into a glass, and chugged it down. The hot liquid tore down his throat and sent a swirl of shimmering warmth through his tired limbs. He picked up two more glasses for his guests.

"Make mine a small one." Skip climbed onto the barstool next to Mandy. "I've got to make it home in one piece. I've also got to be at work by nine in the morning."

Arthur took the drinks and glasses over to the bar counter. Mandy grabbed hers and drank half. Skip had a small sip and said, "I assume Mandy told you how you got back here."

He poured more bourbon for himself and set the bottle on the counter. "I don't know what all this is or who's involved, but I'm pretty certain I stumbled onto something really frightening."

"When I picked up Mandy," Skip said, "she was pretty wrecked. What she told me sounded like something from an international thriller. Two black vans? Half a dozen armed big boys in dark suits chasing you two in a parking garage? Incredible."

"You believe us, don't you?"

"I was skeptical at first, especially when I pulled up that Silicon Valley stuff, but when I saw that van drop you off outside, I began having second thoughts. You'd have to be pretty nutso to make all this up."

"He really thought I was dead," Mandy told him. "They showed him footage that was obviously altered."

"You mentioned film footage before, at the shopping center. Where were the cameras?"

"They probably had them set up in their vans."

"Surveillance?"

"Apparently they've got cameras everywhere."

Skip frowned. "You're talking unlimited camera access?"

"Possibly."

"Public buildings?"

"They were able to get the tape from Robert's Orlando office," Mandy said. "That's a public building."

Skip picked up his drink. "This sounds pretty intense. We might even be talking Government Intel. And since every damned file I've pulled from the databases has been confidential Eyes Only, we're talking cover-ups."

"Why would anyone need me for a cover-up?" Arthur asked.

"That's a damned good question."

"Did you ever find anything on that man with the red flags in his file?"

"I managed to pull up a fairly detailed sheet on George S. Bradford. It took hours, but I got it."

"How much trouble did you get into?"

"I knew I was treading on forbidden ground, so I was especially careful. I waited until everyone went to lunch, then used a few special permissions codes accessible to a couple of the higher-ups to pull up Bradford's file. Apparently he was with the FBI for nearly twenty years, heavily involved with tracking and surveillance methods and systems."

"Vanessa was married to an FBI man?" Arthur asked.

"A few years ago, Bradford got chummy with Leo Jenkins, a German scientist working with robotics for the last forty years. He was one of the first to design robotics that were used in data centers in the late-seventies and was snatched up by our government to come over here and work on advancements in data processing."

"I take it Bradford and Jenkins went into some sort of partnership?"

"The evidence says they met at a social event."

"This was after he'd divorced Vanessa?"

"DeAngelis and Bradford divorced in '15. A couple of years later, Bradford was transferred to

Orlando's FBI branch. We don't know if Vanessa followed him here, just that the two of them came to Orlando around the same year. Bradford had already been getting tired of Government bureaucracy and wanted to break out on his own. His interests lay in security, tracking, and surveillance, so he was kind of limited, and had resigned himself to consider starting up his own surveillance agency. When he met Jenkins, things changed dramatically. Jenkins wasn't fond of bureaucracy either, and claimed he'd been tricked into coming over here from Germany to work. When Bradford and Jenkins began their working relationship, a world of opportunity opened up for both of them. Using Bradford's FBI background and connections, Jenkins began working on various methods of robotic tracking systems that could be sold to the private sector over the open market."

"Tracking systems? Like the one she stuck in me?"

"I'd wager the one DeAngelis implanted you with was personally designed and programmed by Jenkins himself."

Arthur finished his second drink. The subject had come up. Like it or not, he had to tell them the facts while he was still in a conscious, alert state. "News flash: they fitted me with another one. It was before they brought me back here."

Skip's eyes grew. "Then you were in a fugue when they brought you back."

"Apparently."

"That would explain why you moved like a zombie once you got out of the van."

"As I told Mandy, they're planning to use me again."

"We've got to find it and take it out as quickly as possible." Skip got down off his stool.

"It won't be easy without a scanner," Mandy said.

Skip had his cell in his hand. "I know someone who can get one, but it'll probably take at least an hour."

"I don't think we have that much time," Arthur said.

"It would help if we knew where they put it," Mandy said. "I have a feeling they used a different site."

"I couldn't find any fresh marks anywhere else."

"A hypodermic doesn't leave marks. That is, if it's used properly." She moved closer. "We've got to find it."

He sighed. "There just isn't enough time."

"Did they mention specifics?" Skip asked. "Tell you anything that could help us?"

"The only one I talked to was Vanessa. She was vague about most everything, but she did tell me things that would shed some light on this."

"We've got to get our hands on a scanner." Mandy was getting upset. "We've got to find that stupid thing and take it out. And we've got to do it *right now*!"

"Those things she told you," Skip said anxiously. "Remember any of them?"

Arthur's mind had turned blank. The panic had already taken over. *Focus. Think clearly. Visualize. The dark room. The TV screen. Google Earth. The mountain of muscle. Oscar.*

Everything became clear. But just as the words on the screen flashed before his eyes, everything went dark.

***

He awoke in the front seat of his car, staring at the living room bay window of his condo.

The early morning fog had lifted. Shards of sunlight blinked innocently at him through the pines lining the path across the complex, promising a beautiful morning.

He turned away from it. Stiffness raked through his limbs, sending a heavy tingling down his spine, and making him instantly wary of the previous night's events. He wondered how long he'd been sitting here. Where he'd come from. How long he'd been gone. He stared suspiciously at the front door, expecting it to mysteriously turn into some other building he'd never seen before.

As his head cleared, foggy images detailing last night drifted past. A strange house. The body of a man sprawled on the living room couch. A gun in Arthur's hand as he stood close by, staring at nothing.

The realization thrashed through him. Once again, someone had been murdered, and once again, the gory details eluded him. Was this because he hadn't committed the murder in the first place? He sincerely hoped what Mandy had told him was true. And why shouldn't it be? If he *had* murdered this person, he should remember every detail.

As his mind searched for clues, it brought back other things, details that happened earlier. He had decided to kill himself and had gone out in heavy traffic to accomplish it. He might have even done it if Mandy and Skip had not entered the picture.

They followed him and stopped him, then led him back here. Last he remembered, the three of them were inside, discussing what was happening, with Arthur trying desperately to remember the details.

Another blackout. It only made sense. It also explained why he couldn't remember anything else. He wouldn't have voluntarily left the two of them in the middle of a discussion. It would have taken something completely out of his control to get him away from them at that moment.

And what did they do during all this? Where were they now?

The sound of a vehicle jerking to an abrupt stop behind him made him turn sharply.

Mandy, her features taut and pale, got out of Skip's dark sedan. Skip sat behind the wheel, frowning at him.

Arthur knew he should be happy to see them, but their grim expressions suggested this reunion would be anything but joyous. He got out of the Caddie and pushed the door shut behind him. As he approached the sedan, he expected Mandy to smile.

She didn't, and his mood grew even darker. "How'd you guys know I was here?"

"We've been following you all night," Skip said.

"All night?"

"Since you left the condo," Mandy said.

"But what happened? Where'd you two--"

"Not here," Mandy said. "Come with us."

The taut expression on her face jolted through him. He stood there numbly, his gaze settling on them both.

"There's no time." Mandy gestured impatiently and opened the back door of the sedan.

***

Battling the hectic morning rush hour traffic on Semoran Boulevard, Skip reached Florida Hospital on Lake Underhill Road in just thirty minutes.

Neither Mandy nor Skip had spoken on the way over. Arthur remained silent as well. He guessed what was going on and used the silence to obsess over his new chip, hoping they'd be able to find it before his next blackout.

Skip dropped them off at the front entrance of the hospital, then drove off. Mandy pulled Arthur inside, marching him past Reception and down the hall, past orderlies pushing gurneys and nurses guiding elderly patients in wheelchairs.

Mandy stopped at an examination room not far from the tiny room where the other nurse had treated and dressed the cuts on his lower back. She opened the door. "Go on in, I'll be right back." Then left him alone.

He sat in the chair in the corner, staring at the antiseptic white walls. His head swam with images. He envisioned a group of doctors and nurses coming in, making him strip, then strapping him down to the table. He envisioned himself blacking out again. Awakening in his car in front of his condo. Getting out, walking inside, and turning on the TV. The news coming on with a story about a group of hospital workers murdered by a mental patient who had mysteriously escaped.

He forced his brain to stop all this paranoia. Things would somehow turn out all right. They had to. Mandy would come back in just a few minutes and find that damned chip.

As if in answer to his prayers, Mandy returned just a few minutes later with a tall, sandy-haired doctor around thirty-five and a petite, Asian-looking nurse a few years older. The nurse led the way, pushing a small instrument table on wheels.

Mandy closed the door, went over to the table, and picked up a hypodermic syringe and small vial. She still didn't say anything, nor did she look at Arthur. He wanted her to smile at him—to tell him everything was going to be all right. When she didn't, he told himself she was just being professional. He watched as she carefully filled the needle. "Take off your clothes," she said.

"Everything?"

"You can leave your undershorts on."

He did as she said.

"Now lie down on your back."

Again, he obeyed. "What happens if...if I black out before--"

Mandy held up the needle. "Any sudden change in your blood pressure, behavior or body language, and you'll be held down and given this."

Her statement had transformed his nervousness into extreme fear. He could go into cardiac arrest and die before they had the chance to do anything else. "It won't *kill* me, will it?" he asked.

"We hope not," the doctor said flatly.

Arthur waited for a sly grin, but the doctor's blank expression didn't change. It only substantiated his lifelong view that doctors weren't the best candidates for guest spots on SNL.

The nurse picked up a large white gadget from the table. It looked like one of those wands they used at airports to hunt for bombs and weapons, but smaller. She brought it over and flicked it on, holding it just a couple of inches from his flesh and moving it up and down the outside of his legs.

Mandy held the needle just a few feet away. Having witnessed her reflexes, he was confident she could give him the injection before he could raise his head from the table. "Anything?" she asked the nurse.

The nurse shook her head and moved the wand between his legs. He focused on his last talk with Vanessa, remembering the throbbing in his gut, the dizziness, and the stiffness in his joints. What nagged him most was anger for what they'd done. Most of all, for letting him think Mandy was dead--

No. There was something else. Something other than the dizziness, the throbbing in his gut, and the intense anger.

The tingling in his left shoulder.

At the time, he thought it was from being manhandled by the two big jerks in the parking garage. Or the mountain of flesh when Arthur had lunged at Vanessa. Now he wasn't so sure. What he was sure about was that everything happening during the last few days mattered and must be remembered.

"Try my left shoulder," he told them.

The nurse moved the wand closer. "Faint."

"Flip over," Mandy said.

Once again, he did as she ordered. The wand was immediately positioned directly over his rear deltoid. A series of quiet beeps filled the room, and a warm wave of instant relief washed down his body.

"Hello, there." The nurse marked the area with a felt tipped pen and flicked off the wand.

"Give him the local." The doctor hurried over to the sink to scrub up as the nurse blotted Arthur's shoulder with a cold antiseptic swab.

***

After the nurse had cleaned and bandaged the tiny incision in Arthur's shoulder, he and Mandy went back out into the outpatient wing.

Skip sat near a front window, his face buried in a dog-eared issue of *American Journal of Nursing*. Seeing them, he tossed the magazine on the table

222

beside his chair. Mandy handed him the chip, which she'd dropped into a small plastic vial.

He held it close to his face. "Hopefully, this little bastard will tell us what we need to know."

Arthur couldn't even look at the damned thing. It was almost like staring at a bullet that almost killed you. But he couldn't help thinking how powerful such a tiny, insignificant thing really was. How such technology had changed everyone's very existence forever.

They were on their way back to downtown Orlando fifteen minutes later, Skip driving, Mandy beside him, Arthur in back, as before. He'd initially felt some relief but was surprised to find himself just as tense as he'd been on the way over to the hospital. The second chip was removed; he didn't expect to suffer any more blackouts. Even so, confusion, anger, and frustration plagued him. The prospect of what he had done the night before haunted him, and he found it impossible to steer his mind very far from it. "Where'd I go when I left the condo?" he asked.

"Sable Point," Skip said.

"You followed me there?"

"We knew we'd better keep a close eye on you," Mandy said.

"We thought we could observe," Skip added. "If you needed help, we were ready to jump in."

"Besides," Mandy said, "we were both curious. It isn't every day you're talking to someone who suddenly turns into a zombie, then gets up and leaves in the middle of a conversation."

If they followed him, they must have been close enough to see what he did. He couldn't believe it. Bile filled his throat, and his pulse hastened. *Calm yourself. Don't let the anger take over.* After a few deep breaths, he regained his composure. The anger kept fighting to come back, but he forced himself to ignore it. "So…you followed me to Sable Point, then sat outside…and actually watched me *kill* someone?"

"You didn't kill anyone," Mandy said.

You didn't kill anyone…

They'd discussed this before. He wanted to believe it but found it difficult to accept. It just didn't make any sense. Why would Vanessa and the Committee go to such lengths?

"You're absolutely sure?"

"We were right outside, watching from the living room window."

"And I just went inside? And did *nothing*?"

"Someone was already there. A man. As soon as you walked in, he stuck a gun in your hand, then left through the back door."

"You didn't see who it was?"

"He wore a ski mask," Mandy said. "And dark clothing."

"He moved like a cat," Skip said. "He was obviously a pro. We didn't even hear him once he came outside. We have no idea which direction he went."

"We stayed in the bushes," Mandy said. "We didn't want him spotting us."

"I guess he was the killer?"

"Obviously," Skip said. "And the murder was executed before you got there."

"Why would he hand me that gun?"

"We've got to find out," Mandy said.

"How?"

"We're going to talk with some people about it," Skip said.

"At the Police Station?"

Skip chuckled. "Not exactly..."

Arthur's heart skipped a beat. A feeling of dread settled on his shoulders.

"Don't worry," Mandy said. "It's okay."

He envisioned himself as a hapless victim running from the authorities. *We're not going to the Police Station, we're going somewhere else. To talk with some people.*

What the hell did *that* mean?

Skip and Mandy were his friends—perhaps his only friends. He'd known Skip most of his life. He'd known Mandy only a few days, but they'd been through hell together, and he trusted her with his life. But since so many things had changed drastically during the last few days, he found himself suspicious of everyone.

He recalled the footage with Mandy and began wondering if she...if Mandy and Vanessa...if everything he had seen had been altered for his benefit, or for some other purpose...

And Skip...that chuckle of his...

Some people, but not the police. Not exactly.

If they weren't headed for the Police Station, where the hell were they going?

The door handle. It was his one sure way to freedom.

At the next red light, he could force open the door and roll out of the car. If he landed wrong, the concrete pavement would crack open his skull and he would spend the rest of his life in a wheelchair, being fed stewed prunes while watching *Little House on the Prairie* reruns. But if he could land on his side and roll, he might be able to--

"Don't!" Mandy practically shouted.

His hand froze just a few inches from the door handle.

"I know what you're thinking," Mandy said. "I also know why you think you can't trust anyone anymore. But this is us—remember? I'm the broad who got you out of that seafood restaurant alive."

Skip shot him a glance. "I'm that guy you got drunk with at our tenth reunion. Remember? Buds?"

"It's gonna be all right." Mandy's small, warm hand tightened around his wrist.

Chapter 19

At just a few minutes before eleven o'clock, Skip found a vacant parking space a few places down from the intersection of Church Street and Orange. He parked and switched off the ignition. "We're here."

Arthur looked around. The usual crowds and tour buses. A small group of Asians bent over a parked vehicle, a map opened in front of them as they chattered away. No one seemed to be paying attention, and no one was approaching Skip's car.

Even though Mandy had been reassuring, Arthur remained apprehensive as well as paranoid. *Some people*. They'd come here to talk to *some people*. Yet they were nowhere near the Police Station.

"C'mon." Skip opened his door and got out. Mandy also got out.

"Where?" Arthur asked.

"Time for a coffee break." Skip gestured to the restaurant directly to his left, at the corner. The large, well-lit sign above the entrance said *Café et le Brunch*. The constant activity going on inside the tinted windows suggested the place was busy.

Arthur didn't move. This didn't make sense. A restaurant? Were the "people" Skip had mentioned waiting in there? Arthur figured they'd be in some sort of official capacity. But that didn't mean they weren't waiting inside, did it? It didn't mean they didn't eat, and it surely didn't mean they had to eat at the Police Station. Such a place might be a good deal. It was crowded; there would be anonymity. And in this situation, anonymity meant safety.

"C'mon. We'll be okay." Mandy was waiting.

His mind reeling, he got out and followed them inside.

The packed, air-conditioned eatery smelled of coffee, cinnamon, vanilla, and bacon. Despite the crowd, an empty booth awaited them at the other end of the room, less than ten feet away from the kitchen doorway. Busboys and waitresses raced down the aisles, carrying trays and orders of croissants, sweet rolls, bacon and eggs, and delicious-looking omelets.

Skip and Mandy slid into the booth. Mandy picked up a menu; Skip did not. Arthur slid in beside Mandy. No one said anything, which was fine. Arthur was nervous about all this and went back to wondering about the man who'd mysteriously shown up at the house in Sable Point.

Dark clothing. A ski mask. He moved like a cat.

Weird, to be sure. Baffling, to say the least. But everything about all this was baffling.

Arthur scanned the crowd. The heavy mix of colognes, perfumes, coffee, and food smells made this nightmare frighteningly real. He began looking for familiar faces, for anyone watching him, their table. So far, no one seemed to notice them. But that didn't mean anything. These folks were good; they knew how to spy on people without being obvious. There could be three or four of them in here. Or five. Or six. They could be sitting at the next table. Or across the aisle.

Stop this.

Resting his elbows on the metal table, he lowered his head and breathed slowly. He wanted to scream. To jump up and run outside. To disappear.

Mandy smiled and pressed her shoulder against him. It made him feel a little better. He began breathing easier, but it wasn't long before the tension returned. He couldn't let it take control. He was being silly again. They'd come here to meet some people. These people might provide answers to this mess. Even if they didn't, the fact that Skip knew them assured him that they would be on his side.

This uncertainty made him feel small and helpless, as he was as a child, and couldn't sleep without the nightlight on. Darkness frightened him. Monsters lurked in the darkness, waiting to find sleeping children and carry them off to their lairs in the caves.

He was no longer a child, but a grown man. And he really should start acting like one.

Mandy nudged him. "It'll be all right."

"They really messed me up," he whispered.

"We've got to make you right again."

Her statement made him start thinking rationally again. What good was revenge if you let your enemy win? "These people," he said, looking at Skip. "Are they going to meet us here?"

"One of them should already be here," he said.

Arthur scanned the crowd again. No one looked suspicious, and no one was watching them. "You sure?"

"He ought to be. He's here all the time."

Moments later, a tall, slender guy with long black hair tied in a ponytail ending halfway down his back and a thick black beard brought over a plastic gray tub filled with dirty dishes. He was about thirty-five and wore a stained white tee shirt, faded jeans, and a heavy-duty black apron. He set the tub rather clumsily on their table and straightened. He stared at Arthur, then Mandy. "This the dude?" he asked Skip, tilting his head at Arthur.

Skip nodded.

"Who's the babe?"

"She's in this, too," Skip said.

He stared at her. "Cool. What's her name?"

"I'm right here," Mandy said flatly. "Why don't you ask *me*?"

"What's your name?"

"Mandy Rhodes."

"Is that short for Amanda?"

"No one's called me that since first grade."

"C'mon." He gestured with his head and quickly disappeared through the kitchen doorway.

Despite his reservations, Arthur got up and waited until Mandy had slipped out of the booth. This dude looked like he had just popped right out of the late sixties through a time warp. They came all this way to talk to a hippie busboy with greasy hair and a beard that hadn't been trimmed in weeks?

Skip, I really hope you know what you're doing, he thought uneasily. His pulse accelerated, and his face grew uncomfortably warm as he followed the threesome through the hectic, cluttered kitchen, toward the well-lit *EXIT* sign over the door at the other end of the room.

***

At the far end of the alley, a single-wide trailer sat just two or three feet away from the brick wall of the neighboring building.

Two old cars—one a Camaro, the other a Charger—were parked behind the trailer. Both were covered with dirt and riddled with dents and scratches. The windows of the trailer were dirty and smudged. Even the curtains were covered in dirt. Like the cars, the aluminum wall was damaged with dents and scratches.

Arthur reluctantly followed Skip, Mandy, and the tall, long-haired guy across the alley. Just before they reached the trailer, Arthur stopped. Another surge of anxiety slammed through him. An ancient, beat-up trailer in an alley behind an eatery. Could anything be more ominous?

How about a man in dark clothing, with a ski mask, who moved like a cat?

Answers, Arthur. You need answers. A slew of them. And if this is where it happens...

Skip waited until his friend pulled open the door and climbed the three rickety metal steps before following him inside. Mandy went up the steps and disappeared inside. With a deep sigh, Arthur followed suit but left the door open. The tension building within him told him not to close it. It would make him feel trapped.

The long-haired guy turned, glanced at the open doorway, and frowned. "Close the door."

Arthur reluctantly pulled the door shut.

The trailer was a mess. The floor was cluttered with strewn newspapers and magazines. Issues of the Wall Street *Journal* and the Orlando *Sentinel*, as well as *Playboy* and *Hustler*, several science magazines, dog-eared issues of *Analog*, *The Magazine of Fantasy and Science Fiction*, as well as *Galaxy*, with a few *Guns & Ammo* and *American Rifleman* tossed in, covered most of the main area. Stacks of magazines were placed beside one another, three or four feet high, going into the hall.

Beat-up filing cabinets lined the rear wall of the living room. A long folding table set up against the front wall was overwhelmed with computer equipment. Monitors, cells phones, TV screens, and various boxes and wires covered the table.

"What a mess," Mandy said. "I take it you fired your maid."

"You're kidding, right?"

"I guess so..."

He gestured to the breakfast nook. "Take a load off." He grabbed a can of Dr. Pepper from the fridge, raised it, and splashed some down his throat. He held it up. "Anyone need a sugar jolt?"

Mandy frowned.

"Got any coffee?" Skip asked.

He jabbed a thumb at the coffeemaker on the sink. It was filled with a very black liquid.

"That isn't exactly fresh, is it?"

"It was when I made it."

"When was that? When Obama was in office?"

"Could've been. I didn't need much of an excuse to stay awake during that administration."

Skip went over and started making a fresh pot. Without turning, he said, "Mandy, in case you and Artie are wondering, this guy's a computer genius, and he's got a ton of contacts. He looks and acts like a moron, does his laundry every leap year, but he's really pretty bright."

"Thanks so much for the accolades."

"What's your name?" Mandy asked.

"Call me Jake."

"Just Jake? Nothing else?"

"Only when he's not using." Skip looked serious. "When he's doing a line, he goes on this "Mister Jake" kick."

Jake slugged more Dr. Pepper. "Can I help if I suddenly turn dignified when I'm high? It must be one of my former lives trying to come back."

"Why are we here?" Arthur found himself growing more impatient by the moment.

Jake nodded. "Dude doesn't like making light of the time/space continuum."

"What?" Mandy asked.

"He doesn't like to waste time. Hell, neither did Einstein."

Skip got the pot going and sat down at the table. "We're here, Artie, because this guy's got some serious contacts, and might even be able to help us out of this mess."

"By himself?" Mandy asked.

"I've got friends in low places." Jake pulled a blunt out of his vest pocket.

"Doesn't the coffee shop frown on that?" Mandy asked. "Or this trailer sitting here?"

"They would if I wasn't the owner." He fired up, gulped down a thick lungful, held it in, and hissed it right back out. "I told the city this is my supply room. They bought it. They fucked me by adjusting my taxes and altering my code, but what can you do?" He took in more smoke and held it in. He raised his brows and held out the blunt.

They all shook their heads.

"Bud and K.C. should be here in a few minutes."

"Jake, Bud, and K.C." Mandy glanced at Skip. "You're not serious."

Jake frowned. "You got something against nicknames?"

"Sounds like a trio of horses," Arthur said, rubbing his eyes.

"They're all assholes," Skip said. "But they know their shit."

"Thank you and fuck you," Jake said.

"You sound like you just popped out of the wrong decade," Mandy said.

Jake sucked in more weed and coughed it back out. "That's what usually happens when your parents grew up listening to their parents listening to Three Dog Night, Janis Joplin, and Led Zeppelin."

"Don't let him kid you," Skip said. "His parents were just as square as mine."

"They *used* to be cool—at least, before they stopped protesting and joined the money generation."

"Haven't heard *that* term in a while," Mandy said.

"It got shitcanned. Actually, it was replaced. The new phrase is capitalism. Or free enterprise."

"That's rich," Mandy said, "coming from someone who runs a money-making establishment."

"Money-making, maybe," he said. "Establishment? Now, that word's been a bummer with me since college."

"You're *so* messed up," she said.

"I'm hip," Jake said. "Half of me gets high on Hendrix and lives in this run-down trailer while the other half spends the rest of his miserable existence shoving processed food and artificially-flavored coffees down people's throats."

"For money," Skip added.

Jake shrugged and stubbed out his roach. "I just bank it and use it to buy vintage cars and Joplin CDs."

"Those are vintage cars?" Mandy asked.

"What would *you* call them?"

"Junk."

"You're cold."

"Just being truthful. They do need a lot of work."

"One of these days," he said. "When I'm not too busy listening to Hendrix. Or selling coffee."

"How else do you spend your time?" Arthur asked impatiently.

"Usually on his laptop," Skip said.

"That's for the Cause." Jake pulled over a chair and sat ass-backwards, resting his slender, hairy forearms on the back of the chair. "We've been fighting them the last fifteen years. Since we graduated from college."

"Them?" Arthur asked.

"Our beloved Government. And their cover-ups. Their lies. The million and one ways they slip things to us, by us, and at us—without our knowledge, of course. Or approval."

"You're a conspiracy nut," Arthur said flatly.

"If you knew about some of the things my buds and I already know, you'd be paranoid as well."

Arthur sighed. "I have more than enough to be paranoid about."

"Muldrake, here, told us about your problem. Bummer."

"I guess you could call it that."

"Tell him why we're here," Skip said to Jake.

Sounds of footsteps. The door opened. Afternoon light filtered in.

***

Two men climbed into the trailer.

Both wore dress slacks, suits, and ties. Each carried a laptop. They were both in their mid- or late thirties. The first one, blond and fair-skinned, wore thick glasses and a bushy reddish-blond mustache. His hair was wavy and worn long, reaching his shoulders. He was about six feet tall, long boned, and slender. The other was an inch or two taller, darker, and slightly balding. His curly, dark-brown hair was worn loosely over his shoulders, reaching his shoulder blades. Like his light-skinned partner, he wore glasses. He also wore a neat goatee, with an elegant mustache waxed at the ends.

"K.C.," Skip said, gesturing to the light-haired man. "Bud," he added, turning to the darker of the two, "this is Artie. I told you his story."

Bud nodded. "And the chick?"

Mandy moaned.

"That's Mandy. She's good people."

K.C. squinted, using the middle finger of his left hand to push his glasses up his long, pointed nose. "You Government?"

"I'm a nurse," she replied flatly.

"Now that we've gotten the familiarities out of the way," Skip said, "we can--"

"Just who *are* these guys?" Arthur asked. "Just because they're friends of yours doesn't exactly give me a warm fuzzy."

"They're good people," Skip said. "I've known 'em for years."

"But who *are* they? Are they government workers?"

"Bite your tongue," Bud said.

"Yeah," agreed K.C. "Watch the insults—at least until after you get to know us."

Jake grinned.

"You don't need to know," Skip said.

"I think I do."

"So do I," Mandy said.

"Listen," Skip said. "The less you know about them, the better."

K.C. shrugged and went over to the folding table in the living room. He found an empty space among the clutter, laid down his laptop, and said, "Tell us what you wanna know."

"For starters, what did Skip tell you about me?" Arthur asked.

Bud shrugged. "He told us what happened. The chip thing, the blackouts—the works."

"But how can you help? What exactly do you do?"

K.C. cocked his head. "You mean, for a living?"

"Let's start with that."

"I'm an accountant."

"For who?"

"Bill's Charbroiled Steakhouse. The one on Colonial and Semoran."

"A *restaurant*?"

Bud looked hurt. "What's wrong with *that*? I do their books and they pay me. Everyone's happy."

"I just thought--"

"How about you?" Mandy asked K.C.

K.C. pushed his hair away from his face. "Right now, I'm managing a liquor store on Orange Avenue."

Arthur couldn't believe this. He asked Skip for help and was brought here to meet a restaurant owner, a bookkeeper for a steakhouse, and the manager of a liquor store. The anxiety came back in a heavy flurry. "Any of you guys have degrees in anything?"

K.C. sighed. "I've got three, actually. One from Berkeley, another from UCLA, and a medical degree from Stanford."

"I've been to Berkeley, too," Bud said. "Also, Yale and Columbia."

Jake said, "Duquesne and Carnegie Mellon, and post-grad studies at Julliard."

"Music?" Mandy asked.

"Among other things. Why? You don't think guys like us can help you?"

Arthur didn't reply.

"What you actually need," K.C. said, "is some serious brainwork from people who aren't associated with the Police Department. Right, Muldrake?"

Skip sighed.

Arthur turned to Skip. "What's this all about?"

"Like I said before," Skip replied, "they're brilliant."

"But what was that bit about OPD? And can these guys honestly help me?"

"If anyone can," Skip said, "these dudes can."

Bud put his laptop down on the table beside K.C. and sat. He opened it up and turned it on. "What databanks do we need to be hacking into?" he asked, attacking the keyboard.

Skip got up and strolled over. "To begin with, I'd say OPD, FBI, and Homeland Security."

"Homeland Security?" Jake frowned. "You sure you want us in there?"

"No. But it might help."

Bud began typing.

Jake went over and sat down at his laptop.

"These guys former agents?" Arthur asked no one in particular.

Skip smiled. "Hardly."

Bud's flat expression didn't change as he pounded the keys. "The three of us all have had close contacts from time to time with special investigators. We've all had prior experience in government investigation, and two of us have been attached to Government task forces."

Every word tore into Arthur like a series of sharp, well-aimed blows.

Bud's expression remained flat. "Judging by what Muldrake has told us, you've stumbled onto an elite group of international terrorists operating in the United States, with various ties to organizations based out of several unfriendly governments."

International terrorists. Unfriendly governments. What the hell?

"And this involves me how?" Arthur was surprised the words came out so coherently.

"Directly." Jake's eyes never left Arthur as he picked up his can of pop.

The word formed a terrifying image. Directly. This involved him directly. Calling him a terrorist, or traitor, wouldn't have made him feel any worse.

Mandy rested a hand on his forearm. The contact somehow revitalized him, and he immediately began thinking rationally. He wasn't a terrorist or traitor. Just some poor schmuck who had gotten involved with the wrong woman. He was no different from millions of other guys.

The anger rushed back, and he sat up and looked Bud straight in the eye. He was shocked to discover the fear inside him had vanished. "Then this is why we're here, rather than at the Police Station?"

K.C. didn't look up from his keyboard. "They tried to get you there, didn't they? At OPD?"

The images flashed by. The man at the reception desk, watching everyone, while the other guy blocked the rear exit. The traffic stop. The message became all too clear.

Bud said, "Orlando Police Department's obviously been compromised."

"What does *that* mean?" Arthur asked.

K.C. shrugged. "It means someone with incredibly deep pockets bought their way in."

Chapter 20

The Police Department. Compromised. Bought. Fake cops. Surveillance. Cover-ups.

The picture had become frighteningly clear.

Arthur sunk down in his seat.

Bud looked up suddenly and glanced at Skip. "Got that implant on you, by any chance? We'll need it."

Skip dug the plastic vial out of his pocket and handed it over. Bud took it, removed the cap, and dropped it into his palm. He picked up a magnifying glass from the table and studied it closely, as a jeweler examines a rare gem. He nodded. "Looks like the typical 2000-IF model."

"IF?" Arthur asked.

"Insertion Friendly." Jake chuckled. "Sounds kinky, doesn't it?"

"Clever." Mandy frowned.

Jake smiled sheepishly. "Er, sorry. Just a little levity."

Mandy didn't reply.

"Anyway, its size and design make it much easier to implant. It can be made operable even when inserted a mere quarter of an inch beneath the outer surface of the skin, and its biocompatible glass coating makes it more difficult to locate." He put it back in the vial and handed it to K.C. "They've been working on that option the last year and a half. We don't know if the Chinese perfected it, or if it was the Russians."

K.C. glanced briefly at it as he picked up his cell. "Chip's here."

Arthur fought to keep the panic away. This seemed all wrong. They were talking so calmly about all this. He'd been implanted with a chip. Without his knowledge. And he still didn't know who these people were. "Is anyone gonna tell me what this is all about? You still haven't told me who you are. Not really."

K.C. stared at Arthur a few moments before he spoke. "Like we've already said--"

"You were vague."

"Real vague," Mandy added.

"For a reason."

"Which is?"

Jake said, "For one thing, we no longer have any official capacity."

"That means we're--"

"Rogues," K.C. said sourly.

"That's a pretty nifty euphemism," Jake said. "Roughly translated, it means those of us who've had our wrists slapped and were ordered to stay away from any hint of government program in the future. Or else."

"Especially hacking," Bud said, typing away.

"Then what you're doing--"

"Could get them sent to the federal pen," Skip said.

"Then they really don't have to do this."

Bud grinned. "Actually, we love this shit. It's really cool to find out stuff not even the government guys know about."

243

"Even though you could end up in a federal penitentiary?" Mandy asked.

"They wouldn't do it," K.C. said.

"How do you know?"

He laughed. "We're too valuable."

"How can you be so--"

"Ever hear of state's evidence?" Jake asked. "We've got so much shit on so many people, by the time we've finished naming names--"

"A lot of important people would be headed directly for the chopping block," Bud said.

Mandy nodded.

K.C. grinned. "It pays to have some valuable shit on the right people."

"I'll bet."

"How'd you get it?" Arthur asked. "I mean, you guys obviously know how to get around clearance and security issues."

"At one time," K.C. said, "we belonged to a special task force assigned by the Under Secretary, NPPD."

"National Protection and Programs Directorate," Bud said.

"NPPD collaborates with all levels of government," K.C. said, "as well as the private sector, non-government organizations, and international bodies. It's in place to prevent, respond to, and mitigate threats to national security that result from acts of terrorism."

"We were a special select group assigned secretly through IP—or Infrastructure Protection, to be more technical," Bud added.

244

"What happened?"

"You don't wanna know."

"I really would."

"Sorry. That was one of the conditions of our butts not being shipped off to a place well beyond the boundaries of the Yellow Brick Road." Bud returned to his laptop, punching keys.

"C'mon over here," Jake said. "You need to see this."

The TV screen in the center of the table lit up with Vanessa's face. It was the same photo Arthur had seen in Skip's office. Bud looked up at him and shrugged. "Know her?"

"Unfortunately."

"Then give us the nasty details."

"She's a cold, arrogant, nasty bitch." He'd said it flatly and didn't care how it sounded.

"Besides that."

"Skip pulled up her file. He said she's from San Francisco--"

"This female is a member of a group we'd love to get our hands on. She's a babe, but she's so bad, we don't really want to get anywhere near her."

"She and her friends have been doing some seriously bad things during the last few years," Jake said. "In fact, this group is so destructive, we've been studying them for several years."

"What is she and her friends involved with?"

"We have no idea what they call themselves now—which makes it even more difficult to gain any intel on them. But it doesn't matter. There are entirely too many radical groups to keep track of nowadays. Since Nine-Eleven, this country's been inundated with them."

"Talk about paranoia," K.C. said.

"Most are foreign nationals that have grown entirely too comfortable on American soil," Bud said. "Her group has been connected with a foreign operative that surfaced in the San Francisco Bay area shortly after the Towers fell. We're reasonable sure it's a German by-product of the old Serbian group, Black Hand, which came into power a hundred or so years ago."

"I thought the Black Hand was what the Italian Mafia called themselves," Arthur said.

"The Black Hand was originated by members of the Serbian army, claiming responsibility for the assassination of Archduke Ferdinand. Of course, this high-profile assassination nearly destroyed their organization, and six of their top-ranking assassins were caught and tried for treason. One or two others escaped and were thought to have been killed, but they surfaced in Germany during World War II. They were working for the Nazis but were not found when the Third Reich collapsed. INTERPOL reported a small group of assassins calling themselves "Die Anbieter," which means "The Providers," surfacing right about the time of the Nuremberg Trials. INTERPOL is reasonably sure this new group was started by those two original Black Hand escapees, who ventured out on their own, staying beneath the radar and eventually creating a global network specializing in political assassination. They had used females in small numbers before coming over here and learned right off how effective they were. Once they started up cells over here, their numbers grew. A rough estimate puts them at around thirty-five percent female. This one--" Bud jabbed a thumb at Vanessa "--is deadly. She may have been responsible for as many as forty kills during the last ten years."

A lump filled Arthur's throat. He'd actually slept with this bitch. She knocked him out and stuck a chip into his flesh. He had been entirely at her mercy. And she was a killer.

"As I said," Bud repeated, "she's one badass female."

"We'd love to help nail her," K.C. said. "Just put in the word to one of our contacts, let them take it from there." He chuckled. "I believe there's even a sizeable reward for info leading to their arrest and capture."

"Dream on," Jake said. "You know how Capitol Hill handles these so-called rewards."

"Why can't you get something on her?" Arthur asked.

"No hard evidence. The woman's as shrewd as they come. She does her job well and is miles away by the time the authorities step in."

The door opened. A tall, skinny, long-haired man in sloppy clothes came in. He wore thick glasses and stopped behind Bud, took the plastic vial from K.C., turned, and left quickly.

"Where'd *he* come from?" Arthur asked.

"Pay no attention to the man behind the curtain," Jake said. "He doesn't tolerate recognition well."

"They told him at Rehab he could stay invisible if he didn't look directly at anyone," Bud said.

"Are you guys serious?" Mandy asked.

"Only when we're joking," K.C. said.

Arthur went over to the door and peered out the small window. Out in the alley, a dirty white van had parked about ten feet away from the trailer. The man opened the back door and climbed in, closing the door behind him.

Arthur expected the van to pull away, but it didn't move.

Bud began punching keys. "What name did she give you?"

"Vanessa Campeon. Skip pulled her up as DeAngelis."

"Naught, naughty, you saucy wench." He shook his head and sighed. "She lied to you. Her real name is Natasha Prosky."

This third name wasn't surprising at all. Everything about her had ceased being real during his escape in the woods. Someone specializing in assassinations would need a drawer filled with aliases. "Obviously Russian," he said.

"She could have been born over there, but nothing about her is clear, so we have to assume nothing can be verified. There were several Prosky's we came across during our investigations. We can't be sure about anything. Prosky is a fairly common Russian name. However, one of the first assassins used by Die Anbieter around 1946, after the Nuremberg trials, was a Leonid Prosky, and this raises our suspicions. Prosky was around thirty-five at the time, with two young children no one ever saw. One source claims Prosky sent them to the United States with a younger brother, who was also involved with Die Anbieter, but that's something else we can't substantiate. Her early years are sketchy at best. INTERPOL doesn't even have a file on her. About six months ago, one of our associates thought he found some useful intel on her in Moscow, but that went sour when the records office mysteriously blew up the night before he had planned to sneak in and copy the files. We have been able to learn a few things just recently, and found she was married to a man named Bradford for a brief period. George S. Bradford."

"Skip, when you pulled his file, wasn't that the one that brought up all those red flags?" Arthur asked.

"Why do you think he got in so much trouble at OPD?" K.C. asked.

Skip shrugged. "I do stuff like that all the time."

"You obviously don't do it right," K.C. said. "Otherwise, you wouldn't be in your boss's office all the time."

"What the hell should I do? Call you guys whenever I want to look up something classified and sensitive?"

Bud nodded. "By George, I think he's got it!"

"What about Bradford?" Arthur asked. "Does any of this have anything to do with that friend of his?"

"Leo Gustav Jenkins." Bud punched more keys. "Man's from Germany. His background is electronics and high-tech gadgets--especially involving robotics and remote systems. He was a major contributor for robotics equipment and technology used in data centers all over the world. We'd been watching him for some time, but he went missing a few days ago, and hasn't been seen since." Bud pressed another key, and an image blasted onto the screen.

It was the face of the man in the white lab coat.

The man Arthur thought he killed with the paperweight.

Chapter 21

Arthur sat forward and rubbed his temples.

It was bad enough that the film footage he'd been shown by Vanessa had proven this nightmare real. However, knowing the man's name made it worse. He had become an actual *person*. A *life*. He was a scientist—possibly a genius. He was an associate of George Bradford and had made significant contributions to the field of electronics. Now he was dead. Arthur hadn't personally killed him, but he was involved. He'd been in the same room with his corpse, had held the paperweight that killed him.

"Something you want to tell us?" Bud asked.

"Yeah." Jake was watching Arthur closely. "You look more than a little bummed out."

"He's dead." Arthur's voice sounded far away. "Leo Jenkins. He's dead."

"You're sure?" Skip asked.

"I saw footage of me standing over him. I…had a paperweight in my hand. There was a pool of blood on the floor. Under his head."

"Footage?" K.C. said.

"Interesting," Jake said.

"Remember exactly what you did?" Bud asked.

"Absolutely nothing."

K.C. picked up his cell again, turned in his chair, and began talking softly.

Bud punched some keys. "His body hasn't shown up anywhere."

"That bothered me, too," Arthur said. "I watched the news the morning after it happened. Nothing came up."

"The body was obviously disposed of," Bud said.

"As I said, I have no idea whatsoever of what I did that night." Arthur's thoughts shifted to the night in the condo when he'd awakened. "I don't think I killed the man, but they had total control over me. I just can't understand how a chip could make me do any of this."

Bud grinned. "There's a lot you don't know about technology, obviously."

"The chip was programmed to send timed messages to your brain." K.C. put his cell back down. "It has the ability to relax certain portions of the cerebrum, placing you in a semiconscious receptive state while feeding you messages, or commands, when you're most vulnerable to subconscious suggestion."

"Like hypnosis?"

"This technology is much more complicated and invasive. It interferes directly with brainwaves."

"A version of it was used during the Cold War in the mid-fifties," Bud said. "Hitler's boys experimented with it more than a decade earlier, using military prisoners and others not immediately slated for the ovens. They had some success but didn't have the time to refine the concept. The Russians were perfecting their own brainwashing techniques at about the same time. When World War II ended, they began sending a few of their

252

most successful subjects here as sleepers. Each would live a normal life until the time came to be activated. In such cases, it would take a phone call and a simple catchphrase, usually a line from a poem, or quote from Shakespeare, Tolstoy or Dostoyevsky, and the subject would awaken and perform his task."

"The Russians have always been more cultured than us," Jake said.

"You wouldn't say that if you'd ever spent time in a Siberian labor camp," Bud said.

"Be serious," Jake said. "Labor camps are not exactly interested in culture."

"Good point."

"The victim moves around in a dormant, semiconscious fugue," K.C. said, "doing what has to be done to complete the assignment. If stopped and questioned, he'll act dazed and lethargic."

"Like Jake, here, after a blunt and a couple of beers," Bud whispered.

K.C. ignored him. "He'll have no idea what was going on. Detaining and interrogating him will be a complete waste of time. It's actually a foolproof method."

"I take it the Cold War hasn't really died."

"That's a matter of intense debate," K.C. said. "In these modern times, it's become a mutual distrust/tolerance type of relationship, with both parties keeping a close watch on each other. The important thing is that we've got a shitload of enemies out there, and since our government policies let them come over here freely to set up house, we have very little power over what they're actually doing over here."

"We need to change our policies," Arthur said.

"Right now," Bud said, "it's important to lock away as many of them as possible. There are too many to deal with at once, so we've got to move carefully. Back to this group you've stumbled upon. Tell us about the footage you saw."

He told them what he could remember.

"Planning Committee." Bud laughed. "Cool. Anyone might think that crazy female's talking about the PTA."

"And you escaped from a building on Rouse Road?" K.C. asked.

"I had to knock Vanessa unconscious to get away."

"Ouch," whispered Jake. "I'll bet you're on her shit list for that."

"No doubt. But even so, they almost got me a few miles down the road, in the woods. This was before I realized they'd been tracking me."

"Describe this building."

"Big, white, and two floors. No signs—not even at the end of the drive. In other words, anonymous-looking."

Bud punched some keys. "The only building of interest in that area is the Central Florida Records Storage Center. Nothing suspicious there, just paper, microfilm, and magnetic media."

"I already pulled that up," Skip said. "Apparently she's high up on the Administration staff. Yeah, it kind of surprised us, too."

Bud punched another key, and the screen brought up Google Earth. A zoom-in went straight to Rouse Road, moving north, until it settled on a white rectangular structure sitting in the woods not far from the road. Another zoom-in brought up the building in question. "Is that it?"

The sight of it made Arthur queasy. "That's it."

"It's obviously a front." Bud nodded.

"Would that mean the storage people are involved?"

"You'd be surprised how easily these foreign operatives slip through the cracks. It's what they do best. For my money, they might be operating freely amongst the Records Storage people without the regulars even remotely aware of what's going on."

K.C. said, "Al-Qaida operatives have been discovered working at a Wendy's in Peoria, Illinois. Money launderers high up in the Russian Mafia were found employed as chefs in popular Italian, Polish, and Greek restaurants in New York City. The list goes on. We'll be here all day."

Bud punched more keys. "I'm pulling up their staff right now. Any idea how long she's been working there?"

"Since 2015," Skip said. "The year she and Bradford divorced."

"And the same year Bradford and Jenkins hooked up." Bud continued punching keys. "DeAngelis is listed, but that's no help. Even if we did ask the Feds to talk to her, she'd act perfectly innocent and would be so convincing, she'd make everyone feel guilty for interfering with her workday. As we've said, she's a professional, and has been able to stay clean for more than a decade. Besides, questioning her would explode in everyone's faces. She'll vanish, her friends would be alerted, and any and all immediate projects would be executed as planned. The Feds would have to start all over."

"They'd be pissed at us again, too," Jake said.

"We should be used to that," K.C. said.

"We are," Jake replied. "I just can't stand it when they send out their goon squad to search our places and take our laptops and anything else they find that they consider interesting."

"They do that?" Mandy asked.

"They've done it twice before," Jake said.

"They actually confiscate your computer equipment?"

"Like rats going after a brick of fresh cheese," K.C. said.

"What do they do then?"

"Go into them to do an extensive search before they scrub them clean."

"That's barbaric," she said, frowning.

"They call it national security," Bud said.

"They can be rough," K.C. added.

"Let's concentrate on the other bad guys for now," Arthur said.

Jake laughed. "I like this guy. He has a way with words."

Arthur ignored him. "We've got to do something." He was beginning to suspect he had ruined everything by letting Mandy and her friends remove the chip. "Once they find out I'm no longer wearing their chip, they'll pull up stakes."

"It's a little more complicated than that," K.C. said. "You know too much."

Arthur stiffened.

"These folks have contacts all over the world," K.C. said. "They have unlimited access to everything. As you yourself said, they've got access to security cameras. Hell, they've penetrated OPD. You actually think they'll pull up stakes because one of their pawns has decided to talk to the authorities?"

The more they spoke, the more uncomfortable he became.

"They've got just about anyone they need at their fingertips," Bud said. "When they want something done, they make a phone call. That's all it takes, and their problem is fixed within the hour."

"They have film footage of me standing over Leo Jenkins, and footage of me leaving Dr. Tannenbaum's office with him lying dead behind his desk. Now they've got footage of me in Sable Point, with another corpse. Don't you think that would be enough insurance for them? Film footage is pretty incriminating."

"One thing you're overlooking," K.C. said. "Film can be doctored, altered, and scrubbed."

Arthur sighed. The message was clear. "I don't have a prayer, do I?"

"We might have something in mind," Bud said. "It's a long shot, but we'll need your complete cooperation."

"You've got it."

"Don't be so quick," Jake said. "This is illegal, for one thing."

"If the Feds find out," Bud said, "they'll have *all* our heads."

"I had a feeling I wasn't gonna like it," Arthur said.

"Actually, we kinda think you're gonna *hate* it," Jake said.

"You really need to know who you're dealing with before you decide anything." Bud removed a tiny thumb drive from his briefcase and inserted it into his laptop. "This is an interview from a former associate of their group who is currently under Federal protection. He gave the Feds details of their activities. Nothing about him can be revealed from this tape. There are only two copies in existence. His identity has been altered. It'll give you an idea about these people and the seriousness of the situation."

"How'd you get it?" Mandy asked.

Jake grinned.

"I know. Don't ask."

"Smart as well as sexy. Someone's a lucky guy."

Mandy didn't look amused.

Arthur sat back in the chair. His heart was thrashing, but he had to go through with this. These people had ruined his life. Listening to someone else who'd been through this same mess and had survived might give him courage. "Bring it on," he said.

Chapter 22

Bud punched a key.

The black screen immediately grew a shade lighter. At the top, a small-watt bulb sprinkled the darkness with an anemic orange haze. A broad-shouldered figure sat hunched over a table, his face blurred out. When he spoke, his altered voice took on a strange metallic timbre.

"They been around a while, a long time," the voice said in a flat monotone.

"How long?" asked the male interviewer, off-camera.

"Who knows?"

"Can you give us a rough idea?"

"From what I learned, they were doin' their shtick during the Second World War. Before that? Who the hell knows?"

"Where did you first come across them?"

"In jail."

"When was this?"

"Early nineties."

"Where?"

"San Francisco. I lived there back then, I was a petty crook—muggings, burglary, even picked pockets. Then I got into some serious shit when the guy I tried mugging fought back. Feisty little bastard, musta been twenty, maybe thirty years older than me, and I was in shape, played football, ran track in high school—that sorta thing. He gave me no choice, so I let him have it. Fucker went down, cracked his head on a fire hydrant. Killed him, right there on the spot. Some rubbernecks saw the whole damn thing and they caught me the next day. Turns out the guy I killed? Fucker was a judge with the San Francisco Circuit Court. Yeah, I really fucked up, and knew I was goin' away for life. You kill a judge, it's like killin' a fuckin' cop."

"Did you go to trial?"

"These two guys came to see me coupla days later, said they were special attorneys for some damn government agency and could get me out if I played ball with them. Hell, I'd play ball with anyone to get out of that fuckin' mess, so I said yeah, I'd do it. I figured they'd want me to tell 'em what I knew about the streets. I did a little dealin' back then and kept up with what was goin' on. Back then, shit was tricklin' in from the Cali cartel. This was about the time Cali and Medellin were fightin' it out, each wantin' to be top dog, so I figured these special attorneys would wanna know this shit."

"Is that what they wanted? Information about the cartels?"

"Bastards wanted me to work for them. Found out later on, they got me outa jail by convincin' some bigshits I was an informer for the FBI. It was one big fuckin' lie, but it sure as hell worked 'cause I was out of that fuckin' hellhole of a jail in an hour. Just like that."

"What happened next?"

"They said there were some business competitors gettin' in their way and they wanted 'em out of the picture. I said, hey, I ain't no duster, and they said, look, we got you outa jail for somethin' that woulda got you life. I told 'em yeah, I appreciate that, but I still ain't no duster. The judge was an accident, and I felt bad about it. They didn't care, just said that if I didn't change my mind, a member of my family would bite the big one. I thought they were just blowin' smoke, so I told 'em where to go. Coupla days later, this DVD comes in the mail. Express Delivery, no return address. I stick it in the machine, it shows my little brother getting' in his prize Camaro just seconds before it blows up. Just like that. I'm sick to my stomach. It's rough, watchin' your little brother getting' blown up—ya know? We weren't close or anything, but it still sucks. Anyway, that's when I figured these jerks weren't fuckin' around."

"So then, you started working for them."

"Fuckin' A. I still got my mom and two sisters, ya know? I hardly ever see 'em, but I sure don't want 'em blown up like (*bleep*) was."

"What did they want you to do?"

"I'd get somethin' in the mail, said a time and a day, an address, and instructions."

"What sort of instructions?"

"Real vague, but you could figure it out. Sorta like, Male, six feet, forty years old, bald...or female, thirty-two, five-six, blonde. At the bottom would be something like, .357 (mouth), or stiletto (jugular). That would be how they wanted it to go. I was s'posed to burn the message as soon as I got it."

"Did you?"

"Did I what?"

"Burn the message."

"Fuckin' A. Think I wanna get another fuckin' DVD in the mail?"

"And this was the entire job?"

"There were other things I had to do, like carry around that fuckin' camera thing."

"Camera thing?"

"They wanted me to wear a special camera hooked up to the top of my ski mask. It was fancy. Kinda small, like one of those bugs the Feds use. Anyway, I was supposed to have it on."

"They wanted this filmed?"

"They also wanted me to make sure that damn camera saw everything before and after."

"Why did they want you to do that?"

"Who the fuck knows? Maybe they wanted to make a movie. I'm tellin' ya, these dudes are fuckin' *crazy*, man. They even had someone else there when I showed."

"There were *two* of you doing the job?"

"I'd do the job. The other dude would just stand there like a zombie."

"Was he watching? Or making sure you did the job?"

"He wasn't doing anything, man. He just stood there. They even told me to hand him my weapon after I did the deed and wiped my prints off it. Weird, man."

"Did he say anything when you gave him your weapon?"

"Dude just stood there like a zombie. Christ, it was so weird! I nearly lost my lunch when I first handed over the gun, but these jerks were payin' good jack, so I never said anything."

"Weren't you curious about who these people were?"

"Like I said, I kept my mouth shut. My family, remember?"

"Tell us more about this other man, the one standing there like a zombie. Was he always the same person?"

"Different dudes each time."

"Was he watching this? Filming it? Did he have a camera with him?"

"Not a damn thing. Just stood there when I handed over the weapon. I'm tellin' ya, there's somethin' seriously scary about these dudes. I mean, it was like they weren't even there. You could flash 'em your dick and they'd just stand there. Anyone could tell they didn't see a damn thing. Zombies, like I said. But I just figured they were there for a reason, so I didn't bother, just made sure the camera got everything before I left."

"Do you think they were some sort of decoy? In case someone saw something and called the police?"

"Maybe."

"Why do you suppose you were filming everything?"

"I don't *know*, man. I keep tellin' ya these dudes are *fuckin' scary*. I mean *totally nutso*! You don't wanna piss 'em off, ya know? Not askin' questions turned out to be the smartest thing I ever did. Besides, when you check your bank account the day after a hit and find out your balance has gone up five K, you stop tryin' to be curious."

"Tell us more about these people."

"Like I said, they never told me much, but I kinda learned a few things along the way. I saw a couple of 'em on TV, one of those political debate shows, and I got this really screwy feeling that these dudes were actually politicians."

"What else did you find?"

"One time they sent me to this really fancy place, right off Taylor Street. A men's club, they called it. I went there one night with a coupla guys who picked me up outside my efficiency. I had to dress up, and they told me not to say anything unless someone spoke to me. No one did—which was all right, 'cause everyone there acted real snooty and didn't even notice me."

"Why were you there?"

"One of those rich dudes was pointed out to me. I was s'posed to remember him, then sneak out to their grove the following weekend and dust him. They got this huge playground sorta place out in Monte Rio, in the middle of the woods, where they get drunk and do whatever they can't get away with in town."

"You mean women? That sort of thing?"

"I didn't see chicks out there, man. If there were any, they had 'em stashed somewhere. Anyway, I had to sneak out in a canoe, and a coupla dudes were waiting for me when I reached the other side of the river. Weird place—cameras rigged in the trees and guards everywhere out there."

"Who helped you?"

"They never said who they were. They were dressed like the hired help, so I figured they'd been paid off, too. Or maybe they were workin' for the same folks I was, I dunno. As soon as we climbed up the bank, they handed me a shirt and pants just like they were wearin' and told me to change."

"No camera this time?"

"Wearin' a camera woulda been stupid, man. Anyway, we snuck through the woods and went out where they had all these tents set up. I had to make it look like a heart attack. It wasn't too hard. There was a lot of drinkin' goin' on, and I figured out what he was drinkin' and got him a Scotch rocks, which I laced with something they gave me earlier, the day before I went out there. Dude went right to sleep, and I figured no one would notice he was dead till much later on, possibly early morning. By this time, I'd already made tracks. Same dudes that brought me in led me back out, and I was back in that canoe a half-hour later."

"Did you ever find out who you'd murdered?"

"Never did, but you gotta remember that they always kept me in the dark. I figured it was better that way. The less you know, the less you can be blamed for."

"How many people did you eliminate when you worked for them?"

"Too damn many to keep track of. I was doin' about one a week back then. You figure it out this way, you can get sick to your stomach. I worked for them for about eight years. Do the math."

"What made you get out?"

A pause. The figure lowered his head and rubbed his scalp. Then he sat up and groaned. "They had me dust...a little *kid*. Nine, maybe ten years old. A fuckin' *kid*, for Chrissakes. Can ya believe that? They had me do a *fuckin' kid!*"

"Did you want to take a moment to--"

"That's it, man."

"But we haven't--"

"I *said*, that's *it*, goddammit. I'm *done*, here. Turn that shit *off*. *Off!*"

The screen went blank.

A pause, then: "Interview concluded."

***

Arthur couldn't speak, couldn't breathe.

All the air had been sucked from the room. His feet had gone numb, and he could no longer feel his butt or extremities. He had ceased to exist. Had become a zombie, a nonentity.

Just stand there, the bigger kids told him at the playground half a lifetime ago, while choosing up teams for softball. Arthur was smaller than most of the other kids, and not good enough to play with the bigger boys. *Go after the ball when the catcher misses it. Fetch it when it goes foul. If it goes into the woods, find it.*

Now, years later, as a grown man, he had become useful in a darker, more horrific vein. *Hold this while I get away. Take my gun so I don't get caught with it.*

He'd never felt so helpless. Or stupid.

266

"Now we know for sure." Mandy patted his arm. "You're no murderer. And you didn't kill Robert."

Relief was no longer the main issue. This was infinitely worse than the inferiority complex he had developed as a child.

"They made me a stooge." The words came out hotly, filling his throat with bile.

"Better than being a murderer," Skip said.

The statement provided little solace. Vanessa and her brood had turned him into a piece of furniture. It couldn't get much worse than that.

K.C.'s cell buzzed. He picked it up. "You ready, then?" He turned to Bud. "Put him on."

A balding man around forty-five years old appeared on the screen. He wore a shirt and red striped tie. The collar was opened, the knot of the tie loosened and pulled halfway down. He sat behind a desk, facing the camera. He was punching keys on his laptop.

Arthur didn't want to ask who this man was. He strongly suspected he was about to hear even more chilling news.

Bud said, "This dude has been with us for several years, monitoring enemy groups while building intensive profiles on them. He'll ask you a few questions. Ready to talk?"

Arthur knew he didn't have much choice. "I guess so."

"You're on, Ralph."

The man looked up from his laptop. "There are several things we need to know," he said in a loud, low-pitched voice. "Some of these things will require your cooperation. Others will present themselves as we learn what is involved here. Do you understand the position you are in?"

"Completely."

"Then you will cooperate?"

"I have no choice."

He nodded. "We'll need to start with Leo Jenkins, whom we've been watching closely for the last several months. Jenkins was highly respected in the electronics field, specifically robotics, but he was also skilled in the development of multiplayer online games. He worked extensively with individuals who later branched off onto their own and created successful companies. Jenkins contributed his ideas to some of these companies while secretly perfecting his own online ventures. When he teamed up with George Bradford, whose experience lay in electronic surveillance, Jenkins' path veered slightly off-course. However, what he came up with two years later was quickly bought up by foreign nationals."

"I don't understand," Arthur said.

"Jenkins's twenty-year background in robotics came into play when Bradford left the FBI. They met at a convention in San Francisco. Something to do with the Silicon Valley crowd, we assume. Bradford and Jenkins apparently decided to become partners in a new venture. Bradford saw the genius in his new partner and decided to use his knowledge to its fullest potential. For months, he and Jenkins worked with microchips, bugs, and trackers, incorporating standards each had learned about remote control. Jenkins also held degrees in Chemistry and Medicine, had studied Kinesiology, and was quite knowledgeable about the central nervous system."

A chill swept through Arthur. He had a feeling all this was about to hit home. "What does the central nervous system have to do with all this?"

"In simple terms, he found a way to program brain waves into performing specific functions."

"Through a *chip*?"

"Jenkins devised a plan to develop a group of remotely programmed individuals for military use. They were called RPS. He'd wanted the U.S. Army to buy the patent and use the program to fight the war in Afghanistan. To this day, the public knows nothing about any of this, of course."

"RPS? What's that?"

"Remotely Programmed Soldiers."

"Is that even possible?" Mandy asked.

"If Jenkins and Bradford had been given the contract, they might have actually accomplished it. Jenkins would have been able to program and control a soldier's movements from the time he stepped off the chopper onto enemy soil until the instant he was shipped home. However, the funds needed would have been enormous, so the Department of Defense passed on it."

"What happened with the contract?"

"Someone else found out about the program and sabotaged it. We think it was Natasha Prosky. We were able to obtain footage of the San Francisco convention. She was in attendance. Going by what sources we've been able to obtain, Prosky never strayed very far from Bradford. She knew about her ex-husband's goals and figured he'd eventually hit pay-dirt. She'd gleaned all she could about data storage, memory cards, and USB flash drives from her first husband, Richard Summers, during the time he'd worked for SanDisk in San Francisco. She probably learned about surveillance and security from Bradford during their brief marriage. Since she regularly attended these conventions, it wasn't odd that she went to that last one. She might have even bugged Bradford during the event, enabling her organization to monitor and listen to everything the men said to one another."

"Wouldn't Bradford suspect such a thing?" Arthur asked. "He was a surveillance expert, right?"

"If he was drinking, his guard would be down," Ralph said. "Every photo of him showed him holding a glass."

"She probably kept feeding him drinks," Mandy said.

"She knows what she's doing," Arthur said. "When her brood found out about the contract, they undoubtedly used her to get it signed over."

"I wonder how she did it," Mandy said.

"No one knows," Ralph said. "Just that it happened very quickly. She might have used a strong-arm, for all we know. Or maybe it was strictly a money issue. Die Anbieter has unlimited resources. Unlimited capital, as well."

"Bradford and Jenkins both knew what they were up against," Arthur said. "Especially Bradford, since he was married to her."

"As I just stated," Ralph said, "they might have been bought off."

"Without any say whatsoever in Jenkins' plan?"

"According to our reports," Ralph said, "Bradford wanted to head the project. Since he was ex-FBI, he wouldn't appreciate how his ex-wife bullied or outsmarted him and would fight to be in charge."

"What happened?"

"He went missing shortly after and was never heard from again."

"What about Jenkins?"

"Being a scientist, Jenkins was undoubtedly scared into playing ball, and bullied into working on developing the concept further. But that obviously didn't work out for very long. Jenkins was a perfectionist and wouldn't accept how things were going or how the group was handling it. The group wouldn't tolerate this and would have him eliminated. Maybe they simply grew tired of having to deal with Jenkins or decided he might eventually talk to the wrong people."

"Maybe they decided they no longer needed him," Mandy said.

"These are definitely the same people who blackmailed the guy on the tape into killing for them for eight years?" Arthur asked.

"This group has been operating under the radar for much longer than eight years," Ralph replied. "They've got the resources to have refined Jenkins' design, using kidnap victims as subjects, implanting them with chips, then programming them to perform simple functions. Once these tasks were perfected, they moved on to the more complicated."

Arthur's anger flared up again. "You mean you guys *know* all about this?"

"We've had suspicions," K.C. said.

"What about these decoys? Have you ever caught any of them?"

"Two," Bud said.

"We tried questioning them," Ralph said. "We used hypnosis, injections—every conceivable method we know of. The two men obviously knew nothing. Like you, they were under the assumption that they'd experienced strange dreams."

"Are they still--"

"They both escaped while being escorted to another facility."

"How'd that happen?" Mandy asked.

K.C. shrugged. "From what we were able to discover, two of the guards involved in the transport were never seen or heard from again. We have to assume they'd been planted."

"And the decoys?" Arthur asked.

"Vanished as well."

"What have you been able to find out about this chip thing?" Arthur asked.

"A GPS was included in the chip for constant monitoring," Ralph replied. "The subjects were called RCK's, or Remote-Control Killers. Once they were able to kill on command, another batch was turned out with the specific function of being a decoy—showing up at the right time and location to provide an alibi in case the killer was discovered or detained. These decoys were considered necessary. The assassins were vital to their programs."

"The guy on the tape wasn't programmed, was he?"

Bud said, "He was used in the nineties, and came to us not long after the Towers fell. RCK's didn't start popping up until two years ago. Ever since, Die Anbieter has been extra diligent using decoys. The RCK's are crucial and must be protected."

It was as just he'd suspected: he was expendable. Nothing more than a scapegoat. A distraction.

"Any idea who these assassins have been targeting?" Arthur asked.

Ralph said, "These people have been operating freely in this country since the mid-fifties. An investigation would be a waste of time and manpower. Too many people have died in the last half century. It would take an entire agency a decade to handle such a monumental task. Calls from the conspiracy nuts alone would bog down the systems in days. We'd have to look into all suspicious deaths, starting with the Kennedy Administration, and take it all the way to the present. As an example, nearly two hundred people have died under mysterious circumstances during the Clinton Administration. Bankers. Witnesses. White House councils. Bodyguards. Fundraisers. Investigators. That administration alone would gobble up enough manpower to keep us busy for years."

"Now I think I understand what we're up against," Arthur said.

"You gotta realize this sort of thing has been operational for a long time," Bud said. "You'll find that just about every photo of every high-profile political assassination will show at least one suspicious person at the murder scene. Take the JFK assassination. The man in the doorway of the book depository. To this day, many swear that was Oswald."

"Decoys were used centuries ago," K.C. said. "The concept is very old. It has always been extremely vital to shift focus. Good assassins are hard to come by. In most countries, they're a much sought-after commodity."

Flashes of disjointed images raced across Arthur's vision.

"Something coming to you?" Mandy asked.

"I was able to glimpse my page just before they put me under that last time. I had only a few seconds to do it, but I forced myself to memorize as much as I could. DK showed on that page. So did Subject, with something else after it." He struggled to remember. "Subject, subject... What was after— *yes.*" The image scurried by in blurry letters. "Auxiliary Team B. RCK-7, DK-2. I'm sure that's what it was."

From the screen, Ralph attacked his keyboard. "Sounds like you were attached to one of their hit teams. The RCK nailed it. The DK could be a classification, as well. It could stand for Decoy, or Decoy Killer."

Decoy. Alibi. Stooge. No matter what it was called, it meant the same thing. Expendable. Disposable. He was no more important than a box of Kleenex. Important at the time, but to be disposed of and forgotten immediately after use.

Even though he hadn't killed or hurt anyone, he felt no relief. But what serenity he did experience was short-lived, eclipsed almost immediately by the anger, the hurt, and the disgust of what Vanessa and her brood had done in three short days.

K.C.'s cell buzzed. He picked it up. "Got it?" He nodded. "Good work. We'll pick it up from here." He put the phone down. "Lasky's been able to crack the encrypted code of the program."

Bud began punching keys. Ralph's image immediately vanished from the screen.

"What program are you guys talking about?" Arthur asked.

"Lasky's our resident geek," Bud said, furiously working the keyboard. "He can hack into anything." One last punch, and the screen opened with a blue page filled with columns upon columns of small white numbers.

"What the hell's *that*?" Arthur asked.

"The contents of your program."

It took him only seconds to realize what Bud was talking about. *Your program. The chip.*

Near the bottom, a small white hourglass slowly drained. Beneath it, a column of six figures changed constantly, one per second, in a rapidly descending mode.

"What's that?" he asked.

"From what we can gather, it's a countdown," K.C. said.

"To what?"

"Your next activation."

Chapter 23

A little after two, Mandy, Skip, and Arthur left the trailer, followed Bud and K.C. outside, and approached the large van parked next to it.

No one said anything. Arthur knew they sympathized but could not possibly understand the horror consuming him. Their silence told him they had no words to relieve his inner torment.

Your next activation. With what had already happened during the past few days, this shouldn't have shocked him. Even so, the phrase had delivered the same chilling effect as if he had just been told a bomb was ticking away inside him.

The chip had been removed. This in itself should have solved all his problems. But in this case, it had done nothing to eliminate the dilemma. The program had not stopped or abbended, but kept running, just as any clock or timing device would. And each tick brought him one second closer to oblivion.

He shuddered to think what Vanessa and her deadly brood would do when they learned what had happened. Would they send one of their remote-control assassins to kill him while a decoy stood off to the side to take the heat? How long would he have to wait? A week? A month? A year? Would they contact him first to tell him their plan? Would they do it by phone? Email? FedEx? Would they use Vanessa?

After all, he was her pet project. She had picked him personally. He was damaged goods. A loner. A grieving man ready to make the final plunge. The perfect tool. Nothing could possibly go wrong.

But something went incredibly wrong and would cause unforeseeable disaster for them. This would reflect on her, make her look bad to her peers. She wouldn't tolerate this humiliation. He could see her showing up at his door dressed to kill, eager for one last coupling before giving him his final injection later on, while he slept.

He felt as if he were fading away. Somehow, the concept seemed fitting. He had been slowly fading away since Vanessa entered his life. Decoy. Chump. Stooge. A shadow one sees only when he is looking in one specific spot. No longer a human being, but a mere illusion in the darkness. Something that isn't really there.

"How long...do I have?" The words escaping his throat sounded like they had come from someone else.

K.C. glanced at his watch. Earlier Arthur had seen him program something onto it. Perhaps a timer option. "A little less than seven hours."

Seven hours. It sounded like a long time. But since it involved what was undoubtedly the remainder of Arthur's future, it might have been a mere fifteen minutes.

"That'll make it around midnight, then?"

Both Bud and K.C. nodded.

Midnight seemed fitting. There was something eerie and ghoulish about one's fate taking place at midnight. There was also something eerie and ghoulish about the people who had sealed his fate. They were bright. And knowledgeable. And had no problem with technology. He couldn't imagine their not knowing what was going on.

"I probably have less than an hour, tops," he said, more to himself than anyone else.

"How do you figure?" Bud asked.

"They've always kept a close watch on me."

K.C. shrugged. "So?"

"They know I'm here. With you guys. They know what we did. What we're doing. Planning."

"You're looking at this all wrong," Bud said. "Your last meeting with them convinced them you knew what you were up against and quite possibly realized you could do nothing to change the status quo. They would assume you decided to be a good boy and cooperate. This group is undoubtedly arrogant enough to think they've got all the bases covered."

"Don't they?"

"Not necessarily," K.C. said.

"What about the chip?"

"What about it?" Bud asked.

"It's got a GPS. They know where I am. They know I'm here. All this has been for nothing. They--"

"It's been taken care of," Skip said. "The GPS was re-routed. For all they know, you've been home all afternoon."

He wanted to believe them, but a big chunk of his mind didn't want to trust anyone anymore—not even Skip. "You can actually *do* that? I mean, just go on in there and--"

"Once you hack into a program," Skip said, "you can do whatever the hell you want."

"He's right," K.C. said. "Even if it's got antitheft software and the latest blockers."

"Then…they think I'm home?"

K.C. and Bud nodded.

Somehow this didn't sound foolproof enough. "What if…what if they send someone over there? They'll discover I'm not there."

"We've got someone watching the building," Bud said.

"And there's no way they'll know if the chip has been tampered with?"

"Anti-tampering software," Skip said.

Once again, fear and doubt jumped out at him. *The GPS was re-routed. We've got someone watching the building.* It sounded convincing, but the fear just wouldn't go away. It was because of Vanessa and the people she worked for. An organization operating under the radar for so many years would never leave anything to chance. Re-routing the GPS and watching someone's building didn't sound foolproof—not in this context.

"Let's do this," Mandy urged.

He wanted to tell her how frightened he was, but she already knew. But instead of intensifying the fear, this caused more anger to plunge through him. He was *the man*. He was supposed to be strong. But he'd somehow become weak and vulnerable. The good guy. The perfect stooge. He

280

was damaged and could be taken advantage of. He had retreated inward and was so full of grief, he would never notice what was happening to him. And someone who wouldn't notice would never retaliate.

His fear vanished, and an intense anger filled his being. Good guy, my ass. The good guy they selected for their selfish purposes was about to turn into a serious badass.

Fired up, he followed Mandy through the side doors of the van.

***

The seats had been removed from the van and substituted with a padded metal table covered with a white cloth, two chairs, and a smaller table littered with medical supplies.

A man and a woman in white lab coats stood behind the table, watching them. The man, tall, portly, and partially bald, studied Arthur with small, smoldering dark eyes. The woman was tall, slender, and blond. She also gazed intently at him.

Medical instruments were laid out in neat rows on the white cloth. Rolls of gauze, bottles of antiseptic, scalpels and hypodermics sat among the mix.

Arthur sighed deeply. Hypodermics meant one thing. So did scalpels. What other humiliation were they about to put him through?

He turned to Mandy. "Any idea what's going on?"

"No, but something tells me this isn't going to be pleasant."

Her statement sent terrifying images racing through him. Torture scenes from movies he had seen rushed by. Skin being sliced open, gouged, and pulled apart. Chills gripped him, and he froze two feet from the doorway.

"It can't be any worse than what you've already been through," Skip said.

The man in the white lab coat gestured. "C'mon in. We're ready."

Arthur didn't move. This felt no different from the dark room in the unmarked building on Rouse Road, when Vanessa and the other guy discussed "the doctor."

"I'll be right here," Mandy whispered. "I won't let them do anything I wouldn't let them do to me."

The realization tore through him. There was no other option. This was all because of Vanessa. Because she had picked him. He felt his hands becoming fists again. Before even realizing it, he'd entered the cramped area.

"Remove your shirt," the doctor said. "Then lie face-down." He pointed to the table.

Arthur gave Mandy a blank stare, then found himself gazing dumbly at the medical instruments lined up on the table, just inches away.

"Bear with us," Bud said from the doorway. "We've only recently decided on this strategy."

Although he didn't have much of a choice about all this, he did feel like he should be the one in control. If so, he had no intention of letting them off so easily. "Before I do anything, tell me about this…strategy."

282

"I was told this procedure would only take fifteen minutes of my time." The two vertical lines forming between the doctor's dark brows accentuated his frown.

K.C. squinted at his watch. "The clock's ticking, gentlemen."

The flare of anger made him spin around. "I don't care what the damned clock's doing. I won't make a move until I know what you guys are up to. I want to know now. This second. In plain English."

K.C. gazed at Arthur, then shrugged. "It's really very simple. We've got to put the chip back in."

***

Put the chip back in.

They wanted him to go through this again. They knew what he had been through, but obviously couldn't sympathize. Or maybe they didn't want to. They weren't total idiots, just people with a job to do, and not many ways of getting it done. But in this case, he didn't care. One trip through hell was more than enough.

"You've got to be kidding. Out of your fucking minds."

No one replied, and he wondered if they had heard him. In his shock, he might have only imagined speaking. At the moment, he found himself imagining several things. Like walking away. Turning his back on everyone here. Driving back to the condo and drinking himself into a blind stupor. He even envisioned himself just sitting there on the living room couch, grinning stupidly as Vanessa came into the condo.

But even though his thoughts were running wild, he couldn't tolerate letting them put the chip back in.

"It's the only way," Bud said.

"Think of something else."

"This is the only way we can possibly gain the Intel we'll need to go up against this group."

"Look, I had no say in carrying that damned thing around the first two times. I've got a say this time."

"We've got to get this going." K.C., damn him, consulted his watch again. "By the time we finish it, make our calls, then get you back--"

"I've already told you guys what I think about the damned time. Their chip nearly killed me. If you implant me, I'm going through it all over again."

"We're hoping you will," K.C. said. "It's integral to our plan."

"Your plan." They were beginning to sound no different from Vanessa. "It's gonna put me at risk again."

"Not as much as you think."

The doctor shook his head and glanced at his watch. The nurse standing beside him, looking uneasy, snuck a quick look at Arthur and turned away quickly.

Arthur ignored both of them. "And just how do you intend to stop those psychos from discovering what you're doing?" he asked K.C. "Have you forgotten that it comes with its own program? And when it's activated, it instantly turns my brain to Jell-O?"

"Once the chip's implanted," Bud said, "we'll send you back to your place and monitor every move you'll make."

"And when I black out and turn into Zombie Boy again?"

"We'll be right there."

Had he heard him correctly? "You're going with me on my next assignment?"

The men nodded solemnly.

Now he *knew* they were crazy. "You'll be in the *car* with me?"

"We'll be...close by," K.C. said.

"Close enough to see what's going to happen?"

"Yes."

This sounded more and more incredulous. "You're sure I won't die?"

K.C.'s expression did not waver. "We'll make every effort to make sure you're in as little danger as possible."

His statement wasn't reassuring. "I've seen the news. Read the papers. I've heard about all sorts of government cover-ups and conspiracy flicks. It always ends the same. The Government uses a private citizen to help them with hostile groups. The citizen does what he's supposed to and still ends up dead. Or a vegetable. Or he just disappears."

"You'll be as safe as possible at all times."

"Why doesn't that give me a warm fuzzy?"

"You'll be safer than you were before. We can guarantee that."

That statement hit home. He hadn't been safe at all during the blackouts. While in a semi-unconscious state, he had operated a moving vehicle, snuck into buildings and private residences, and stood dangerously close to armed assassins. Viewed that way, he couldn't expect a guarantee of complete safety—especially when placed in the same situation.

But no matter what they said or what assurances they gave, he couldn't ignore the obvious. He had never had much faith in anything the Government said or did. Every word coming from Capitol Hill was saturated in double talk, vague references, politics, and four-dollar words. In this case, they'd spelled it out in simple terms. *We've got to put the chip back in.* Short, precise, and direct. But this was only because they didn't have time for their usual long-winded rhetoric. They had time only to put the chip back in and take him back to the condo, then sit in their vans, drinking coffee while waiting for the fireworks.

"Should I?" He turned to Mandy.

"What else can you do?" She seemed tense.

He tried to ignore the darkness gathering in her eyes. Skip's eyes were also dark, and for one brief instant a spark of fear glinted in them. The Government guys appeared just as grim as always, and the doctor and nurse had gone right back to studying their watches.

"I'll do it," he said. "On one condition."

"Go ahead," Bud said.

"I want Mandy to assist."

The doctor turned to his nurse, who shrugged. "Very well. Let's get this under way. I really need to be back at the hospital."

"Okay with you?" he asked Mandy.

She smiled, and the darkness in her eyes disappeared. "I might as well do *something* constructive while I'm here."

The nurse picked up a bottle of alcohol, cotton balls, and pair of plastic gloves, and held them out. "There isn't time to scrub. I assume there's a sink in the trailer, but…"

Mandy grabbed the alcohol, unscrewed the cap, pressed a cotton swab against the opened end, and tilted the bottle.

"We'll need to insert the implant in the same general area," the doctor said.

Rubbing her hands with the swab, Mandy frowned at Arthur. "Why aren't you stripping?"

"Nervous, I guess."

"I'll be right here."

"Make sure the doc doesn't screw up, okay?"

Chapter 24

Arthur awoke from a deep, dreamless sleep and immediately forced his eyes shut from the glare of the overhead lighting.

He tried to push himself up, but a heavy numbness in his arms prevented him from moving, and dizziness washed over him, forcing him back down.

He closed his eyes and waited patiently for normal feeling to return. He moved his shoulders, and a tingling flowed up his arms, settling in his upper back. He opened his eyes again, just slightly this time, to let them adjust to the bright light. When his confidence returned, he turned on his right side, pushed himself up on an elbow, and scanned the area.

The doctor and nurse had gone. The instrument-covered table was also gone. The two agents sat at a table outside. Bud played Solitaire with a deck of cards while K.C. spoke to his cell. Mandy sat in a chair just a few feet from the table. As soon as she noticed him getting up, she rushed over and felt his pulse, then rested her palm on his forehead. He wondered where Skip was. He also wondered how long he had been sleeping. He felt as if he had been gone for hours.

"How long have I been out?"

Mandy smoothed out his hair. "A while."

Something didn't make sense. "What did you guys give me?"

She shrugged. "You were exhausted. We decided to let you sleep."

Despite the initial aches and pains, he had to admit that he felt much better. He obviously needed the rest.

Delicious smells drifted into the room. Skip came over wheeling a table covered with several white bags.

"What's that?"

"Dinner," she replied.

"Who's paying?"

"We aren't."

"I see Lazarus is finally up," Skip said, wheeling it in.

Strong aromas of charbroiled steak, melted garlic butter, fresh coffee, and cooked herbs and spices quickly filled the confined area. Arthur's mouth watered. Only then did he realize how long it had been since he had eaten last. He could barely sit still and watch Skip and Mandy opening the bags.

***

It was dark when Skip parked beside Arthur's Caddie in front of the condo.

Arthur crossed the front lawn, shuffled up the walk, and reached the front door without incident. His left arm and shoulder continued to buzz. So did his butt and legs. Although it had been hours since the surgical implant, he felt as if he'd been thrashed with a baseball bat. The local they'd given him—or "regional," as Mandy had called it—had been a doozy.

Something didn't make sense. The shot had been for his shoulder area, yet he'd conked out—and stayed unconscious—for hours. True, he'd been extremely tired. It was a long, exhausting day—a long, exhausting couple of days, in fact. It was only natural that he succumbed to the exhaustion as soon as he lay down. But why so long? It had been just after three when they'd given him the shot. According to his watch, it was now after ten. Seven hours? For a minor anesthetic?

"Aren't we going in?" Skip asked.

Arthur opened the front door, reached in, and flicked on the living room lights. But instead of going inside, he stayed right there. His feet had turned to stone.

"It's safe," Mandy said.

She was probably right. So why did he think someone could be waiting inside for him? It made no sense. Bud and K.C. had assured him their own guys were watching the place. Even so, the darkness of the hall beyond the living room disturbed him. Why? Because it concealed monsters? Creatures? Huge men in dark suits waiting to pounce on him?

"I feel like I did when I was a kid, and afraid of the dark." He felt foolish and ashamed as soon as he'd said it.

"From what they told us," Skip said, "they've had six different agents keeping an eye on this place around the clock."

"And there are two out there watching us right now," Mandy added.

He gazed at the palms, bushes, and palmettos, noting every parked vehicle, dumpster, and pine tree bordering this section of the property. It was a warm, quiet night, and no one was about. He heard only distant Semoran Boulevard traffic and the evening breeze whispering through the palms. He saw no vans in the lot. Just a couple of SUV's, a short row of parked cars, and half a dozen pickups silently staring at the buildings. If anyone was out there, they'd become part of the darkness.

"Let's go in." Mandy nudged him. "I'm thirsty after that steak and baked potato."

Her touch seemed to dissolve his fear. He edged through the doorway and crossed the living room. The place was silent and empty, making him feel foolish again. A drink would fix that. He headed straight for the liquor cabinet in the kitchen, grabbed a bottle of Jack, found three glasses from the drainer, and placed them on the counter. As Skip and Mandy plopped down on the stools, Arthur poured and set the bottle down.

"A toast." Skip picked up his glass.

"To what?"

He shrugged. "An abrupt end to all this?"

Mandy frowned. "Sounds dark and ominous."

"You do it, then."

She held up her glass. "Here's to Arthur finally breaking their stranglehold."

"I'll gladly drink to that." Arthur drained his glass. He replenished the drinks and glanced at the wall clock in the living room. 10:19. Less than two hours to go. His thoughts raced again, but this time, instead of wondering where they would send him, he began agonizing once again over those seven lost hours. He tilted his glass and drank.

"Better watch it." Mandy shook her head.

"Afraid I'll get drunk?"

"What happens if you're pulled over while you're blacked out? It could get ugly fast."

He put down the glass, went back out into the living room, and collapsed in the armchair. His limbs and butt continued to tingle, and he went right back to thinking about those missing seven hours. "What kind of shot did you give me? It sure hit me hard."

Mandy came over and sat on the sofa, facing him. "As I told you before, you were exhausted. Your resistance was down. Lying on that table relaxed you, made you fall asleep."

"You're sure?"

"Of course." Her gaze shifted to Skip, who turned away and raised his glass again.

Something strange was going on. Mandy had never avoided his eyes before. And Skip seemed uncharacteristically quiet and nervous. They were keeping something from him—he could feel it. He could even sense the tension in the room. It was as if something evil were lurking nearby.

A knot tightened in his gut. The darkness in Mandy's eyes had returned. But even as his suspicions grew, he realized how ridiculous he was acting--how totally absurd. The last time he suspected Mandy and Skip, his suspicions had blown up in his face.

Now he was doing it again. This time, however, his fears somehow seemed more credible.

But why should they? Because his friends were avoiding his eyes?

He was tired, scared, and frustrated, and wanted all this to end. It was only natural that he was imagining all sorts of weird things. But how could he possibly suspect them? How could he possibly think they'd hurt him?

The darkness in their faces did not change. And neither did his suspicions.

10:41. Time was moving unusually fast.

Why would they turn on him?

Money? Most people responded to money. But would Mandy? Would Skip? Both made good money. Would they consider turning him in for a sizeable lump sum?

No. They wouldn't. They wouldn't for one moment consider working for Vanessa and her brood.

Despite his rationalization, the little voice inside him said: *Everyone has a price...*

He had to go off by himself, think this out. But he had to do it without arousing their suspicions. There was still more than an hour to go before midnight. If Skip and Mandy were in fact working against him, he couldn't stay here. He had to get away, find someplace safe. Once he went under, he had no control. They could deliver him wherever they wished, and if they'd bargained with someone for his capture, he'd be completely at their mercy.

He could make a trip to the bathroom, lock the door, and slip through the window. It was only a foot wide and would be a helluva squeeze, but adrenaline would help him through. If he could kick out the screen, he'd be able to--

"What's wrong?" Mandy asked.

"Wrong?"

"You're staring."

"I've...got to...use the bathroom."

"Know where it is?" Skip asked.

"Of course I know where it is." His left eye began to twitch.

"Then why aren't you going?" Mandy asked. "And why are you acting so nervous?"

"I've had a rough day, and..." *Damn, the room sure is getting warm.* He reached up to loosen his collar. His fingers shook; they'd grown cold. He glanced at the clock again. 11:01. Still plenty of time to get away. He couldn't be here when the next blackout came.

Mandy had gotten up and was moving toward him. She looked worried. If he didn't soon make a beeline for the john, he'd be a sitting duck. His program would activate. They'd make their call and--

The blackness came suddenly, swallowing him up.

***

Arthur woke up on a sofa.

A sofa, armchair, and loveseat took up most of the poorly lit area. The sofa faced a brick fireplace. The dark stained mantelpiece was filled with a large collection of snow globes. Newspapers, magazines, and half a dozen thick candles covered the glass surface of the cocktail table in front of him. The wall on his left displayed color photos of family gatherings and studio portraits. A small ceramic lamp sat on the marble surface of the end table on his right.

Certain details surfaced as his head cleared. The Feds knew where he was. Using the tracker they'd implanted in his arm, they'd followed him here. They were probably outside in a van, listening with their high-powered gadgets.

Tracker. Implant. Dark images rushed past, and the scene with Mandy and Skip returned. *"You were exhausted. Your resistance was down."*

They had been tight-lipped and mysterious. Something had obviously happened while he was lying on that table.

K.C. had calculated that Arthur's next activation would be around midnight. But that wasn't the case, was it?

What time was it when it happened? 11:15? 11:30?

It was shortly after 11:00. K.C. had been wrong. And if he'd been wrong about that, what else had they messed up?

It made no sense. They couldn't miscalculate something that simple. The program had obviously been altered, and the Feds knew about it. They had to. They'd hacked into it, knew what was going on. They had access to the best hacking software in the world. They'd surely be able to view any program.

So why didn't they tell him?

The clock above the mantelpiece said 11:33. He'd only been gone twenty minutes or so. That wasn't enough time to drive here, come into this house, and perform his usual decoy job. Even if this place was only a block or so from the condo, there hadn't been time for whatever Vanessa's group had planned. Even if it was, why hadn't he come to in front of the condo? Did this have something to do with an altered program? If so, what other surprises did he face?

If Vanessa's crew had learned about his talk with the Feds, they would want to set him up for murder. And if they could alter the activation time on his chip, they could also change the destination. They could match anything the Feds did. They might even have sent them on a wild goose chase.

He could be on his own. The thought of it made his blood chill.

No one's out there to help you, no one's watching you, and no one but Vanessa and her brood knows what's going on. Whatever happens will happen, and nothing can stop it.

The panic rushed back. He jumped up and squeezed past the sofa and cocktail table. If the car wasn't outside, he was dead. This would be the perfect frame-up. With a body lying around, he'd only have a few minutes before--

He tripped and went sprawling, landing face-down on the lush carpet. For tense moments he lay there, dazed, his nerves quivering. *Get up. Get out. Now!*

He pushed himself up. Something caught his eye in the anemic orange haze of the lamp. He turned. His heart climbed up his throat, and he gagged.

A man and a woman, both dressed in their nightclothes, lay on their backs in the doorway, gazing with wide-open eyes at the dark stucco ceiling. Their throats had been sliced. Dark circles of blood covered the area around them.

Choking back hot tears, he turned away. A soft, high-pitched squeal trickled out of his throat. He wanted to throw up. And scream. And cover his eyes, all at once. He couldn't move, remaining on all fours while the slender dark-haired figure walked briskly down the dark hall toward him.

Chapter 25

Vanessa wore a white blouse, black skirt about two inches below the knee, and open-toed black pumps. Her hair plunged heavily over her shoulders. A thick, long knot had pulled loose and dangled near her face, brushing her right eye.

Under normal circumstances, Arthur would have been aroused. However, these circumstances were far from normal. This woman was a cold-blooded killer. He'd kissed her, slept with her. Shared his bed with her. But now he found himself nauseous, frightened, and disgusted in her presence.

Her presence baffled him. This was a murder scene. She was one of the psychos calling the shots. Showing up at the scene and placing herself in jeopardy would not be a smart move.

His head swimming, he forced himself to stop rationalizing and scrambled to his feet. Her presence brought back the anger and the disgust. It brought about other things, as well. He wanted to wrap his hands around her neck and squeeze until her eyes popped out of their sockets. He wanted to make her gasp for breath—to choke her until her tender flesh turned blue. He wanted her to collapse at his feet and lie there, like discarded trash. She really was trash and should be dead. For what she'd done to him and countless others like him, she should not be allowed to live.

He wanted her to know how much he hated her, how much she nauseated him. He wanted to ruin her life just as she had ruined his. He found himself struggling for the right words, the right phrase—anything that would hurt her, make her realize what she had done...yet the only words trickling out of his mouth were, "What are you doing here?"

She placed her hands on her hips. "Arthur, did you really think you could go to the Government people and tell them about us?"

They knew. Despite the care the Feds took with their leased offices, their anonymous vans, their hacking software, and their secret dealings, Vanessa and her people knew everything.

"You're not going to deny it, are you?"

He lowered his gaze to the floor. "I guess not."

"Why did you do it? Did you really think you could talk to them without us finding out?"

"I wasn't thinking too much about it at the time."

"That was very stupid of you, Arthur."

Her statement tore through him like a tongue of flame. It took him a few moments to find his voice. "Maybe..."

"Then why--"

"When your life has gone down the tubes, you're willing to do anything to get it back on track."

"What did you tell them?"

"Everything I knew."

"That couldn't have been very much, could it?"

She was obviously sent here to clear it all up. He decided to be vague. It might make her uncomfortable.

"I don't know. Was it?"

She sighed. "I didn't tell you much, so nothing you told them will help them at all."

"Maybe not."

She watched him closely, her gaze settling on his forehead. She was trying to penetrate it, see what was inside. He quickly discovered he was enjoying this. "We'd really like to know what you told them. Arthur. Not that we're worried, of course. Just curious."

They were worried, all right. He could see it in the vertical cracks splitting her brows. His afternoon with Skip and his friends must have caused quite a stir.

"Like I said, I told them what I know."

"You know precious little, Arthur."

"Then why are you so curious about it?"

She didn't speak.

He had to keep her talking. If the Feds were listening, this could be his best chance to help them nail this group. "Who were these people?"

"What?" She frowned. "What are you talking about?"

"These people." He pointed to the two corpses. "The two unfortunates who used to live here. They've become corpses. Care to elaborate on why they're no longer among the living?"

She flung it aside. "They are inconsequential."

He fought down the explosive surge. He couldn't believe this woman could be so heartless. "They're dead. You killed them. You and your pack of sadistic savages."

300

"Arthur, you're being melodramatic."

"You and your reptilian friends slither around, murdering people and getting away with it. You've been doing this since World War II, and it's got to stop."

She stiffened. "H-How did you know, Arthur?"

He suddenly realized he'd hit pay-dirt. "How did I know what?"

She didn't reply. He figured she didn't want to say anything else about it.

"Why are these people dead?"

"How do you know…about…about--"

"*Tell* me, dammit!"

She sighed. "The husband needed to be, well, stopped."

"From what?"

"It's inconsequential. It has been handled."

"For what purpose?"

"He was an attorney prosecuting a useful client."

"Useful? To whom?"

"The client is a successful Southern Florida developer."

"So?"

"This developer has important connections. It would be inconvenient if he were prosecuted."

"So then, you just decided to kill the attorney?"

"It wasn't that simple."

"What was so complicated about it?"

"Arthur—"

"Tell me!"

"He was to be offered a large amount of money to mishandle the case. A mistrial would have been all that was necessary." She shrugged. "He refused."

He refused. This meant certain death. You don't go against Die Anbieter without suffering the ultimate consequence.

Something was wrong. If she suspected her statements were being taped, she wouldn't have told him anything. Once again he wondered if Bud and K.C. were out there. Or listening. Or capable of listening. "That's more than you've ever told me before."

"You asked, didn't you?"

"I've asked questions before, but you never answered them. Until now."

She smiled, and the fear came back, rippling through him. "There's no one listening, Arthur. No one waiting in the shadows. It is just you and me."

Panic threatened once again, but common sense told him to keep it at bay. Vanessa had already proven she was a successful liar. Her lie about Mandy had convinced him not to believe anything she said.

"We're not idiots, Arthur. As soon as you went off the grid, we made major adjustments to your program. We changed its time schedule and killed its present program, then installed a different program to automatically kick off. This one is foolproof. It repels bugs and hacks—every conceivable intruder program developed during the last ten years. It also rerouted the GPS in the chip. Answer your question?"

"Unfortunately." His heart sank.

"Anything else you'd like to know?"

Despite his disgust, his growing fear, he had to keep himself together. He still needed to find out everything he could. He wasn't about to give up. Not yet. "Then this poor man had to die because he didn't accept the bribe?"

"A great deal of money was at stake."

"That's all it boils down to?"

"Money rules the world, Arthur. Everyone knows that—especially now, since most of the larger, more powerful countries have gone global and rely on one another to survive."

"What about his wife? Did you have to kill her as well?"

"It would have been awkward to let her live. Inconvenient. They were close. He most assuredly told her about the bribe."

Awkward. Inconvenient. Let her live. The disgust ripped through him. "You people are nothing more than a pack of psychotic bastards."

"You are naïve, Arthur. This is the modern world. Certain things have to be done a certain way if civilization is to survive."

"Whoever told you it was up to you to decide how things must be done?"

"We've been handling things for many years."

"By killing people."

"It is the most efficient way most crucial situations are resolved."

There had to be some way of crippling these psychos. He couldn't just let this go. Not without a fight.

"Arthur, I've been sent here to inform you that you are required to answer several questions."

"I already told you, I--"

"You need to tell us everything you told the Government people. You might have forgotten certain details of your talk with them. We need to know exactly what you told them as well as what they told you. It will be necessary for us to use technology to induce you to recall your interview in detail."

"Technology?" The word made his pulse accelerate.

"We have the latest scientific methods at our disposal."

Torture? Unlikely. Truth serums and other chemicals worked far better and more efficiently than removing fingernails with pliers or shoving hot pokers into unprotected scrotums or eyeballs.

"And then?" He really didn't want to know but figured he should hear the rest of it.

"You will then be sent on one last errand."

Chills swept through him. They were going to drug him, interrogate him, then send him back out. If he were correct in his assumptions, he wouldn't come to until the cops showed up—possibly through an anonymous tip. And then he would spend the rest of his life in prison for a murder he didn't commit.

"I think I get the picture."

"I knew you would, Arthur. You are very intelligent."

"Not intelligent enough to stay out of this, apparently."

"You've been a sound investment. But like most short-term risks, you have also become a liability. As a result, we've got to let you go. I'm sure you'll understand. We've got a business to run..."

He began measuring distances. If he could slip past her, he could run down the hall, find the front door, and escape. Unless one or two of their big boys were waiting outside, he could hide out in the bushes until morning, then find a phone and call someone--

That was the problem. He had no idea who to call. Bud? K.C.? He didn't know their number. It would take time to get to them and even more time to find out where he was. Mandy? Skip? After their strange behavior in the condo, he felt he could no longer trust them.

He had to face facts. He was totally alone.

"I know what you're thinking, Arthur."

He knew she was bluffing. He was much too confused to be thinking of anything specific.

"You're thinking of freedom. Of getting away."

He shrugged. "It's only natural—don't you think?"

"I'm watching your eyes. They're the mirror of the soul. But I promise I won't let you get by me like that last time."

The eyes. What was it about that phrase that made him think of Mandy?

"Besides," she said, smiling, "you're just not the type."

He blinked. "The type?"

She shrugged. "Confrontational. The type to stand up and fight. You see, this was what attracted me to you in the first place. One of the main reasons we selected you for our DK program. You were not only safe, honest, and law-biding, you were also non-confrontational. This happens to a person after a horrendous loss. You've been internalizing since the death of your wife. Turning away. Moving inward. Finding escape within yourself. Your type is much easier to deal with. We don't have to worry about resistance, or sudden outbursts."

He found himself growing angrier with every word she spoke. Non-confrontational. She might have been talking about a drooling mental patient sitting in a padded hospital room after being given a lobotomy.

"How about that whack to the forehead I gave you a couple of days ago?" Despite the makeup, the area was still slightly swollen and discolored. Under the circumstances, it made him very proud. "What would you call that?"

"An accident, Arthur. You'd panicked, obviously. I'll wager you had no intention of doing that, and probably felt very badly afterward."

His thoughts went back to what she said before. *The eyes.* Then he remembered. The eyes were not only the windows of the soul, but also the body's most vulnerable areas. Mandy's favorite targets. Focusing on them and then attacking them enabled her to overtake several huge men in just seconds.

He took one step toward her.

"Don't try it, Arthur. I honestly don't think you know what you're doing."

"Get out of my way."

Vanessa laughed. "Please, Arthur. This really isn't you."

Her laugh rocked through him. It was the ultimate insult, suggesting he was helpless, and wouldn't hurt a fly. Maybe he was—before the chip. And the blackouts. And the fact that they had taken over his life—and were ready to destroy it very shortly.

He lunged, and she sidestepped. At that same moment, something big and solid slammed him in the ribcage, knocking the wind out of him. He nearly collapsed as a hot swelling of pain crushed through him in tingling waves. Doubling up, he saw her lower her arm. She'd apparently used her elbow, and he knew right then that she could take care of herself. It only stood to reason. When you worked for killers, you were obviously required to be trained as one as well.

"Arthur, I'm way out of your league." Her voice rang flat. Using both hands, she pulled the heavy knots of hair away from her face.

Measuring distances, he lashed out with his right foot, catching her sharply behind her right knee. Gasping, she lost her balance and fell into the floor lamp near the wall. She went down hard, landing on her tailbone with a loud grunt. Her hair gushed forward again, covering her face and breasts. She pushed it over her shoulders and stared up at him. Her eyes were wide-open and glazed. "Arthur…what's gotten *into* you?"

Looking down at her, he felt a huge sense of triumph. She sat dazed, her hair unkempt, her skirt halfway up, one of her pumps lying on its side, three feet away.

"'Bye, Vanessa." He moved toward the hallway. "I'd like to say it's been nice, but I've never been a very good liar."

Just as he took his first step, Vanessa raised her right arm and held her forearm horizontally, her watch just inches from her face. Her gaze stayed on him. "I'm sorry it has to be this way, Arthur."

Before he could react or even anticipate her next action, she brought the watch closer to her mouth. "Oscar, activate the new program for DK-Seven."

Oscar. A chill rushed down his limbs. Dammit to hell. The name resonated into his consciousness only a moment before the world instantly went black...

Chapter 26

He awoke strapped to a chair in a tiny, damp room.

A small-watt bulb hung from a cord a few feet above his head, diluting the darkness with a faint orange haze. The room was cool, but his face felt hot, as if encased in plastic.

His limbs and torso had gone numb. Thick leather straps pinned his wrists to the padded arms of the chair. Another strap encircled his chest and another, his waist. The tightness of the straps prevented him from looking down at his feet, but he could tell by their numbness that his ankles were similarly fastened to the metal legs of the chair.

Despite the circumstances, he felt strangely at peace. Frightening images swam past his vision, but instead of surrendering to the panic, he enjoyed this strange solace. He didn't even care who'd brought him here. The only thing that mattered was the peace and quiet. He closed his eyes and enjoyed the emptiness, the quiet and stillness, and the comfort and security of the chair.

He tried dozing off, but his mind betrayed him, bringing back dark images. Vanessa. Two dead people lying on the floor, their throats cut. The chip in his shoulder. Blackness. Helplessness. Oscar. Die Anbieter.

I'm sorry, Arthur. It has to be this way.

He was brought here to tell them everything he told the Feds and everything the Feds told him. He had no choice; they were going to use their latest scientific methods to make him cooperate. He would then tell them everything Vanessa had done to him. He would tell them about the guy with the blurred-out face who talked about killing someone every week for eight years, until Die Anbieter ordered him to kill a ten-year-old kid. He would tell them about the attorney dying because he was too honest to accept their bribe. And that this man's wife had to die, too, because she talked to her husband. He would tell them everything he knew about the man named Leo Jenkins. And George S. Bradford. And Richard Summers. And the three men who had followed Mandy and Arthur to the seafood restaurant. He would tell them about Denise…and their life together…and how she died…and how he had become the type they were looking for because of her…and the grief that had nearly killed him and turned him inward.

Scientific methods, Arthur.

His right forearm was exposed, the shirt sleeve pulled almost to the elbow. In just a few moments, Vanessa would come in to insert a hypodermic into his flesh.

The process was necessary. It would be done to avoid problems. Even though he was non-confrontational, they still couldn't take chances. He had managed to knock Vanessa squarely onto her ass. Twice. The first time was an accident, the second, deliberate. Their safe, non-confrontational investment had snapped, and must be dealt with.

This was much safer and less time-consuming than torture. Just activate the program, send the subject into temporary oblivion, bring it here, strap it down, and administer the shot. Wait a few minutes for the drug to be absorbed into the subject's bloodstream, then ask the necessary questions. Once everything is recorded, release the subject for its last mission and let it enjoy one last glorious nap before the cops are brought in to arrest it for first-degree murder.

One last errand, Arthur.

A door opened somewhere off to the right. He heard the squeaking of tennis shoes moving quickly. Two figures in white gowns emerged from the darkness—a tall, broad male about forty, and a small, slight female with a shock of blond hair.

My God.

Mandy approached him, a grim expression on her pretty face. She held a hypodermic in her hand.

The realization tingled like a bucket of ice water to the face. Mandy was going to give him the shot. It didn't make any sense.

Or maybe it did. Her suspicious behavior at the condo made all the sense in the world. It wasn't all in his mind. His paranoia really did have merit.

Die Anbieter had gotten to them. They no doubt made Mandy and Skip an offer they couldn't refuse.

He couldn't let them do this. He had to escape. To break free of these straps and fight his way out of this nightmare.

He began tugging furiously at the straps. He wanted to upset the chair and kick at them, but then remembered his ankles were strapped to the chair as well. No leverage. But he had to do *some*thing. He couldn't let Mandy inject him without a fight.

Her doctor friend moved quickly behind him and placed his hands firmly on Arthur's shoulders. Arthur continued thrashing, slamming his head back in a feeble attempt to knock the man off-balance.

He quickly succumbed to exhaustion from his efforts. Dizziness washed over him, and he had the strange sensation that he was floating. As his vision turned cloudy, he thought he saw the blurry image of Mandy moving toward him again.

He tried one last time to pull away, but more dizziness overtook him. Mandy said something he couldn't understand. His hearing had gone just as useless as his vision. Then the darkness rushed over, consuming him.

***

He awoke in a bed.

No straps this time, just some tingling in his left shoulder and right butt cheek. He felt groggy and weak. The last thing he remembered was his pitiful scuffle with Mandy and the doctor.

This had to be a hospital room. Everything was white—walls, door, sheets, the table next to the bed. The heavy antiseptic smell sealed the deal.

He wondered if this was a prison hospital. Or where Vanessa's people had sent him to be picked up by the cops. Either way, he would be restrained. Otherwise, the folks in charge would make sure to place an armed guard in here with him. But he was alone.

Suddenly curious, he pulled his arms out from beneath the sheet, then raised it. A hospital gown, with nothing pinning him to the bed. As far as he could tell, he could get up and sneak out of here.

He forced himself to sit up and found he could only raise his head a few inches. Instant dizziness wrestled him back to the mattress. They obviously gave him something to make sure he didn't go anywhere. No wonder they hadn't bothered to strap him down.

He lay back down and closed his eyes. A few moments later, he heard the door opening. Mandy, dressed in her nurse's uniform, came right in.

This didn't have the feel of a casual visit. She was probably the one they selected to tell him his fate. Vanessa might have decided this method would be most upsetting to him. So be it. He was much too tired and disgusted to care.

Mandy grabbed his wrist and took his pulse. He turned away. She finally let his arm drop gently to the mattress. "How're you feeling?"

He saw no darkness on her face, no betrayal. Whatever he had seen in her eyes that night in the condo had vanished.

"Did you hear me?"

"Yeah." Confusion filled his head. Surely she hadn't asked him that. Was she so dense that she had asked such a ridiculous question? He didn't know her that well, but he knew Mandy was not dense.

"Well?"

"Angry. Hurt. Betrayed." The words shot out of his throat like bullets. "How the hell am I *supposed* to feel?"

"Angry, hurt, and betrayed." She shrugged.

His sudden fury ebbed just as quickly. He hadn't expected her to agree so easily. "I'd like an explanation," he said coldly.

"Agreed."

He waited, but she said nothing.

"Well? What do you--"

"You'll get one as soon as I get an apology."

An *apology*? For her turning on him? Giving him an injection? He couldn't believe her nerve. "What the hell for?"

"For fighting us, what else? We came to rescue you and there you were, acting as if we were--"

"You came...to *rescue* me?"

"We figured they'd already injected you by the time we found out where you were. Luckily, they hadn't."

"*You* gave me the shot. Didn't you?"

"Now why would I do something like that?" She watched him in silence for several moments. Her jaw dropped. "Don't tell me you thought...no, you couldn't *possibly* think I was working for them..."

Her tone made him feel guilty. "You...you had a hypo...in your hand!"

She sighed. "I was going to give you a stabilizer for the serum. It would counteract the effects. But when you began fighting, it became

314

much more difficult to examine you. Fortunately, you passed out."

"I passed out?"

"Right there on the floor. Doctor Bell did all he could to hold you down, but you managed to knock over the chair anyway. You also managed to smack him in the chest with your head. It slammed him against the wall. Then you knocked your chair over. I tried catching you, but I was at an awkward angle and couldn't maneuver very well in the confined space. What did they give you? We didn't find anything out of the ordinary with a blood test."

"I woke up in the chair. Then you and the doctor came in, maybe five minutes later."

"Why were you fighting us so much? This is *me*—remember?"

"You and Skip…you were acting so *suspicious* at my condo…just before I blacked out."

"K.C. and Bud told us to be evasive. You weren't supposed to know anything that happened while we had you on the table. It would have ruined their plan."

He was afraid to ask. "Wh-What did they do?"

"We implanted you with two chips."

"*Two* chips?"

"The original, plus one of their own. They implanted theirs deep in your right butt cheek. They didn't want you to know what they were doing, so we gave you a general."

"The chips. Are they still--"

"They were removed."

He studied her face, looking for more darkness, deception. Her gaze was dead steady. He wanted to believe her.

She sensed his doubts. "I was right there during the procedure. I made sure both were removed."

Her expression was sincere, but he found this difficult to grasp. "Why two chips?"

"I'll let them explain it." She ran a hand lightly along his left cheek. "You need rest. When I come back, they'll be with me. I had to threaten them with physical violence to keep them away this long." Then she touched his forehead and winked. He wanted to curse himself for not trusting her.

"Promise you'll come back soon?"

She smiled. "I'll be back before you can even miss me."

He must have been much more exhausted than he realized. He didn't even remember falling asleep.

***

When he finally awoke, Mandy was sitting beside the bed.

She told him K.C. and Bud were chomping at the bit to talk to him. She also said he didn't have to talk to them if he didn't want to.

"Send them in." He quickly realized that he was more concerned about what happened than anything else.

Mandy ushered in the two agents. They both looked like they'd been working too many long hours. Their eyes were blood-shot, and K.C. hadn't shaved.

"You can start off by telling me all about that second chip you didn't want me to know about." He knew he sounded harsh but found that he was angry for what they had done and needed to hear their explanation.

"It was the only way we knew to monitor you without their knowledge." K.C. sat in one of the two chairs against the wall, on Arthur's right. "Our chip contained an alternate program, with several vital features. One feature included a sensor that rendered it dead if scanned or probed. It was also GPS-enabled."

Bud took the chair next to his partner. "We followed you from your condo to the attorney's residence in Orlando. After your scuffle with Prosky, you were placed in sleep mode and driven by van to a vacant building in West Orlando. The building was an old high school that closed down when a new one was built a few years back. We figured they were going to give you the serum there and interrogate you before sending you off."

"Why there?"

K.C. shrugged. "Privacy, most likely. They used a small storage room. The block walls made it dark, isolated, and quiet."

When they mentioned the attorney's home, he wondered how soon they'd gotten there. "You couldn't prevent the murders?"

Bud frowned. "Coroner put their TOD at shortly after ten-thirty, which was nearly half an hour before you showed up."

Arthur rubbed his temples. "Then you missed the killer?"

"We got there in plenty of time for that part of the job," K.C. said with the hint of a smile.

"Then you were able to catch him."

"Her."

"Their assassin…it's a *she*?"

"Prosky."

He couldn't believe it. "*Vanessa* killed the attorney and his wife?"

"You sound surprised."

"I didn't think she did *any* of the dirty work."

"Die Anbieter is a vicious group," Bud said. "Don't forget, it was fashioned from charter members of the Black Hand. For Prosky to reach her obvious high level, she would have had to earn her status by proving herself. Wet work was just one of her many skills."

Suddenly nauseous, he lay back. He had made love to a cold-blooded killer. He couldn't believe he'd been so incredibly stupid. "I invited her into my bedroom."

"You didn't know," Mandy said.

"She's actually a killer? An assassin?"

"Not any longer," Bud said flatly. "She's dead."

He couldn't speak right off. His throat had gotten dry. He had to clear it first. "H-How did--"

"Cyanide. She'd been carrying it in a fake molar. Common practice for spies in the fifties and sixties during the Cold War. The Russians used it extensively. It was virtually foolproof—which was

318

why it was so popular. Death occurs in less than thirty seconds."

Cyanide. In her molar. Her tooth. He had kissed her. Passionately. Arthur began shaking.

"Arthur?" Mandy gently touched his wrist. "What's wrong?"

"She...kissed me." He felt as if a steel spike had been forced into his chest. "When we were in bed. She could have killed me. The cyanide...it might have...leaked..."

"It was sealed tight," K.C. said. "Two concentrated drops placed in a special miniscule pouch positioned in the artificial molar. The only way to get to the poison is to crack it open. The tip of a fingernail usually gets the job done."

She'd brought a lethal poison into his bedroom. The realization had turned his blood cold.

But now a different realization rocked through him. The cold-blooded assassin that had nearly ruined his life was dead. Gone. But instead of experiencing genuine relief, he felt only anger. And repulsion. And disgust. She died too easily. Too conveniently. He should have been the one to have done it. He should have done it at the attorney's house. For all the anguish and torment she had caused, he should have been given the pleasure of watching her die.

"You never liked her, did you?" Mandy asked softly.

"Not even when we were in bed together. She was too cold, too distant."

"Assassins are forbidden to form emotional attachments," Bud said.

"They're trained to kill people. Prosky was a professional."

"She made me feel like a moron."

"From what we've been able to come up with," Bud said, "she most likely did in both Bradford and Jenkins."

"Did she talk, by the way?"

K.C. shook his head. "She didn't say a word."

"It wasn't necessary," Bud added. "Our chip was enabled with audio capabilities. Its sound was relayed from one of our satellites. We heard what she said to you in the attorney's home. Every word."

"Did you ever find out about that building on Rouse Road?"

"It's a legitimate records storage center. Since Prosky was high up with them as well, she had no trouble claiming several rooms. Her security clearance reached high level. Hell, she could have brought in a terror cell and used their lunchroom to conduct a meeting."

"Did you find anything there?"

"Not a damned thing," K.C. said. "Every room used was cleaned out. The filing cabinets contained nothing useful."

"No wonder they've been able to operate for so long."

"They've built a huge, powerful network on a global scale," Bud said. "We estimate at least a thousand of them operating in this country alone, and they're recruiting unsuspecting people like you constantly."

"Any idea how busy they've been lately?"

"We've had numerous reports of witnesses, attorneys, politicians, and other government people dying under suspicious circumstances over the last two years," K.C. said. "Presently there are more than a dozen individuals being held in police custody in association with several of these crimes."

"Decoys? Or were they the trigger men?"

"We can't tell," Bud said. "None of them are aware of any involvement."

"What about implants? Surely you can tell--"

"We've been studying yours since you were brought in," K.C. said. "We've learned quite a few things about it, unfortunately."

"Unfortunately?"

"Once the chip is turned off, it's untraceable. And it's made of a biodegradable material that dissolves within thirty minutes."

"Dissolves?"

"After a complete shutdown," Bud said, "the program decomposes."

"You mean totally?"

"Within forty-five minutes," K.C. said flatly, "there is no trace."

Chapter 27

The next few days passed quickly.

Arthur wasn't allowed any contact with anyone as WITSEC went through its necessary procedures to provide him with a new identity. According to what he was told, any contact would jeopardize his life as well as the lives of his former associates. A new identity meant starting from scratch. Die Anbieter was still out there, operating at full capacity.

Once he left Winter Park, his condo would be cleaned out and sold, as well as his Caddie. He was allowed to keep whatever he could fit into one suitcase, provided he took no photos or any other hints of his past with him. Unbeknownst to anyone, he snuck a small wedding photo of himself and Denise and placed it in his pants pocket.

The most difficult part of all this was walking away from Mandy. After the last talk with Bud and K.C., he saw her only twice. Once he was taken from the hospital, he never saw her again. She had ceased to exist, becoming just another memory, along with Skip and everyone else he'd ever known. He tried several times to get in touch with Bud and K.C. but had no success with that as well. His escorts were closemouthed, telling him virtually nothing. And he was not allowed near a phone.

The word was final: Once everything had been finalized, the man named Arthur Sills was officially dead.

As soon as he'd finished packing, he was escorted outside, driven by a government sedan to Orlando International Airport, and given a one-way ticket to Columbus, Ohio. Why they had picked Columbus was anyone's guess. He figured they knew what they were doing, so he didn't question it.

Neither the driver nor the tall, somber-faced man who had accompanied him to the plane spoke as Arthur joined the line of passengers waiting at the boarding area. Everything seemed unreal, almost dreamlike, as he gently but firmly detached himself from the crowd—as well as the place where he had lived nearly all his life—connecting him to his old life.

Just before he slipped through the doorway that would take him down the ramp leading to the plane, he turned for one last glimpse of the man who had dropped him off.

He had already disappeared in the crowd.

***

A tall, well-dressed guy in his mid-thirties and an attractive redhead pushing forty met Arthur in the terminal when his plane landed at Port Columbus International.

They both flashed badges, but before he could read either, they'd already hustled him outside and into the back seat of a shiny black SUV sitting at the curb.

The inside of the cab smelled like leather and coffee, plus a lingering scent of *Obsession for Men*. The man got behind the wheel. The woman slid in beside the driver and opened her large black leather handbag. Before anyone had the chance to say anything, the SUV started up and immediately jerked out of its spot.

"Anyone want to tell me what the hell's going on?" Arthur realized these were Government people, but the suspense was aggravating. "I know this is secret cloak-and-dagger shit, but it's kind of traumatic and confusing. No one's talked to me in two days. It's like I'm really not here."

"Your name is Louis." The woman handed over a tan cowhide wallet. Her nails were long, polished, and cultured. He caught a glimpse of a silver horseshoe ring on her left pinkie. "Louis Hailey."

"The guy who wrote *Roots*?"

"That was Alex," the driver said, frowning. "And the last name is spelled differently."

"You're forty-two," the woman said. "You're unmarried. You went to Ohio State, majoring in Liberal Arts. We were told you're a crackerjack computer analyst, so we didn't think it would be very bright to stick you in a computer room. Even the dumbest of assholes would find you out."

"I'm thirty-eight." He didn't appreciate losing four years.

"Open your wallet."

He opened it. An Ohio driver's license with his latest photo and a different date of birth jumped out at him. He couldn't stop gazing at it. It was unreal, seeing his face with a different name and stats.

"See?" She shrugged. "What'd I tell you? Says you're forty-two, right?"

"It's wrong."

"It's a cover, ace. New identity--get it?"

"Why couldn't I be thirty-five?"

"Better to look younger for your age than older."

He still didn't like it, but she had a point. "I guess that's all right, then."

"We're glad you approve," the guy said flatly.

He decided not to take their sarcasm personally. Uprooting and moving people around had to be nerve-racking. He could only imagine the aggravation and resistance they faced daily.

He found a Visa credit card, a social security card with a different number beneath his new name, a United Health Care card, and a dental card. A registration card under his name, for a one-year-old Dodge Challenger, was also included. He checked the date and found it had been issued recently. "A Challenger? It's slightly sportier than my Caddie, don't you think?"

"Don't ask questions," the woman said.

"By the way, what do I call you guys?"

"Ma'am and Sir will be just fine," she said. "I'm the Ma'am."

The driver raised his hand. "I'm the Sir. Just in case you were wondering."

Somehow that just didn't cut it. "I'd feel funny, not knowing your names--especially if something happened, and--"

"Better tell him something to shut him up," the driver said. "His voice is kind of soothing. You don't want me falling asleep at the wheel again."

"That's right," she said. "Last time you did that, it turned out to be a really bad day. I'm Smith," she said, winking at Arthur. "He's Jones."

Her wink suggested he stop the questions and join their little game. "Ah.   Easy to remember. Your first names?"

"We're both named Marshal."

He nodded. "Okay, then. Now that we've gotten past the formalities... Tell me about this Challenger thing. How'd I rate such a cool car?"

"Apparently the Government considers it a token of their appreciation for what you did in Orlando," Jones said.

"A Dodge Challenger isn't cheap."

"It's the Government," Jones said. "We all know how generous they are."

"Especially with the taxpayer's money," Smith added.

"In other words, I paid for it."

"By George, methinks he's got it!"

He sat back in the seat. The heavy southbound Interstate traffic moved along at a frantic clip. Northbound wasn't nearly as bad, possibly because they were moving away from the big city. Since the lunch hour hadn't quite ended, he expected heavy traffic. The chaos reminded him of I-4.

"Where are we headed?"

"It's a nice area," Smith said. "One of the more established communities in Westerville. Most of the residents are older, so you won't feel that much out of place."

"Thanks a lump."

"You prefer the younger crowd?"

"I'm just a little miffed at losing four years of my life."

"You'll get over it," Jones said.

Smith shifted in her seat and used an elbow to prop herself up on the console. Her large green eyes settled on him. "I know this'll probably be difficult for a layman to understand, but you're not really four years older."

"Only on paper," Jones added.

"I think I got it now, thanks." He closed his eyes and thought once again about what he had left behind. He lived in Central Florida most of his life, but other than a few childhood memories and losing Denise, his only regret was leaving Mandy. In the few days they spent together, he had experienced a closeness he hadn't felt since Denise.

"How safe will I be?" He couldn't help wondering.

"We have a pretty good record," Smith said.

"How good is pretty good?"

"Since '71, WITSEC has protected, relocated, and given new identities to more than eight thousand witnesses, and nearly ten thousand of their family members."

A fair number, but it still didn't ease the tension. "And how many of these people are still alive?"

"There are two categories for this," she said. "The first includes those who've followed our guidelines. The second includes those who didn't."

"How about those who did?"

"A hundred percent."

"And the others?"

"You don't wanna know."

Half an hour later, they reached the Glenwood area and cruised down East Walnut, a quiet street with a small-town feel—much like the area in Winter Park. He suddenly felt the rest of his life might not be so different after all.

They pulled off the main drag, where the brightly painted white wooden sign, *Whispering Grove—a quiet, peace-loving community*, showed pleasantly beside a cluster of trimmed bushes a few feet off the shoulder. The road swerved around several units of two-story, brick bungalow-type condos nestled in lush groves of buckeyes, flowers, and large trimmed bushes. Jones veered left, taking the SUV down another winding drive of condos, where they reached the rear of the property, at a cul-de-sac fronting a two-unit tan brick building. Behind it, a tennis court rested comfortably in the sloped grassy area about a hundred yards from the woods.

Arthur found the area quiet and serene, and discovered that he felt less tense. The shiny light-blue Challenger sat in front of a two-car garage beneath the unit on the left. A gleaming gray Charger sat beside it.

"Is that my neighbor's car?" he asked.

Smith turned sharply in her seat. "Didn't we tell you not to ask questions?"

"I think you might've mentioned it."

"Don't forget it."

"Guess I'm just curious."

She pushed some heavy red tresses away from her face and gave him another dose of those big green eyes. She handed him a ring of keys. "Two are for the car. The other two, the condo. Don't lose 'em. You might wanna make spares. There's a mall not far from here. It's got a hardware store. There's a cellphone in the condo registered in your name. Our numbers are in the phone's address book, contacts three and four. We'll give you a couple of days to settle in. Then we'll pop on over to discuss job opportunities. Sound like a plan?"

"I guess."

"*Please* don't do anything stupid, then call us and expect us to bail you out, okay?"

"I'll try not to be a pain in the ass."

She opened her door and shot him a quick frown. "Something tells me you're not gonna be too successful at it." She went to the back of the car, lifted the trunk, and pulled out the suitcase. She left it on the pavement outside his door as she got back in the SUV.

Without another word, they drove off.

As he watched them disappear around the bend, he felt a heavy throbbing emptiness filling his being. He was alone, in a strange place. He knew no one, and the only two people who knew anything about him had just vanished in the dust. He felt helpless and vulnerable—much like the day his mother dropped him off in front of the school on his first day.

He had survived Vanessa's organization of killers—which was something to feel good about. But when he realized he would have to keep on surviving, and that there would always be the slim chance they could find him again, all feelings of elation vanished. From this day forward, he would spend the rest of his life alone.

That realization caused a deep depression to descend upon him. He couldn't let it consume him. Not now, not ever. The trauma with Vanessa had turned him into a fighter. From now on, he would continue to be one.

Pulling in a giant lungful of cool Ohio air, he picked up the suitcase and marched bravely up the paved drive, then up the steps, to the front stoop. He found the right key and unlocked the door. Then, holding his breath, pushed it open.

Standing in the entrance in her bare feet, wearing a short-sleeve red tee shirt and faded jeans, was Mandy.

EPILOGUE

Stunned, he let the suitcase drop onto the ceramic tile. His throat felt hot and constricted. "M-Mandy?" He was surprised his voice worked.

"My name is Julia." She smiled and extended a hand. "Julia Greer. I'm thirty-six, divorced, and live in the condo next door. And who might you be? I don't think I've ever seen you before. Are you new to the area?"

He felt his right hand moving awkwardly in her direction. The shock of her touch sent a flurry of chills racing up his arm. She was real. Mandy was actually standing there. This was the second time she had come back into his life, and the feeling was indescribable.

"Are you gonna tell me your name or what? I don't have all day, you know."

He cleared his throat. It was as dry as dust, but the words eventually came out. "Louis Hailey. You can call me Lou."

"Hello...Louis."

Reluctantly he let go of her hand. He still couldn't accept the fact that she was standing there...that she'd been brought here as well...and that they were together again. His eyes filled, and she became blurred and distorted, as in a dream.

"You've really got to do something about that," she said, sighing. "If you cry every time I try talking to you, I'm gonna eventually get a complex."

"It's really...they actually...*sent* you here?"

She shrugged. "I insisted."

"Really?"

"Someone's got to keep an eye on you. Besides, they stuck me in the same program. It was kind of necessary, given the circumstances."

He couldn't speak. A warm tear drifted down his left cheek. He made no move to wipe it away.

"You're not gonna do anything stupid, are ya?"

"Define stupid."

"Like, maybe, a hug? A long, wet kiss? Maybe even a little groping around?"

She had to be kidding. "I wouldn't consider *any* of that stupid."

"Normally, I wouldn't, either."

"Normally?"

"You left the door open." She frowned. "There are three old ladies out there, taking their afternoon stroll. I'd strongly suggest closing it. We wouldn't want to give anyone a heart attack, would we?"

That didn't seem to matter. He wanted only to stand there and gawk at her.

"Sometimes you're *so* helpless…" She rushed right past him and pushed the door shut. Then she turned and, without another word, wrapped her arms around his neck.

***

His new job was Assistant Manager of Shop Mart, the local supermarket in Glenwood.

He did the weekly time sheets and handled the payroll money when it came in. The front wall of his smallish second-floor office, a large window

332

overlooking the store's four aisles, enabled him to monitor its daily activities.

His boss, Elaine Ramsey, managed the store. She was fifty-eight, tall and skinny, and treated the employees as if they were members of her own family. She was fair, but ran a tight ship, and took no nonsense from anyone. She was impressed by his work ethic and brought him coffee whenever she was getting a cup for herself.

Julia usually dropped by in the afternoons, and they had lunch across the street, at one of the cafes in the area. There were two others in the four-block radius, but the one they liked the most was the Glenwood Café. It had a courtyard out front, with nearly a dozen small round tables and green umbrellas over each. The place offered dozens of brands of coffee and served croissants, sweet rolls, and the best homemade cheesecake in the county.

After work, they had supper and spent the evening together on the couch, watching Netflix. On weekends they took strolls to one of the local parks and fed the pigeons or watched a movie at the local theater. Some would consider their life boring and monotonous but wouldn't understand what they'd been through.

Julia dyed her hair. No longer a striking blond, she'd become a stunning redhead. Louis let his own dark hair grow longer, and recently began sporting a beard. Julia liked his new look, saying it made him look sexy and authoritive.

They never mentioned Vanessa or what happened during the terrible week that almost destroyed their lives. In fact, they didn't mention Orlando at all. For them, the subject was dead. There really was no reason to rehash any of it. The past was dead and buried.

The future had become the only thing worth caring about.

OTHER WORKS BY DAVID BERARDELLI:

THE APPRENTICE
THE WAGON DRIVER
STEPPING OUT OF MY GRAVE
ESCAPE CLAUSE
FATAL INNOCENCE
COLORS
IN ANOTHER REALM
BEYOND RECOGNITION
THE NIGHTMARE COLLECTOR
HIDDEN
BEYOND GUILT
A RIPPLE IN TIME
YESTERDAY'S JOURNEY
ENLIGHTENMENT
REDEMPTION
AWAKENED

Titles available through:
Fiction4All

OTHER WORKS BY DAVID
BERARDELLI

www.ingramcontent.com/pod-product-compliance
Lightning Source LLC
Chambersburg PA
CBHW010830250626
47157CB00010B/3231